DIAMOND

PART 6 OF THE
LOVE, LIES & LUST
SERIES

MZ. ROBINSON

STREET ESSENCE

Robinson

Published by:

G Street Chronicles
P.O. Box 1822
Jonesboro, GA 30237-1822

www.gstreetchronicles.com
fans@gstreetchronicles.com

Cover design:
Hot Book Covers, www.hotbookcovers.com

ISBN13: 978-1-9384421-5-5
ISBN10: 1938442156
LCCN: 2012950161

Join us on our social networks

Like us on Facebook: G Street Chronicles
Follow us on Twitter: @GStreetChronicl
Follow us on Instagram: gstreetchronicles

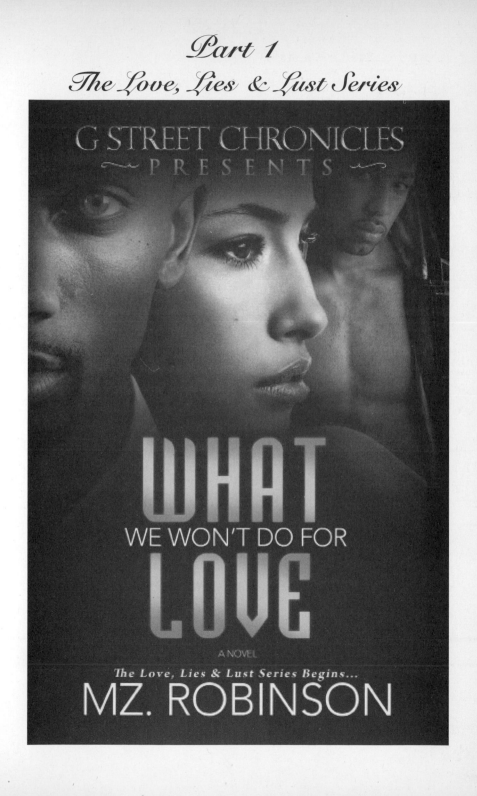

G STREET CHRONICLES
~ PRESENTS ~

WHAT
WE WON'T DO FOR
LOVE

A NOVEL

The Love, Lies & Lust Series Begins...
MZ. ROBINSON

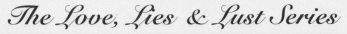

Part 2
The Love, Lies & Lust Series

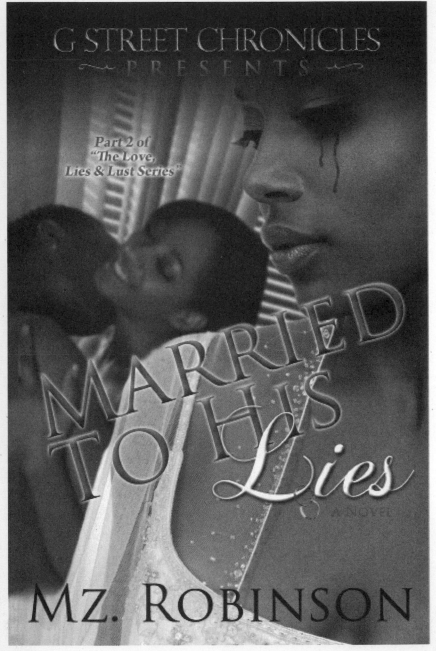

G STREET CHRONICLES
~ PRESENTS ~

Part 2 of
"The Love,
Lies & Lust Series"

MARRIED
TO HIS
Lies

A NOVEL

MZ. ROBINSON

Part 3
The Love, Lies & Lust Series

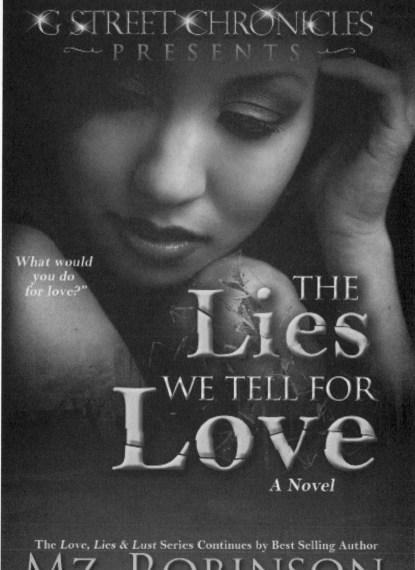

G STREET CHRONICLES
~ PRESENTS ~

"What would you do for love?"

THE
Lies
WE TELL FOR
Love

A Novel

The *Love, Lies & Lust* Series Continues by Best Selling Author

MZ. ROBINSON

G STREET CHRONICLES
PRESENTS

Love LIES AND LUST

PART 4 OF *THE LOVE, LIES & LUST SERIES*

MZ. ROBINSON

G STREET CHRONICLES
~ PRESENTS ~

NO ORDINARY
LOVE

PART 5 OF THE
"LOVE, LIES & LUST" SERIES

MZ. ROBINSON

G STREET *Essence*

"The vision I have for myself is like a grain of sand when compared to the plan of divine greatness He has for me.."

~Mz. R

Dedication

I dedicate this book to Lasheera Lee, the Olivia Pope of the literary industry (minus the whole hooking up with the President thing). *Smiles*

Lasheera you have a beautiful spirit and you are truly a blessing to all who know you. I am eternally grateful and thankful for all that you do. You give unselfishly and you have taught me so much. Thank you for your motivation and encouragement. May God's blessings overflow in your life.
~Mz.R

Acknowledgements

To my Lord and Savior, my Alpha and my Omega: Thank you for continuing to nurture my gifts and talents. Thank you for your mercy, grace, and loving kindness. I am so unworthy but you are truly a merciful God and I'm very grateful.

To my Mother: Mommy, we made it to book 9! It has been a difficult journey but I thank God for you hanging in there with me and encouraging me when I thought I didn't have the strength to "type on". I love you and KNOW that the best is yet to come. WE claim it and WE thank Him in advance.

To my Father: Daddy, thank you for continuing to encourage me throughout my journey. It hasn't been easy but nothing worth keeping ever is. I love you Daddy and I'm happy to have you as my father.

To my uncle Kenneth "Bay" Leslie: You are still a man of your word and one of the realest I know. I love you.

To my family, the Leslies, Turners, Caudles, and Masseys: I LOVE YOU ALL!

To my cousin Tammy: I love you and seeing you pop in on FB was a pleasant surprise.

To my Bestie Banita Brooks: We are still rocking and rolling together and I'm thankful for it. I love you sis.

To Rena: Thank you Na-Na for all your support!

To George Sherman Hudson: It has been an unforgettable journey full of ups, downs, and a lot in between but truly everything happens for a reason. I want you to know, I listen even when you think I'm not and I have not forgotten any of the lessons. Thank you for everything. G Street is forever inked in my heart.

To Shawna A.: Thank you for all that you do, seen and un-seen. Your story is incredible and your dedication is amazing. Thank you!

To Ella Curry: Thank you for your kind words and being a light in the industry. It was a pleasure meeting you.

To the D.I.V.A.S:

Andrea Wheeler, thank you for the support and just being you! You are a wonderful woman and your motivation and encouragement has been a blessing. I am anxiously awaiting my visit to Wheeler World. Thank you Sweetness!

Denia Turner, my Vegas Diva, thank you for staying down and always making me laugh. #Late nights and early mornings!

Robyn Traylor, I will never forget the first time we met; you were truly team Mz. Robinson. Thank you, for your support and encouragement.

Shanika Dewey Greenleaf, thank you for your support and encourage-ment and allowing me to laugh at your expense. There is never a dull mo-ment with you and RJ and the two of you keep me smiling.

Jewel Horace, you are a "jewel" in every sense of the word. Thank you for your continued support and encouragement.

JeaNida Luckie-Weatherall, I love your determination and your faith. You are a beautiful example of a woman who is determined to win no matter what life throws her way. Thank you for your support and I know healing is on the way.

Timiska Martin-Webb, thank you for riding with me and showing me mad support since day one.

Natasha Potts, thank you for spreading the word and always trying to bring a friend in. Tasha, you are a sweetheart who deserves nothing but the best.

Susan Vincent, thank you for embracing my crazy and always asking for more!

Keisha Woods, thank you for the laughs, sometimes the tears, support, and the love. I hope you don't turn against me after book 7. Hint...hint...lol.

Shelia Jones Weathersby, thank you for the support and always trying to find a way to keep the Love, Lies, and Lust series going. I swear if it were up to you Damon would still be running around at 90years old. Lol.

Samantha Pettiway, I know we haven't chatted lately due to work and life but I am still very thankful for your support and our connection. You ROCK Naturalista!

Lisa Bryant, hey Lisa B.! I'm so happy we connected and I thank you for all of your support and encouragement.

Lashunda P. Cato, thank you Peaches, for your support and rocking with me.

Naomi B. Johnson, thank you for your kind words and encouragement.

Barbara Love, thank you for being an inspiration and your continued support. XoXo.

Leslie Gray, I've always known that women name "Leslie" can be trouble and you have yet to prove me wrong. Lol. Thank you for your encouragement and support!

Me'Tova Hollingsworth, Thank you for your support and dropping in and making me smile!

To: Lisa Dewey Chambliss, Jo'Lynn Dewey Pierre, Jo'Licia ·Dewey, Brittany Dewey, MarQuita Drayton, and the entire Dewey family, Thank you! Thank you to: Ayanna Butler, Karen Gilyard, Karamel Hibbler, Cheri Walker, Toni Zardies, Nelly Hester Alejandro, Pamela Perry, Althea JustBeing Me, LaBrina Jolly, Danielle Churcher, Nikki Johnson, Nekisha White Bell, Amy Ackerson, Justin Davon Price, Sha Cole, Stacy Johnson-Leonard, Jacole Laryea, Yvonne Stovall, Qiana Drennen, Courtney Lawson, Sharon Alsobrook LeGrande, Anya Alsobrook, Nicki Brownsugar Williams, Helen Richards, Davan Holt, Kerrisha Brown, Angela Clark, Mary Green, Shawnte Avery, Lee Regan O' Neal, Natoya Taylor, and Stephaine Marie.

To all the members of Books and More with Mz. R, I love you! To every one on the Mz. Robinson fan page, and the Love, Lies, and Lust series fan page, Thank you!

To each and every group and book club that has shown me love: Thank you! Sending a special shout out to:

Kenya Ervin and the Soul Sistahs Book Club

Oosa Book Club

Page Turner's Book Club
Just Read Book Club
SIRR

To my Editor: Autumn, thank you, it is always a pleasure working with you.

To Hot Book Covers: Thank you for another HOT book cover!

To each and every blogger, blog talk radio show host, and promoter: Thank you!

To the following talented authors: To Fire & Ice (trouble makers...lol), Katavious Ellis, Janie Peterson, Kim Carter, Honey Honey, UrbanNovelist Eureka, Thomas Long, Aleta Williams, Real Divas, Nika Michelle, Charmaine Galloway, Ellen Sade, and $paid: Thank you for connecting and much love.

If there is anyone I forgot, please, blame it on the voices in my head and not my heart! To every one with a hope and a dream remember to P.U.S.H.

Chapter 1

I watched as the low fuel indicator illuminated in the dash of my Honda Civic, an indication that I needed to refuel immediately or I'd have to hoof it. I knew I should have stopped for gas before work that morning, but it had been my intent to leave my job at the Holiday Inn before rush-hour traffic and get gas then. Of course my plans were canceled when my co-worker, Tina, came dragging in late for her shift, looking and smelling like she'd been rolling around in a tub of liquor. The heifer didn't have an excuse or even offer an apology. I wanted to check her ass and express my dislike with her obvious lack of consideration, but instead I grabbed my purse, clocked out, and left without saying a damn word. I knew there was no use in expressing my feelings; if I opened my mouth and let my thoughts roll off my tongue, I'd most likely end up pounding the pavement again, checking the want ads. I'd been working as a desk clerk at the hotel for a little over a year, and although it was far from my dream occupation, it was a legit job that paid the bills. In moments like that, though, I wished I'd chosen to further my education after high school or at least pursued some sort of trade or career. Of course, after graduation, there were other responsibilities that required my immediate attention, so higher education had to be put on hold anyway.

The loud chirping of my cell phone drew my attention to the center console and advised me that my brother was calling. "What is it this time, Randall?" I grumbled to myself, debating on whether or not to answer. I loved my brother, but lately, he'd only been calling when he wanted something, and it seemed as if he wanted something all the time. I was torn between sending him to voicemail and answering before I finally concluded that it could possibly be an emergency. "Hello?" I answered.

"Hey, sis. What you up to?"

"Headed to the nail shop," I said. "What's up?"

"Check this out...I need to hold twenty until next week."

"What happened to the twenty I let you hold two weeks ago?" I questioned, agitated.

My brother had been nickel-and-diming my pockets every chance he got, asking for gas money or with help with his bills. The man was single, with no children, yet he claimed he never had a dime to his name. I was beginning to think there was more going on with him than poor money management skills.

"Yeah, about that..." he said. "They cut my hours at the carwash, so I've been running short, but as soon as things pick up, I'm gonna run you your money."

I knew he was lying. According to an associate of mine, who also worked at the carwash, Randall hadn't been to work in days, and even when he did bother to show up, he was practically useless. Nonetheless, I decided to entertain his lame excuse for his lack of funds. "Randall, if you're not making enough to carry your weight, you need to look for something else and—"

"Look, Diamond, I didn't call to listen to no lecture," he blurted out, cutting me off. "If you got me, I 'preciate it. If not, just have the balls to say so. You can kill all that extra. I swear you startin' to act just like Mama, thinking you talkin' to a child instead of a grown-ass man. Damn it, sis!"

"A grown-ass man would know how to handle his business," I snapped back. "Don't call me gettin' loud, Randall. I'm trying to help you."

"Can I hold it or what?" he blew loudly into the phone. "A simple 'yes' or 'no' will do."

"All right," I said, offended. "No."

Click.

He hung up, but I knew it would be only a matter of days, if that, before he called again. Sometimes it was hard to believe that Randall and I were even related. I believed in hard work and earned every dime I spend. Randall, on the other hand, would have gotten somebody else to breathe for him if he could; he was just that damn lazy. I don't know what branch of our family tree he'd fallen from, but it was obvious that the limb was as sorry as hell.

I pulled into the parking lot of the Conoco gas station and parked in front of pump 8. I reached over to the passenger's side, opened my handbag, and removed my wallet. The digital 6:32 on the face of my stereo deck reminded me that I had less than thirty minutes to make it to the nail salon before they closed.

Normally, I arrived at least an hour before closing, out of respect for the nail technicians, because I knew they hated last-minute walk-ins, but this time they would have to deal with it. My nails were long overdue for a full set, and I wanted to treat myself. I removed my keys from the ignition and climbed out of my car with my wallet and keys in hand.

As I stepped across the parking lot, walking toward the gas station store, I noticed two vehicles parked in front of the door, a snow-white Lexus with dark-tinted windows and an all-black Tahoe. I watched as the driver of the Lexus opened his door and stepped out, a dark-skinned brother. He shut the door of his Lexus, and then climbed into the passenger side of the Tahoe. A few seconds passed before the door of the Tahoe reopened, and the man got out and climbed back behind the wheel of the Lexus.

Dumbasses, I thought to myself. It was plain as day that the parties in the vehicles were engaged in some kind of illegal transaction, and my instinct told me it had something to do with drugs.

I stepped past the Tahoe and entered the store. After grabbing a bottle of juice and a little something to snack on, I paid for my items and exited the minimart.

The driver-side door of the Tahoe opened, and a majestic man with light brown skin stepped out. He was attractive and neatly dressed in slacks and a button-down shirt. He was approximately six-three, with a toned, but not overly powerful, build and a neat Caesar cut. "How are you today?" he asked.

"Good," I said, walking by him.

"Excuse me," he said from behind me.

"Yes?" I questioned, turning to face him.

"May I talk to you for a moment?"

"I'm in a hurry," I said truthfully, "and I'm not interested."

"You're in a hurry?" he repeated smoothly. "I understand that, but how do you know if you're interested or not? You haven't even heard what I've got to offer. Why don't you get to know me first, then decide."

"I guess you have a point, but I'm sure I'm not interested."

"Are you married?"

"No."

"Do you have a man?"

"No."

"What kind of men do you like?" he probed, penetrating me with his dark brown eyes.

"Men who *work*," I said sarcastically, letting him know I'd seen his little illegal interaction before I'd entered the store and that I was not digging what he had going on. Granted, I could have been completely off in my assumptions about him and the other man, but my gut feeling seldom ever let me down.

His eyebrows inched up while the corners of his lips turned up into a small smile. "What does it matter if I work or not? Why do men work? For money, right? I've already got money. I don't need to work."

I wanted to argue, but I unfortunately didn't have time. "Look, I gotta get to the nail salon before they close," I said, walking to my car.

"Heh. The nail salon? Is that why you're in a hurry?" he asked, following behind me.

"Yes," I said. I popped open the cover for the gas tank, and then unscrewed the cap.

"What are you getting done?"

"Why?"

"Let me get that," he said, stepping up to the pump.

I stepped back, allowing him room to pump my gas. "Thanks," I said.

"Well? What are you getting done?"

"I need a full set," I said impatiently, "but at the rate I'm going, I'm not gonna make it before they close."

"What's your name?"

"Diamond," I said smugly, pointing to the gold-plated name badge I wore.

He looked slightly embarrassed and extremely cute at the same time. "Sorry."

"No problem."

"In any case, it's nice to meet you, Diamond," he said politely. "They call me Gator."

I looked at him strangely, wondering how such a nice-looking brother had ended up with an unattractive nickname. "What's your *real* name?" I questioned.

He smiled. "Leon Douglass."

"Well, it's nice to meet you too, Mr. Douglass," I said curtly. "I wish I had more time to chop it up, but I really have to go."

He finished filling my tank, screwed the cap back on, and then closed the cover. "I'll make you a deal. Gimme a few more minutes of your time, and I'll make sure you get your full set before the night is over."

"How? You do nails too? I thought you said you don't need a job…and you don't look like the nail salon type."

"No, I don't do nails, but I'll make sure I get yours done."

"Listen, I'm sure you're a real nice dude and all, but—"

"No buts," he said. "Just a few minutes, Diamond."

I considered it for a moment, looking him over, glanced at my watch, and decided there was no way I was gonna make it through traffic in time. I figured if he didn't come through, I could always hit the salon in the morning. "Fine," I said, defeated. "You've got five minutes."

"You never answered my question," he said.

"What question?"

"If I have money, why do I have to work?"

"Because all money isn't good money, *clean* money."

"It might not be clean, but it's all *green*. All money pays the bills," he replied, "and if I can pay the bills and take care of you, isn't that all that matters?"

"*I* work," I advised him, nodding toward my name badge again. "I don't need a man to take care of me." I wasn't the kind of female who overly expressed her independence. I believed a man should always take care of his woman, but that same woman should be fully capable of managing on her own. I wasted no time with any man who expressed what he *thought* he could do for me.

"I like that," he said, nodding, "but a real man wouldn't expect you to work."

I smiled sheepishly, trying not to fall for his bullshit.

"Finally…a smile."

"Don't get used to it," I said, walking around to the driver's side door. "You've had your five minutes, and I'm leaving."

"Fine," he said. "I'll see you tonight at dinner."

"Dinner? I don't remember you asking," I said with a frown, "nor did I agree to go out with you."

"You're right. Diamond, will you join me for dinner?" he asked seductively.

I looked at him, contemplating whether or not I should accept. There was something intriguing about the man and the way he carried himself. I knew his failure to deny his career choice was also an omission of guilt, but I was helplessly drawn to his confidence. I remained silent while attempting to make a decision.

"Take some time and think about it," he finally said. He reached into his pants pocket and removed a business card holder. "The top one is my number," he said, handing me two cards. "The second is for a salon on Madison Boulevard, Divaz. When you get there, ask for Erica. I'll let her know to expect you…and I'll be waiting on your call."

Damn. Hook, line, and sinker, I thought, looking down at the cards.

* * * * *

I'd heard several things about Divaz, the salon Gator had referred me to, one being that they provided excellent service the other that their rates were as high as hell.

The moment I walked through the door, I was greeted by a slender woman of Hispanic descent, with deep-set, dark brown eyes and long, dark hair that draped down over her shoulders. She was dressed in a yellow romper with a plunging neckline and hot pink six-inch heels. "Welcome to Divaz," she said in a thick Spanish accent. "My name is Mariah."

"Hi. Um…I'm here to see Erica," I said, observing my surroundings. There were four large leather massage chairs along the left wall of the salon, four manicure tables positioned along the right, and two tan leather sofas in the waiting area. One of the booths was occupied by another Hispanic woman and her client.

"Your name?"

"Diamond."

Mariah scanned me from my eyes down to my shoes and then back up again.

I frowned, unappreciative of the unwarranted onceover. Don't get me wrong, I loved receiving attention from other women; to be honest, I loved women almost as much as men. However, the attention Mariah gave me had nothing to do with admiration. It was obvious from the snobbish smirk on her over-painted red lips that she didn't like what she was seeing.

"You're not what we were expecting," she stated sourly.

I instantly took offense. *What in the hell does that mean, not what they were expecting?* Granted, my work uniform seemed out of place in that upscale salon, but I was holding my own in my khaki pants and cotton shirt. Hell, it was my personal opinion that I could make any ensemble look good. From my flawless, sienna complexion and deep-set pecan-shell eyes, to my luxurious black, curly lashes and succulent, full lips, I was a work of art—no filters and no makeup required. My hair, however, was another story. I was rocking eighteen inches of Yaki that I flipped and swung like it was my own. Yes, I wore it out of pure laziness, but at least I had hair.

Other than on my head, there were a couple places on my body that could have used a few renovations, those being my chest and my ass. I had perky B-cups and just enough ass to squeeze but not enough to hold on to. There was a time in my life when I longed to have a body like the porn girls who shook their shit in videos, but I got over that. I was a queen, and queens come in all shapes and sizes and don't have to pattern themselves after anyone. Besides, what I lacked in ass and titties, I made up for in attitude. At five-four, I was what some might have considered short, but I carried myself like a six-two female. I had confidence that some mistook for conceit and a charisma others mistook for arrogance. I usually got the respect I wanted, but Mariah wasn't giving it to me, and I thought about checking her ass for the way she came at me, but instead I chose to hold my tongue.

"Mariah, *no seas grosero,*" the other technician spoke loudly.

"I'm not being rude," Mariah said, rolling her eyes. "I'm just stating a fact. Gator normally goes for women who are a little more…glamorous." She grinned at me mischievously, an indication that she was referring to herself.

"Hmm. Well, he didn't mention your name at all," I announced sarcastically. "Clearly, Gator didn't see the need for me to know about the hired help."

The customer sitting with the other technician laughed loudly.

Mariah lowered her eyes to tiny slits, and her forehead creased in anger. "First off—"

"First off, when I have a guest, you come get me immediately," someone interrupted.

We both looked up at the woman who had joined us in the room and interrupted Mariah's verbal retaliation. She'd come from the back of the salon and was standing with her hands planted firmly on her hips, staring at Mariah, chastising her with her eyes. She was a plus-sized beauty, with dark skin and short, tapered hair. She was wearing snug-fitting jeans and a low-cut shirt with "The Bomb" spelled out on it in red letters.

"I-I was just about to come get you," Mariah tried to explain.

The woman waved her off and approached me. "You must be Diamond," she said. "I'm Erica." She stepped past Mariah and extended her hand to me.

"It's nice to meet you," I said sincerely.

"C'mon." She motioned and turned on her heels. "Let's go to the back, and we'll get you taken care of."

I cut my eyes at Mariah, flashed her a victorious smile, and then followed Erica through the door that led to the back of the salon. The area was decorated much like the front, except there were only two massage chairs and one booth.

There was a woman sitting in one of the chairs, soaking her feet. She had skin the color of cinnamon and mysterious, slanted eyes, with a wide nose and full lips. She wore her hair in a chin-length bob that perfectly framed her full face. Her fitted wrap dress stopped just above her knees, revealing her toned legs. She looked up at me and smiled.

"You have to excuse Mariah," Erica said, taking her seat behind the manicure table. "She's got a big mouth and doesn't know when to shut it half the time."

"So I noticed," I said, sitting down across from her.

"Gator's somewhat of a celebrity around here," Erica explained, "not to mention that he has a few admirers. He's like a little big brother to me, the reason I opened this shop. Hell, if it wasn't for his encouragement I don't know where I'd be. Mariah's just one of his jealous fans."

I wondered if Mariah's admiration for the man was one sided or if Gator had given her a reason to be salty toward other women. I knew men tended to tell only the portion of the truth that suited them. In some rare cases, innocent friendship was mistaken for love, but far more often, the lines of friendship were crossed, and the female was led to believe she was entitled to more.

"In the case of some, the admiration is one sided," the other woman in the room chimed in, as if she'd read my mind.

I cut my eyes in her direction, wondering if she was also one of Gator's admirers.

"I'm Venetta," she said.

"Hi. I'm Diamond."

"My brother was right," she said with a smile. "You are a cutie."

I looked at her, attempting to see a family resemblance between her and Gator, but the only thing the two of them seemed to have in common was their gift of flattery; they clearly both had a way with words. "Thank you," I said, wondering if it was merely a coincidence that I'd ended up at the salon at the same time as the man's sister being there, or if it was all some big plot to coerce me into going on a date with him.

"This is merely a coincidence," she stated, reading my mind again.

"I was just wondering."

We talked during my visit, and Venetta told me she was married and had a twelve-year-old son, Emerson, E. for short. She was thirty-three; three years older than Gator, and they'd been born and raised in Union Town, a small town in lower Alabama. They'd relocated to Huntsville a few months after their mother was murdered at the hands of a boyfriend. "I was sixteen years old and had $400 to my name," she explained. "I didn't have a clue how the two of us were going to survive or even where we were gonna live. I just knew we had to get out of that town before we went insane, so I packed up my mama's old Buick with as much of our stuff as I could, and we hit the road. When we got here, I lied about my age so I could work in bars, till Leon went to work."

"Didn't you have any other family to help you?"

"None we could depend on," she said with a sigh. "We never knew our father," she explained, "so we never missed him. For as long as I could remember, it'd always just been me and Gator and our mama, but that had always been enough. When Mama was killed, we only had each other to hold on to."

There was a distant longing in her eyes that nudged me to ask more about their mother, but I refrained for fear that it might drudge up some unpleasant memories or pain. Instead, I chose to tell her a little about me. "I was born and raised here in Huntsville," I explained. "I'm twenty-three, no man and no kids."

"Only twenty-three? I thought you looked young," she said, her eyes wide. "Well, at least you're legal."

We both laughed.

"Anyway, you know what they say about age," she said with a shrug. "Besides, I can tell you have an old spirit."

"I've heard that before."

"It's true," she said. "Do you have any brothers or sisters?"

"An older brother," I said.

"So, you're the baby in the family, huh?"

"Yes, but sometimes it feels like the other way around," I confessed, recalling Randall trying to bum twenty bucks off of me.

"And your parents?"

"My father passed away last November," I said sadly. "My mother still lives here."

"I'm so sorry to hear about your daddy," Venetta said softly. "I know what it is to lose a parent that you love."

"Thanks."

There was a brief moment of silence between the two of us.

"So…what do you think of my brother? What was your first impression?" she probed.

"No offense, but he's a hustler," I said without hesitation.

"A hustler? Hmm. You say that like it's a bad thing."

"Isn't it?"

"Hustlers come in many forms, girl. I'm a mother and wife who balances staying fabulous with taking care of my family, so even I'm a hustler. Our mama was a maid who sometimes worked ten-hour shifts for a hotel chain, came home and spent time with me and my brother, slept for two hours, then went to clean private residents before returning to the hotel. I guess she was a hustler too."

"And your brother?"

"Leon is a provider and a protector," she explained, "a mentor to some, an entrepreneur, and—"

"A hustler," I cut her off and laughed, and she laughed right back at me.

"What do you think he does for a living?" she asked, raising her eyebrows.

"You tell me," I said.

Venetta smiled and shook her head. "We both know you know," she said. "If you didn't, you wouldn't be here."

"He held me up so long I couldn't get to my normal nail shop before they closed," I admitted. "That's the only reason I'm here."

"I highly doubt that," she said. "Leon saw something in you worthy of his time and attention."

"So I should feel special?" I said sarcastically.

"You may not now, but you will, once you learn more about him and the kind of man he is."

"We'll probably never see each other again," I stated. "Considering his line of work, he's not my type."

"We'll see about that," she said, batting her eyes. "We shall see."

Twenty minutes later, I sat there admiring my nails. Erica was the bomb, and my pink and white French tips were perfect. I originally requested brighter colors and designs, but Venetta convinced me simple was better.

After promising them I would see them again, I thanked them and then left through the front door. I debated about calling Gator and taking him up on his offer to join him for dinner, but a little voice inside kept telling me I should avoid him. I chose to send him a simple text message instead:

Thank U 4 hooking my nails up. ☺

You're very welcome. What time should I pick U up 4 dinner?

I think it's best that we don't.

I would ask why, but that would make me seem doubtful.

Doubtful?

Yes. I know I'll get my chance. So until I do, take care, beautiful.

Conceited much? LOL

Not conceited. . .just convinced.

Chapter 2

Three weeks later...

Scanning over the reservations for the night, I observed that the hotel was booked for the whole weekend. I wasn't surprised, considering it was King of the Hill weekend, an annual motorcycle race. The city would be packed with out-of-town guests.

I looked at the metal clock hanging on the wall, pleased that I had less than an hour until the end of my shift. *Tina better be on time!* I thought. I had plans with my girlfriend, Shaundra, for the night and intentions to keep them one way or the other; I didn't give a damn if my manager, Ashanti, had to come in, somebody was going to work Tina's shift if she didn't show up, and I was determined that it was not going to be me.

The *whoosh* of the automatic sliding door opening drew my attention. Looking up, I smiled slightly at the sight of Gator. He was dressed in a dark suit with a mint-green shirt and gold tie, along with a clean pair of alligator shoes.

"Hello," I said, trying hard not to focus on how good he looked. Although I hadn't seen him since the day we'd first met at the gas station, I had received several *Good Morning* texts, along with the occasional phone call to ask me how I was doing. Conversations with him were always pleasant, and despite the desire I heard in his voice to see me, he never asked. I had come to the conclusion that the two of us were going to be nothing more than phone pals, and I had almost forgotten how attractive he was. However, at the sight of him, my memory was refreshed instantly.

By the way he was dressed, I assumed he had plans for the night, and I silently wondered with whom. "Hello," he said, walking up to the front desk.

There was a light, but masculine, scent that accompanied him as he stood in front of the counter with his hands in his pants pockets. *Damn, he smells good.*

"How are you?"

"I'm good," I said. "And you?"

"I'm doin' good," he said, "but I'll be doing much better in approximately thirty minutes."

"Why is that?"

"That's when you get off," he said, "right?"

"How do you know that?"

"I have my ways," he said, smiling slyly.

"Care to share?"

"A gentleman never reveals his sources."

"Like a magician never reveals his tricks?"

"Something like that."

I frowned.

"I called every Holiday Inn in the city until I found out which location you work at. It took a little persuasion, but one of your co-workers let me know when your shift ends. I hope you don't mind. I just really wanted to see you."

Part of me was flattered that he had put forth so much effort to research my life, but another part was apprehensive of the hustler; I wondered if his ass was a stalker, and I was somewhat pissed that someone I worked with had given out confidential information. "Interesting," I said, not sounding too impressed.

"That you are," he said.

I blushed slightly. "So you came to keep me company until the end of my shift?"

"I did," he said, "and then I'm taking you to dinner."

"How do you know I don't have plans?"

"You do," he stated confidently. "Like I just told you, you've got plans with me. I made reservations for dinner."

I loved the arrogance in his voice and the determination in his eyes; both equally sexy. "I actually have plans with my girlfriend," I stated honestly.

"And what will it take to change those plans?"

"I was kinda looking forward to our girls' night out," I said and it was the truth. I'd been pulling a lot of double-shifts at the hotel lately and had had little to no time to spend with my friend. I loved making money, but I needed a break, an opportunity to get out and shake my ass.

"I've got another deal for you. Join me for dinner, and if you don't enjoy yourself, I'll pay for you and your friend to go wherever you like."

I contemplated his offer. I hadn't been on a date with a man in over a year, and although there were some I could have gone out with, I always refrained. After my father's passing, I came to realize that I needed to put my life and my priorities in perspective, and having a man in my life, or any sort of serious relationship, was thrown to the back burner. Making money was a priority, so I'd busied myself with that. Still, despite the fact that I was content, there was something inviting and charming about Gator's offer that I didn't want to resist, so I finally agreed to go out with him. "I'll need to go home and change first," I advised him. I had packed an overnight bag before leaving home, with the intent of changing at Shaundra's after work, but looking at Gator's attire, it was obvious that my leopard-print bodysuit would not be appropriate.

"Deal," he agreed.

After my shift, I called Shaundra to inform her of my change of plans, and she was actually thrilled for me. "We'll get together tomorrow, "she said. "Besides, I got my own cutie I wanna spend a little time with."

"Blair? That dude you met at the gym?"

"That's him, Mr. Chocolate Thunder." She giggled. "Have fun, girl, and don't worry about being good, because I sure as hell won't. I'll talk to you later."

"Okay," I agreed.

I told Gator to follow me to my apartment so I could shower and get ready for dinner. Inside, I stood in front of the floor-length mirror in the corner of my bedroom, admiring my reflection. I was dressed in a red, strapless, above-the-knee sheath dress and large, gold hoop earrings. My ensemble was sexy but classy, hopefully perfect for the evening. I bumped the ends of my hair, then stepped into my gold, open-toed heels, grabbed my handbag, and left my bedroom.

Gator was sitting on the sofa in my living room, flipping through the leather-bound album I kept under my coffee table. When he looked up at me with appreciation in his eyes and a smile on his face, I knew I had chosen the right dress. "You look beautiful," he said, standing.

"Thanks."

"I was just looking at your pictures," he stated, pointing at the album. "I hope you don't mind."

"No, it's cool."

"Are these your parents?" he questioned.

I walked over to the couch and looked down at the slightly faded picture of my mother and father. The photo had been taken when my mother was six months pregnant with me. The two of them were sitting on a small park bench, wearing smiles on their faces, with their arms wrapped tightly around one and another. "Yes, that's them," I said proudly. "My father was Oscar, and my mother is Anna."

"I can see where you get your beauty. Your mother is gorgeous."

"Thanks. That picture was taken before I was born," I said. I leaned forward, then flipped to the back of the album, where there was a photo of me, my mother, and my brother, a picture taken the previous Christmas. "This is Mama now."

The more recent photo showed the three of us in my parents' living room, standing in front of my mother's Christmas tree. There wasn't much difference in my mother's appearance. She still had the same mocha-colored skin and doe eyes, but her smile was much smaller.

"Is that an old boyfriend?" Gator asked, referring to Randall.

I laughed out loud. "No! That's my brother, Randall."

"Now that you mention it, you do slightly favor him," he said.

"Yeah, we've got the same eyes, I guess, but I look more like my mom. He takes after our daddy."

"Where was your father? Not home for the holidays?"

"Uh...that was a month after he died," I said, wincing and holding back a tear, "our first Christmas without him." I stared at the photo, reminiscing about how difficult that day had been for me, for all of us. A wave of sadness coursed through my body, causing me to tremble.

"I'm sorry, Diamond. If you don't mind me asking, how did he pass?"

"Heart attack," I said lowly.

"I'm sorry," he repeated.

"Me too." I sighed. "You woulda liked him. He was super cool and funny."

"Tell me more about him," Gator said, easing down on the sofa.

"What about our reservations?"

"They'll wait for us," he said, looking up at me. "Trust me. What did your father do for a living?"

"He owned an auto repair shop, off of Meridian Street," I said, sitting down beside him. "It was called Tinsley's Auto Repair."

"I've heard of that place," he said, nodding. "Your father had a good reputation in the city."

"That he did," I said proudly. "He was a good man, a hard worker who did a lot of his jobs for free or next to nothing. He wasn't in it for the money. He just loved what he did, and he loved helping others. He was one of the best men anyone could ever meet and the best father anyone could ever ask for."

"So, the two of you had a good relationship?" Gator concluded.

"We did." I sighed again. "Daddy tried his best to keep me and my brother out of trouble, but we're both so damn hardheaded. On the day he died, we got into this huge fight about my choice of friends. He was telling me right, but I just snapped at him about me being grown, and then I stormed out. Later, Randall stopped by the shop and found Daddy on the floor of his office, dead." I paused, attempting to fight back my tears. "I never got to apologize or tell him he was right. I hate that. I hate that my last words weren't, 'I love you.'"

"I'm sure he knew you did," Gator said empathetically.

"I know," I said, forcing a smile. "It just hurts that my last words to him were so harsh."

He reached out and stroked my forearm gently with the tips of his fingers, causing the fine hairs on my arms to stand up and tiny flutters to waft through my stomach. I looked at him, caught up in the comfort of his eyes, lost in the understanding within his gaze. There was a peaceful moment of silence between us, until Gator finally pulled his hand back.

"I was twelve when my mother, Sara, was murdered," he said, clearing his throat. "So, I know how it feels to lose a parent."

"Now that you mention it, I remember. Venetta told me, and she said the same thing," I said, remembering my conversation with his sister.

"I was there with her, with Mama, the night it happened," he continued solemnly. "I talked to her and held her in my arms until she took her last breath."

I listened quietly as Gator recounted to me the events that had led up to his mother's murder. Prior to Sara's death, she'd met a man named Raymond, whom Gator and Venetta both thought was an ideal candidate to date their beloved mother. Unfortunately, Raymond turned out to be a woman-beater.

"I came home and found Mama and Raymond in the middle of an argument," Gator said. "The bastard had been drinking heavily. I could smell the alcohol from the door. Mama was lying on the living room floor, curled up like a baby, and he was just standing over her, hittin' her repeatedly. I can still hear the sounds of his fist pounding against her flesh. I can still hear her whimpering." He paused, and then rose from the sofa, walked over to my living room window, and stared out the partially open blinds, into the dark night. "I attempted to pull him off of her, of course, but he was bigger and stronger and just knocked me outta the way like he was swatting at a damn fly. I was just a kid then, but he called me weak, said I was nothin' but a piece of shit, born to a whore. He kept beating her, cursing the whole time. I was angry and hurt. I felt weak and helpless, absolutely useless. Mama looked over at me, and her face was bloody and bruised, her eyes red and swollen from her tears. I saw the pain in her face and felt the hurt in her eyes, but that woman somehow managed to pull herself up off the floor and stand in front of Raymond like a bull ready to charge when he put his hands on her baby, on me."

I hung on Gator's words, envisioning the events as he continued on.

"Raymond just laughed and taunted her," he said. "He threatened to beat my ass like he was beatin' hers, but Mama warned him not to lay another finger on me or he'd regret it. While the two of them went back and forth, I crawled away and finally got up and ran into the kitchen. Raymond yelled after me, demanding that I come back and stand up to him like a man, even though I was only twelve. I made it to the kitchen drawer and grabbed the biggest butcher knife I could find. When I turned around, he was standing there with a smug grin on his face. 'Do it!' he said. I raised the knife, telling myself I had it in me to take the man's life. He laughed. He knew I couldn't do it. He grabbed me and pried the knife from my hands. Mama came up from behind him and started beating him in his back, ordering him to get the hell away from me, and he...that was when he did it. He didn't even blink twice. He just turned around and took that knife and..."

I watched Gator as he fell silent, undoubtedly lost in his memories, trapped in his own world. I stood and walked over to the window, then placed a comforting hand on his shoulder and stared at him. The pain was evident in his beautiful features, as evident as if he'd been wearing a scarlet letter on his chest.

Once he was able and ready to carry on, he explained that Raymond stabbed Sara three times, once in the neck and twice in the chest, then dropped the weapon on the floor and ran out of their house.

"Did they ever catch him?" I asked, referring to the authorities.

"No," he said. He turned and looked at me intensely. "*They* didn't, but I sure as hell did eventually." There was an eerie, almost frightening undertone in Gator's voice that told me things hadn't turned out well for Raymond when the two of them had run into each other again. "You know," he said, stepping away from me, "maybe you should go out with your girlfriend tonight instead."

"Why?" I asked, confused.

"I-I just think it's best. This probably wasn't a good idea," he stated, staring at me. The change in his demeanor was unsettling, and I knew he felt vulnerable and exposed after sharing such an emotional, intimate part of his life with me. It was clear that he wasn't accustomed to opening up like that, and as crazy as it seemed, that only made him more attractive.

"You don't talk about your family much do you?" I coaxed.

"In my line of work, the less people know about you and your loved ones, the better," he stated flatly.

"So why do you do it?"

"I was...pulled in," he said, ready to open up some more. "I accumulated a debt, and my only option was to repay it or die. I chose to live. After that, it became a lifestyle, one that pays better than your average nine-to-five. Once you know how it feels to have real money, you'll never be content with minimum wage."

I was tempted to ask just how much "real money" he was working with, but out of fear that he would think I was a gold-digger, I refrained. I truly wasn't impressed, but I sure was curious. After all, I hadn't forgotten that when we met, it was after he'd made a sale at the corner store. In my opinion, any man getting "real money" wouldn't be so blasé as to pull off some local dope-boy bullshit in broad daylight, in the middle of a minimart parking lot.

"I have an idea," I said, kicking off my heels. "Why don't we stay in? We can talk some more, get to know each other a little better."

He was silent for a moment, as if he was considering my suggestion.

"C'mon! You've been stalking me for weeks now," I teased. "You *owe* me a date."

"I don't consider it stalking." He laughed lightly. "I consider it…research."

"That's just a classy way of saying it."

He smiled, then shook his head, and I was pleased to see that his jovial mood was returning. "If that's what you prefer," he said. "I can call D'Alessandro's and have them deliver."

"You were really going to take me there?" I asked, impressed.

"Yes."

"I've only been there once, but I loved it," I said, recalling my one visit to the upscale Italian restaurant on the south side of the city. The first and only time I'd patronized the establishment was when my father had treated me to dinner for my twenty-first birthday. "Do they really deliver?"

"I know the owners," he informed me. "They'll deliver for me."

"Hmm. Well, I was thinking we could do something a little less serious," I stated. "Something fun, to lighten the mood."

"What did you have in mind?"

"I'll whip somethin' up for us," I said, walking toward my kitchen.

"You cook?" he called after me in utter surprise, as if it was impossible.

"Of course I do." I swung open my refrigerator door and frowned when I saw only a dozen eggs, a loaf of bread, a half-gallon of orange juice, and a pack of chicken bologna in a slightly greenish hue, likely past its prime. I shut the door and opened my pantry. *Hmm. I know I said something fun, but this guy doesn't seem like the Captain Crunch or Ramen type.*

"I'd love a home-cooked meal," he said, entering the kitchen.

"Um…okay," I said, sucking my teeth. "We just have one problem."

"And that is?"

"I'm fresh outta groceries." I laughed, slightly embarrassed.

"That's not a problem at all," he advised me, then pulled his cell phone out his jacket. "It's merely a temporary setback."

I waited as he instructed someone over the phone that he needed a delivery immediately, then handed me the phone.

"Tell him what you want and need," he said with a wink.

* * * * *

An hour later, Gator and I were sitting on my sofa, side by side, laughing and talking, basking in the aftermath of the homemade pizza and salad he'd prepared for us.

Thirty minutes after our phone call, an associate of Gator's, someone who worked at one of the local grocery stores, had shown up at my front door not only with the things I'd requested, but also cases of meat and other household items.

Once I had everything put away, Gator had removed his jacket and tie and instructed me to go in the living room and wait until *he* finished dinner. I'd graciously accepted, and to my delight, Gator had put it down in the kitchen and looked sexy as hell while he was doing it.

During our dinner conversation, he advised me that he held an associate's degree in business and was bilingual. I told him that I wanted to go to college or take up a trade, but my family's financial situation would not allow it, so it would have to wait.

"What happened to your father's business when he passed?"

"Mama didn't have anyone to run it, so she closed the shop and sold the building to help cover other bills," I said, shrugging my shoulders. "Daddy was a good man, but he was too kindhearted. That generosity left him in a lot of debt, with not enough income to cover it."

"What about Randall, your brother? He couldn't run the shop?"

"Pssh!" I laughed and took a sip of my tea. "My brother is the poster child for the jobless. He can't hold a job, and even if he could, he doesn't want to."

"Hmm. Maybe he just needs more motivation," Gator suggested.

"If having your own money doesn't motivate you, nothing will," I disputed. "Randall lives under the delusion that the world owes him something. I don't know what it's gonna take to make him understand that life doesn't owe us shit but death."

"Would you like me to talk to him? I can be very persuasive, and maybe I can hook him up with some steady income."

"Some of your 'real money,' huh?" I smirked. It was an interesting offer, but there was no way my enlisting a man who made his money illegally to talk to a man who wanted a free ride could work in my brother's or my family's favor. There was no way in hell working for Gator was the better alternative to not working at all. "I'll keep it in mind," I said politely, not wanting to insult or offend the man further.

"I'm serious, Diamond."

I paused to gather my words so I wouldn't come off as being rude, then finally asked the question that had been plaguing my mind: "I know you've got some pull. You proved that tonight."

"Yes," he said confidently.

"But if that's so, why were you at the store that day, pushing from your car?"

He gave me an arrogant grin, then exhaled. "Things aren't always what they seem, my dear. I wasn't pushing anything," he informed me. "The man you saw me with that day is an undercover cop."

"A cop? Shouldn't someone in your, uh...position try to avoid the police?" I asked, confused.

"Under normal circumstances, yes, but I'm not the norm...and neither are you." He looked at the diamond watch on his wrist, then stood. "I should get going."

I darted my eyes to the iron clock hanging on my living room wall and saw that it was a minute after midnight. A date hadn't ended that early for me since high school, and no man had ever volunteered to leave my place so early. I had to conclude that Gator was different, like he said, or married. I waited until he had his jacket and tie on, and then I stood up too. I wasn't ready for the evening to be over, but at the same time, I didn't want to experience that awkward moment of having to kick the brother out. All things considered, it was best to let him go if that was what he wanted to do. "Thank you for everything," I said sincerely. "I had a great time."

"The pleasure was all mine," he said, walking to the door. "It's still early. If you and your girlfriend wanna hit up a club, my offer still stands."

"Nah, I'm good," I said, following him. "I think I'll slide into my jammies and do some channel-surfing."

"Call me tomorrow, Diamond," he said, staring me in the eyes.

"I will."

Gator leaned in close to me, causing the place between my legs to jump slightly. I closed my eyes like a girl home from her senior prom, anxiously awaiting the touch of his lips against mine. When I felt his lips on my cheek instead, I opened my eyes and felt like a dumbass. I wondered if I'd given him the wrong impression, if I'd led him to believe I was not attracted to him or thought of him as an older brother or something. I waited for him to make another move, to try to plant a better-aimed kiss, but he never did.

"Goodnight," he said, then opened the door and stepped out into the night air.

"'Night," I said lowly before he closed the door behind him.

Chapter 3

*I*t was the first Saturday I'd had off in months, and I wasn't sure when I'd have another one again, so I planned to live it up a little and enjoy myself with my one and only friend. As an adult, I kept a small circle of friends and only spent time with a select few, mostly my girlfriend, Shaundra, and a male friend by the name of Alvin Staten.

Alvin had recently caught a possession charge and would be spending the next three years in County, so we hadn't been hanging out much as of late. While my father was still living, he'd warned me that Alvin was on a one-way bus to nowhere, and although I'd defended my friend right up to the day of my daddy's death, it didn't take long for me to realize that my father knew best.

Shaundra and I met a year earlier, at a job fair held at the Von Braun Center. She was working in the booth for Verizon Wireless at the time, since she was a floor supervisor in their call center. In the beginning, the two of us conversed about the positions they had open and their benefits, but somewhere throughout the course of those dull career conversations, I noticed a physical attraction to her. When she finally asked for my number and asked if I'd like to hang out sometime, I knew the attraction was mutual.

That night, we went to a local club, Fatty's, on the south side of the city, a real hip-hop, hood place, complete with half-dressed females, shaking their asses like they were getting paid, and saggy-pants-wearing, draw's-showing brothers who looked like they wanted nothing more than to get laid. The club was completely outside my element, but I had a good time and was in good company.

After we left Fatty's, we went back to Shaundra's place and had several drinks. The alcohol loosened us up a lot and led to the two of us getting to know each other on a much more intimate level, and we'd been best friends and occasional lovers ever since.

Now, the two of us were set to attend an exclusive, all-white party hosted by the 103.1 deejay, Jo-Ski Love. It was to be held at Crossroads, a nightclub downtown. Shaundra had managed to score VIP passes to the event from Blair, and naturally, I was all for it.

Earlier in the day, I'd thought about calling Gator to let him know I'd had a good time on our date, but I'd decided against it. A small part of me hoped he'd call me instead. When he didn't, I concluded that after actually spending time with me, he'd discovered he wasn't as interested as he originally thought he was.

When Shaundra and I arrived at Crossroads, the first thing we did was hit the dance floor. We moved and dropped like one unit. Once we were satisfied and damn near perspiring, we exited the floor and made our way upstairs to the VIP lounge, on the second floor. It was enclosed in plexiglass, offering a view down into the rest of the club. Those unfortunate souls not lucky enough to be invited into the lounge could easily look up and see what they were missing. One long, velvet-covered sectional couch wrapped around the wall, and large speakers were in every corner. It was also equipped with a fully stocked bar.

Shaundra and I sat there watching the crowd, enjoying our vodka and pineapple juice and listening to Jackie Chain, performing on the stage below. To my delight, with the exception of the waitress and a security guard, there were only four other people in the lounge, despite the fact that the bottom floor was packed with men and women sporting their best white attire. I had chosen a short, body-hugging, one-shoulder dress and red stilettos, and my hair was done up in a weave that stopped just past my shoulders. Shaundra's lace corset dress stopped several inches above her knees and flattered her petite frame. Her low-cut, natural hair was adorned with brown highlights that complemented her bronze skin.

An hour and a half after our arrival, she received a text from her friend who'd scored our passes. "He's on his way up," she said, flashing her eyes at me. "Trust me, baby, you're gonna love him."

I really didn't care if I liked the man or not. My only concern was having a good time.

A few seconds later, a tall man with deep, dark chocolate skin entered the lounge. He was dressed in a white linen shirt and matching slacks, with white, gold-tipped shoes on his feet. His bald head glistened under the dim lights as he stepped over to the booth. "Hello, ladies," he said in a sultry, baritone voice. "I'm happy the two of you could make it." He looked from Shaundra to me, with an expression of admiration stamped on his face.

"Blair, this is my girl, Diamond," Shaundra introduced.

"It's nice to meet you, Diamond."

"Likewise," I said politely. I nonchalantly scanned my eyes over the man's physique and silently decided that Shaundra had done quite well. Not only was he fine, but it was obvious he had some pull at the club. The only thing better than a man who could make things happen is a sexy man who could make things happen.

"Mind if I join you?" Blair asked.

"Not at all." Shaundra grinned and slid to her left on the couch, allowing room for Blair to sit between us.

"So…what's on the agenda tonight?" Blair asked, rubbing his hand over Shaundra's thigh.

In that moment, I realized I didn't have a clue what Shaundra had agreed to in exchange for our entrance in the event. I was so happy to have those tickets that I hadn't thought about what they might cost. I loved my friend, but when it came to men, she didn't always use her best judgment, or her basic instincts, and she was known for getting caught up in bullshit.

"We'll see," she said, batting her eyelashes.

Speak for yourself, I thought. My plan was to sip, shake my ass, and go home alone.

"Hopefully, I'll be able to influence your decision," Blair said, looking at me.

"Humph," I mumbled, then took a sip from my glass.

Twenty minutes later, my mind was made up. Blair had influenced my decision; I'd decided to leave. The man had been working my nerves, rambling about his career in the music industry and constantly name-dropping. It took every ounce of my willpower not to tell him that I didn't give two sweaty fucks about the artists he claimed he knew. Shaundra, on the other hand, soaked up his bullshit like toilet paper on a wet ass. I picked up my glass, tossed the liquid back, and puckered as it went down my throat, burning all the way. It was my third straight shot since Blair had joined us in the lounge, and I was starting to feel a buzz.

"You okay, boo?" Shaundra asked, looking past Blair and at me.

"I'm good." I sighed. "Bored as shit, but good."

"What's wrong, sexy?" Blair asked, slipping his arm around my waist. "Tell Daddy what you need."

Daddy? I laughed hysterically, drawing unwanted attention to myself and realizing I'd gone past buzzed and was walking the drunken trenches.

The music changed, and Twista's "Get it Wet" came blaring through the speakers. Blair looked at me, then leaned over and whispered something in Shaundra's ear. I watched as the two of them went back and forth for a brief moment, and then Shaundra looked at me and gave me a sweet smile.

"Let's go to the ladies' room," she suggested, extending her hand to me.

I grabbed her hand with one hand and my clutch with the other and allowed her to pull me to my feet. She held my hand tightly and led me out through the crowd to the ladies' room. Inside the restroom, she informed me that Blair wanted us to join him for a "private party" at the Embassy Suites. She put emphasis on the word "private," clearly indicating the man wanted to fuck.

"No deal," I said, shaking my head.

"Diamond, I'm sort of diggin' him, baby," she whined.

"Then you go right ahead," I suggested. "Just drop me off at the crib first." I wanted no parts of Blair, but I wasn't about to discourage Shaundra from getting what she wanted after I was home safe.

"I want you to come too," she purred. "Please?"

"No," I said, staring at my reflection in the bathroom mirror. I brushed a loose strand of hair back in place with my fingers, then redirected my attention to Shaundra.

She looked disappointed and defeated. "Please, boo?" she begged again. "He's good people, Diamond. Trust me. Just come with us, and I'll take care of the rest. Please say you'll come."

After she continued begging for several seconds, I finally agreed. If nothing else, I'd at least get a decent meal out of Blair in exchange for my company and for having to put up with all his bullshit. Besides, if I didn't go with her, she would have gone alone, and I knew I wouldn't feel comfortable leaving her alone with that man.

We returned to the lounge, and Shaundra announced to Blair that we would be joining him at the hotel. We waited for him to take care of the tab, and then the three of us departed the club together.

Outside of Crossroads, there was a full moon overhead, casting a strange, silvery-blue glow in the night sky. Although there were several people standing outside the front of the club, there were only a few vehicles maneuvering down the street.

"Where you parked?" Blair asked Shaundra.

"At the old bank, a couple streets over."

"I'm across the street in the garage," he said. "I'll drive you to your car."

"Sounds good," I said, relieved that I wouldn't have to walk on my drunken legs in those stilettos.

Shaundra cut her eyes in my direction. I knew she was expecting me to turn down the man's offer, but it was the best offer Blair had made all night. We would have had to walk at least two blocks to get to her car, and there was no way in hell I was going to put any more strain on my already aching feet. My heels were sexy, but cheap; a bad combination for twerking in the club and then having to walk.

We followed Blair across the street, to the second level of the parking garage. He pulled a set of keys from his pocket, then hit the disarm button on the key fob, unlocking the doors to a black Mercedes C-250 luxury sedan parked in the spot marked "B-4."

"Ooh! This is nice," Shaundra said, climbing in on the front passenger side.

I agreed with her but chose not to express it; instead, I settled in the seat behind her, relaxing against the cool leather.

"Thanks," Blair said with a proud grin. He then shut each of our doors, strolled around to the driver side, and slipped behind the wheel. He revved up the engine, cranked up the radio, put it in reverse, and backed out of the parking space.

The bass coming from the speakers tickled my back, and Tupac's "Ghetto Gospel" brought back memories of my father. My daddy, Oscar, was a God-fearing, God-serving man, but he loved Pac and Biggie with a passion. It wasn't out of the ordinary for me to climb in the cab of his

F-150 and find either of them in the deck. The memories of the times we'd shared brought a smile to my face and made me laugh.

Suddenly, the sound of tires screeching, followed by Blair abruptly cutting his wheel to the right and laying on his horn, jolted me out of my walk down memory lane. "Stupid-ass motherfucker!" he yelled out the window. "Watch where you going in that raggedy piece of shit!"

I looked out the front windshield at the car that had zoomed by us, almost sideswiping Blair's vehicle in the process. The driver proceeded on, like nothing had happened, and stopped at the entrance gate of the parking facility. We watched as the driver briefly exchanged words with the silver-haired man in the booth, then sped out of the parking lot.

"Dumbass," Blair grumbled, pulling up to the booth. "What's up, man?" he said to the guard.

"Ya'll all right in here?" the man asked, peering inside the car. "Looked like you almost had a fender bender back there."

"Yes, sir," I said respectfully.

"Nah, that bitch almost made me bust his head," Blair corrected.

"Hmm. Well, I'm glad it didn't lead to that." The old man laughed. "We don't want no trouble."

"I feel ya. Baby, reach in the glove department and hand me that ticket," Blair instructed Shaundra.

Obeying his request, Shaundra opened the glove compartment and removed the ticket I assumed had been assigned to Blair when he'd originally parked his car in the garage.

The roaring sound of a car approaching pulled my attention back to the windshield. A rusty, green 1972 Chevy Monte Carlo with dark-tinted windows came to a screeching halt in front of the entrance, the same car that had exited the garage moments earlier. In an instant, the back door swung open.

"Oh? This nigga want it?" Blair said, sucking his teeth. "His ass gon' get it real—"

"C'mon, son," the booth attendant said gently. "Trouble is easy to get into but hard to get out of."

I watched the car, waiting for the people inside to make their next move, hoping things were not going to get out of hand. I hated when grown men acted like children, and it happened far too often.

"Naw, fuck that," Blair said. He threw his hands up, providing the unknown parties in the car an open invitation to a confrontation. "What's up?" he taunted.

The sound of a cocking gun sent my heart racing, and fear penetrated me to my core. I looked out the window at the old man, staring at the barrel of the sawed-off shotgun he was holding in his hands with a white-knuckled grip.

"What the—"

The clap of gunfire pierced the air as Blair's words and life were cut short by the bullet that penetrated his forehead. The echo of Shaundra's petrifying screams danced in my ringing ears, and my heart pounded in the cavity of my chest, like a beast trying to free itself from a cage. I heard the gun pump again. Another shot rang out, and Shaundra's body fell against the passenger side door.

The old man looked at me with eyes clear as rain and aimed the gun at me. Silent tears poured from my eyes as I gasped, awaiting the cold darkness that I was sure would accompany death. That moment, however, did not come. I wasn't sure what happened, but the gun must have jammed, because the man stared at me briefly before running and jumping in the awaiting Chevy.

* * * * *

I pushed through the glass double-doors of the North Precinct, still in a daze from the events I had witnessed hours earlier. The sound of the gun and my friend's cries floated in my head like a balloon being carried in the wind. I stood in the parking lot, staring down at my dress, at the crimson stains that were subtle reminders of the horror my eyes had beheld.

After the Chevy drove off, I had sat there, frozen in place, staring out the window. I didn't know how many seconds had passed until one of the pedestrians from the street rushed over to offer their assistance. I remembered stepping out of the car onto the concrete, then opening Shaundra's door. She'd fallen into my arms like a shattered porcelain doll, blood gushing from the lethal wound in her neck. I'd begged and pleaded with her to breathe, but she was already gone. I'd sat on the cold concrete, holding her in my arms, until the man who came to offer his assistance and pulled me away, screaming as loud as my lungs would allow.

When the police had arrived I told them what had happened, what I'd seen and heard, and then I'd willingly traveled with two uniformed female officers to the station. Three grueling hours later, I was free to go.

One of the officers offered to take me home and provide security for the night, but I declined, advising her that I would call my brother and stay at his place. I hadn't talked to Randall since the day I'd refused to lend him money, but I hoped he would come through for me now, when I needed him the most. I dug inside my bag and removed my cell phone. My hands shook uncontrollably while I dialed Randall's number, and the phone rang four times before his voicemail came on. "Randall, call me...please," I begged, and my tears begin to surface again.

I ended the call and tried calling again, but it went straight to voicemail. I didn't want to call a cab, not only because of how much it would cost, but also because I didn't want to go home and be alone. *What if the man comes back to finish what he started? To make sure there are no witnesses?* He didn't know me personally, and even the officers agreed that Shaundra and I were just in the wrong place at the wrong time, caught in the middle of a plot that was clearly set for Blair long before that night, but that didn't make it any easier to cope with.

I began to call my mother, but quickly stopped dialing, knowing she'd be far too worried. Besides that, I didn't want another me-and-your-daddy-told-you-so lecture about my drinking and partying.

I scrolled through my text messages, in a panic and feeling like I needed to call someone, and I just so happened to spot Gator's number. I pressed the call button and waited, practically holding my breath.

"Hello?"

"Hey. It's Diamond. I'm sorry for calling so late, but—"

"I know who you are," he said, "and you're fine...in every conceivable way."

"Thanks. Um, I hate to ask you this," I said, running my fingers through my hair, "but something bad happened." I went on to tell him all the gory details of what had taken place, my voice shaking all the while. It was no easy task to talk through the lump in my throat and all the tears streaming down my face.

"I'm on my way," he said without hesitation.

It took Gator less than thirty minutes to arrive at the station. The moment he stepped out of his car, he took one look at me and pulled me into his arms, allowing me to saturate his silk shirt with my tears. His arms felt like a steel blanket around me, secure and strong. I didn't want him to let me go; if given the choice at that moment, I would have allowed him to hold me forever.

After a few wordless moments of him comforting me, the two of us got in his car and left. I gazed out the window, focusing on nothing in particular as the streetlights zoomed by in a foggy blur. I kept seeing Blair's and Shaundra's dead bodies flashing through my head, haunting me repeatedly.

"Where would you like me to take you?" Gator questioned gently. "Your mom's? Or, if you'd prefer, I can put you up in a nice hotel."

"Home," I whispered, looking at him.

"Okay. What's your mama's address? Just let me put it in my GPS, and I'll—"

"No, Gator. I wanna go home…with you."

He pulled his eyes from the road and looked at me, long enough to gauge my expression.

I nodded, confirming that he'd heard me correctly.

He redirected his attention to the road and signaled to take the I-565 exit. The remainder of our drive was silent, with the exception of my occasional emotional outbreak. By the time we arrived in Cliff's Cove, the nice neighborhood where Gator lived, my throat felt like it was on fire, and my eyes were swollen to the point that they ached.

Gator's home was nestled cozily in the back of the subdivision on a cul-de-sac, surrounded by two empty lots. It was a beautiful red-brick, ranch-style house, situated on a small hill, with a circular driveway in front of it. Inside, I stood in the foyer admiring the simple, but immaculate, design. There were hardwood floors and crown molding throughout, along with wooden accents and black art gracing the walls.

Following Gator through the living room, I observed the leather and wood furnishings. He led me to the master bedroom and opened the door. The gorgeous room was furnished with a king-sized bed with a large cherry headboard, a matching armoire, a dresser with mirror, and two nightstands.

"I'll run you a bath," he stated, turning to look at me. "There are t-shirts in the bottom drawer of the armoire, if you'd like to wear something more, uh…comfortable," he said gently, looking at my bloodied white dress.

I nodded and watched as he disappeared into the master bath. I stepped out of my shoes and looked around the room, admiring the paintings on the walls. Finally, I locked eyes with my reflection in the dresser mirror, and when I did, I shuddered. The image of me standing there, with my little makeup smeared, my hair going every which way, and my stained white dress was simply too much to bear. I pulled the dress up and over my head and quickly tossed it down on the carpeted floor. I stood in front of the mirror again, this time wearing nothing but my panties and the tiny goose bumps that covered my skin.

"Diamond…" Gator called from behind me.

I turned around slowly to face him.

He hesitated momentarily, allowing his gaze to flow across my body, penetrating my skin with the beam in his eyes. "Your water's ready, sweetheart," he finally said, then looked away. He remained silent while walking past me, then exited through the bedroom door.

* * * * *

Physically, my body felt better after my bath, but emotionally, I was still a wreck. I couldn't believe my best friend was gone and that my life had almost been taken along with hers and Blair's. The dark, angry, sad feelings coursing through me were surreal, and there were seconds when I thought and hoped that it had all just been a bad dream, a life-altering nightmare from which I would wake up at any moment. *Why has death come into my life again? This isn't fair…not so soon after…* After the death of my father, I'd naïvely thought it would be years before I'd have to lose another loved one. I knew it was a silly notion, a ridiculous hope to hold on to, but in mourning, hope was all I had.

I entered the living room, carrying my clothes and shoes in my hand, wearing a gray, short-sleeved t-shirt I'd found in Gator's drawer. I saw Gator reclining on the sofa, dressed in sweats and a plain white tank-top that revealed the tight molding of his sculptured arms and chest. "Hey," I said, getting his attention.

"Let me take those." He stood to his feet and held out his arms for my dirty clothes. "You hungry?" he asked, taking the items out of my hands.

"No…but thanks."

"Have a seat," he instructed. "I'll be right back."

After he left me alone, I contemplated sitting down but chose to walk across the floor to the fireplace instead. On the mantel were four white pillar candles, surrounding a framed picture of an attractive caramel-skinned woman and a little boy.

"Me and my mother," Gator said, causing me to jump slightly.

"She was beautiful."

"Yes, she was," he stated, walking up to me.

"And you were such a handsome little guy," I said, looking up at him. "Just like you still are." When he responded only with silence, I said sincerely, "Thank you for everything, for letting me come here and the bath and clothes and—"

"I want you here, Diamond. You're more than welcome...always."

I reached up and stroked his face with my fingertips, searching his eyes. I wasn't sure what I was looking for in those chocolate pools, if anything at all, but something inside of me yearned for him, screaming that I needed him. I wanted Gator to ease my pain, to relieve just an ounce of my sorrow in any way he knew how. Standing on my tiptoes, I pressed my lips to his.

He took a step back and looked at me like a teacher who'd just crossed the line with a pupil, not at all the reaction I'd expected. "I think you should get some rest," he said. "You've had a long night. You can sleep in my bed, since it's the most comfortable, and I'll be right down the hall if you need me." He turned, preparing to leave.

Sleep was the last thing I wanted at that moment; I was terrified of what dreams might come if I did close my eyes. I grabbed his arm, prepared to beg him to stay. "Please," I whispered, pulling him back to me. "Please, Gator? I don't wanna be alone—not tonight." I placed my hand on the back of his neck, guiding his face down, leading his lips to mine.

"Diamond."

"Please?" I begged, the same way Shaundra had begged me to get into Blair's car.

Our lips met again, and this time, he allowed them to linger a moment longer. I parted mine, welcoming his warm tongue, anticipating it with passion and gratitude. Gator wrapped his arms around me, pressing his chest against my breast, devouring my lips with his. I felt a surge of heat in between my legs as Gator trailed kisses down my neck, across my shoulder blade, then back up to my lips again, leaving me breathless in the process.

He released his hold on me, freeing my lips from their pleasurable captivity. "Do you know what you're doing?" he asked. "What you're getting yourself into?"

"Yes," I said, attempting to kiss him again.

"Diamond..." he said, stopping me. The stone look in his eyes expressed the seriousness behind his question. "You've been through a lot tonight, and—"

"I know that," I snapped, running my fingers through my hair. "I was there, remember? I don't wanna think about that, to think about anything right now! Right now, I just want this. I just want you. Please?"

There was only silence for an answer.

Refusing to further humiliate myself, I exited the room and returned to the master bedroom, slamming the heavy door behind me. I sat on the edge of the bed, feeling hurt, afraid, and rejected.

A few seconds later, Gator opened the door and entered the room. He looked like a king as he stepped over to the bed and stopped in front of me. Easing down to his knees, he knelt before me on the floor. In utter silence, I watched as his hands traveled up my calves to my thighs, pushing the shirt up around my waist. Our eyes remained engaged as I pulled the material up over my head and tossed it to the floor. His eyes cruised my body slowly, taking in every inch of my skin. He grabbed both of my ankles and lifted them up to his lips, forcing me to push back on the bed. He parted his lips slightly, then exhaled, blowing warm air across each of my toes before kissing and sucking them one by one. After he'd tended to all ten digits, he pushed my thighs apart, then slowly moved his way up, leaving a trail of warm kisses along my inner thigh. My lower region tingled as Gator blew on my clit and stroked its hood with his thumb. I shuddered as he flicked his tongue across my clit with one swift stroke, then returned to tantalizing blows. He rubbed my chocolate knob softly, making small circles with his thumb, pushing my hormones over the edge. I stared into his dark eyes, anxious for the moment when he would dive in. If anticipation had been fatal, I would have been dead. Flutters erupted in my stomach as he trailed kisses from my knees up between my thighs, until finally burying his face between my legs. He rolled his tongue back and forth inside my pussy, causing chills to course through me from head to toe.

"Mmm…" I moaned, running my fingers over his head.

Gator pulled away, just long enough to remove his clothes, then climbed back on the bed. He kissed me softly while positioning himself between my legs. He stroked and dug deep inside my pussy, rotating his hips, serenading my lower walls with his dick. He held my right leg in his palm while I locked my left leg around his waist. Elevating my hips, I arched my back, and rotated my hips, throwing it back. He dropped his grip on my leg, then grabbed my waist with both hands, lifting me up off the bed.

"Shit!" I groaned in pleasure and wrapped my arms around his shoulder, my legs around his waist, while pressing my face against his neck. I closed my eyes while flexing my pleasure muscles, holding on to his man for dear life.

"Do you know what you're doing?" he asked again, then grunted lowly. He flipped me back onto the bed, and increased his thrusting speed. He beat the corners of my pussy viciously, causing me to scream out in ecstasy. "Do you?" he asked again.

"No…" I moaned. "No!"

* * * * *

"I can help you find the person responsible," Gator stated, stroking my back.

The two of us lay in each other's arms, basking in the afterglow of what I could only describe as true lovemaking.

"How?"

"I have my ways."

"What happens after you find him?" I asked curiously.

"What do you want to happen?"

"Justice."

"Then justice will be served," he said. "However, my idea of justice might be different than yours."

"I'll take my chances."

"So…what happens next, Diamond?" he asked, tightening his arms around me.

"What do you want to happen?"

"You to give me your loyalty and love."

"I think I can do that," I said without hesitation.

"You may want to think about it Diamond. I take both of them seriously."

"If my loyalty and love is what you want, Gator, they're all yours."

Chapter 4

When the police finally located the man responsible for my best friend's murder, they discovered that he'd been tortured and mutilated to the point of being unrecognizable. I didn't necessarily agree with the methods Gator had employed, but part of me felt some bittersweet satisfaction that justice had been served, albeit a crueler justice than I would have imagined. His cohorts, the other men in the rusty, green car, were later apprehended; as it turned out, they had been disputing with Blair over a breached contract. Truly, Shaundra and I had just been in the wrong place at the wrong time.

While losing my girlfriend was my greatest regret from that night, some good came out of it. Her tragedy led me to grow closer with Gator, the best man I ever known next to my father. Six months after that tragic night, the night Gator and I had made love for the first time to soothe my pain, Gator had asked me to be his wife, and I'd accepted without a second thought.

"Diamond, you know nothing about that man!" Mama ranted, pacing back and forth across her living room floor.

"I know I love him, Mama, and that's enough," I explained.

"You've known him six months, Diamond. That isn't love. It's just... lust."

I had been attempting to explain to my mother for the last half-hour why I was going to marry Gator, and I'd hoped she would offer me her blessing. That hope had fizzled out within the first sixty seconds of our conversation.

"What does he do for a living? Who are his people?" Mama raged. "I know nothing about him."

"Mama, he's good to me," I pleaded. "That's all that matters."

"Money doesn't make a man good, Diamond. And furthermore, what's he plan to—"

The front door opened, and Gator stepped in, interrupting our conversation. I'd originally asked him to wait in the car for me, but much like my pleas for my mother's approval, my request had fallen on deaf ears. "Mrs. Tinsley," he said, standing with his hands clasped in front of him. "Diamond is going to be my wife. It would please both of us if you would give us your blessing and agree to share in our new life. However, if you choose not to do so, I will respect your decision, but it won't change a thing. Diamond and I are getting married, no matter what anyone else has to say about it."

Oh shit, I thought, as few people I knew had the nerve to stand up to my mama.

Mama stared at him like he'd lost his mind. "You do *not* have my blessing," she said firmly, "and you never will."

"Thank you for your honesty, ma'am," Gator said politely. He extended his hand to me. "Enjoy your evening, Mrs. Tinsley."

Speechless, I took his hand and followed him out the door.

"Diamond, if you leave with that man, you are no longer part of this family!" Mama yelled after me.

Gator held the car door open while I climbed in. "Our flight leaves in an hour," he said, sliding in behind the wheel. "Are you sure this is what you want, Diamond? I'm not the kind of man who just lets people drop in and out of his life. Once you become a part of my world, there's no turning back. Baby, if you're feeling even an ounce of doubt that this is what you want, you need to let me know now."

I stared into his beautiful brown eyes, concentrating on every word he said. "I want this." I smiled. "I want it more than anything I've ever wanted before."

"For life?"

"For life." I leaned in and kissed him softly on the lips, anxious to see what our future would hold. It pained me that my mother was so upset, but Gator had all the love I'd ever need. If I'd ever been sure of anything, I was sure of that.

Chapter 5

Five years later...

I sat in the corner of Club Delight, relaxing against the soft leather booth and sipping on my third glass of Kinky for the night. The bright electric blue and neon green lights flashed around the room, creating a spectacular show, while the bass blaring from the stereo speakers ignited my inner desire to move my hips. I maintained my composure and watched the crowd. On any given Friday night, the exclusive club located on the island of Ambergris Caye, was packed with an array of partygoers, and this night was no different. The dance floor was a melting pot of men and women representing almost every nationality, shaking their asses and turning their glasses up. On all four sides of the dance floor were long runways, flanked with spotlights, each housing two metal poles.

I was sitting in the VIP section near the stage with Jonah, my husband's second-in-command. He'd been assigned to accompany me until Gator arrived. Jonah was a tall brother with skin the color of dark chocolate, two hundred pounds of modest, but lean muscle, with a round face, full cheeks, and low-cut hair flowing with deep waves. His long, curly eyelashes and big, brown eyes made him look more like the boy next door than a bodyguard. He was dressed in dark slacks and a button-down shirt, a dramatic change from his normal jeans and polo shirt.

A loud *gong* resounded throughout the room, indicating that it was now midnight, time for all those hogging the dance floor to step off and make room for the real entertainment. At the stroke of midnight, the music changed, the lighting softened, and the atmosphere became more sexually exhilarating. The dancers hit the stages and began to slither around their respective poles. The deejay, a slim Rastafarian with shoulder-length dreads, made his traditional midnight announcement that it was time to slow the party down. I watched as the crowd on the floor dissipated and eight bikini-clad female dancers strutted out in a single-file line.

I held my glass up for Jonah to pour me another drink and shot glances from one stage to the other, until my eyes landed on a tall, cinnamon-complexioned female. She wasn't on stage, but was sitting in a booth near the exit door. I'd seen her in the club before, and upon further examination, I recognized her as the assistant manager. Our eyes locked momentarily, until I redirected my attention to the voluptuous eye-candy that now gyrated and bounced against the poles.

Out of the eight dancers, one in particular stood out, a far cry hotter than the rest. She had skin the color of milk and hair the color of night; it swung past her shoulders and stopped in the middle of her back. The shimmering gold two-piece outfit she was stuffed into could hardly contain her large, round breasts and ample, perfectly sculptured ass. I followed her every move, admiring how she rolled her wide hips back and forth atop her stilettos as she pranced and slid around the pole. She grabbed the pole with both hands, then pulled herself up off the floor. She slowly spread her legs apart, stretching them out until they were parallel with the pole. She held that position while the crowd went wild, tossing bill after bill onto the stage. I admired her strength as she balanced her body without struggle or hesitation, like an acrobat, entirely suspended in midair. When the tempo of the music changed, she slowly inched her legs up, then locked her ankles around the metal pole before releasing her hands. She hung upside down, rotating her hips and bouncing her crotch against the pole, grinding like she was riding a dick.

"That's one bad chick," I whispered in appreciation.

After the dancers completed their sexy show, each stepped seductively off the stage and dispersed out into the crowd. I watched as they approached the onlookers, undoubtedly on a mission to secure an additional paycheck for the night.

The female who had captured my attention stepped up to a distinguished-looking gentleman dressed in a tan linen shirt with matching pants. He appeared to be in his mid-thirties, and from the way he extended his arms to greet her, it was clear that the two of them had a connection outside the customer relationship. She leaned in and welcomed his embrace, then kissed his cheek before sauntering off, toward the other woman I'd noticed earlier.

"Gator texted," Jonah said, getting my attention. "He's running behind, but he'll be here as soon as possible."

"Of course," I said sarcastically.

In the five years Gator and I had been married, I had grown accustomed to his late arrivals and early departures; they came with the package. The first two years of our union had been better than I ever could have imagined. Not only had Gator showered me with gifts, but he'd also given me his undivided attention, day in and day out. Of course there were rare moments when he was called away for business, but those moments had always been far and few in between. But the more money Gator made, the less time I received. I knew what I was signing up for when I said, "I do," and I loved the benefits of being his wife, but it was frustrating at times as he grew busier and busier.

On this particular night, Gator and I were supposed to be celebrating our anniversary, but I tried to make the best of it. *I guess my frustration's a minor sacrifice in comparison to the lifestyle he's giving me, right?* From trips around the globe to jewels and a wardrobe that would have made a supermodel want to slit her throat from envy, I had a life most couldn't even afford to dream about. Still, even though it was only the first anniversary Gator had missed, I feared he would eventually start skipping them all.

"Why didn't he text me?" I questioned, slightly annoyed. I looked at my phone, which was sitting right there on the table in front of me, utterly silent, with no missed calls or messages. I hated it when Gator talked to me through his employees, as if he didn't have time to contact me directly.

Jonah pressed a button on his phone, then secured it back in the case on the waist of his pants.

I looked at him, still awaiting his response. "Well?"

He exhaled, then lowered his eyes. "Would you like another drink?" he asked, ignoring my question.

Jonah had grown accustomed to my temperamental outbursts and rarely ever entertained them. He knew that no matter how much I vented, the bottom line was that I would cooperate and always do what my husband requested, not because I was fearful of the repercussions of doing otherwise, but merely because I understood that living the good life sometimes meant compromises. I, just like Jonah and everyone else, would choose compromising over broke anytime.

"I'm good," I said, standing. I knew I was quickly approaching my limit, and the last thing I wanted to be was drunk. "Let's go."

Jonah immediately rose from his seat, then stepped back, giving me room to slip out of the booth. He extended his elbow to me, allowing me to wrap my arm around his before escorting me through the crowd toward the entrance.

We were almost at the door when the dancer I'd been eyeing earlier stepped in front of us. "Excuse me," she said in a thick Spanish accent. "Leaving so soon?" She stared at me with eyes the color of spruce tree needles, puckering her full lips.

"Yes," I said politely.

Jonah moved to step around her, but the woman blocked his path. I looked at him, gauging his expression. His eyebrows inched up, and his lips grew tight. I could see in his eyes that he disapproved of the move the woman had made. I, on the other hand, respected her aggression and her bravery. It was obvious that she was new or had yet to be familiarized with my family name; otherwise, she would have been aware of Jonah's reputation and would never, under any circumstances, have gotten in his way. I tugged lightly on his arm, letting him know to remain calm and that I wasn't ready to walk away.

"You're new here," I said, observing her facial features. She had a heart-shaped face with slightly slanted eyes and a wide nose. Unlike her body, her face wasn't beautiful, but the way she looked at me with those bluish-green eyes pulled me right in.

"I am. This is my first night," she said, batting her eyes at me.

"You did an excellent job."

"I'm flattered that you noticed." She smiled sweetly.

I nodded and smiled back at her.

"My name is Lisette," she said. "And you are?"

"Leaving," Jonah answered before I could respond.

I looked at him and shook my head. It was unlike him to be so short with a female. Obviously, the woman had stepped on his male ego when she'd hindered our departure.

"Seems your husband doesn't like me," Lisette said, cocking her head to the side. She licked her bottom lip slowly, then smirked while looking at Jonah. "It doesn't matter though. I'm only interested in you, not him," she said with an obviously suggestive, seductive undertone in her voice.

I felt the place between my legs moisten as the two of us continued to stare at each other. "Uh…this is not my husband," I said, "and my name is Diamond."

"Diamond?" she repeated. "A beautiful name for an exquisite woman. You know what they say."

"What?" Jonah said gruffly.

"A Diamond is a girl's best friend."

He rolled his eyes and shook his head. I knew that flattering the patrons was one of the duties that came along with Lisette's job, but my instincts told me the attention she was showing me was much more than part of her hustle.

"We should go," Jonah said, looking at me.

I looked from him to Lisette, trying to decide whether or not I was ready to end my conversation with the woman. I was ready to leave the club, but I was not ready for my flirtatious banter with Lisette to end. "Give us a moment, would you, Jonah?" I said, releasing my grip on his arm.

"Diamond, I think we oughtta—"

"One moment," I said sternly, cutting him off.

He hesitated before stepping away and leaving the two of us alone. He stood by the entrance of the club, watching me, close enough to get to me in the event that something happened but far enough that he couldn't overhear our conversation.

"Protective, isn't he?" Lisette laughed.

"He's just doing his job," I said.

"Lucky man. Must be a pleasure to protect such a lovely piece of art," she purred.

I smiled slightly. "That man who greeted you when you stepped off the stage…" I said, changing the subject, "…was he your husband?"

Her eyes lit up, and she smiled; I assumed she was pleased to know I'd been watching her. "Just a friend," she said. "It's difficult to keep a man when you're…well, in my line of work."

"Understandable," I said.

"Besides," she said, "I prefer the company of ladies." She scanned her eyes from mine down to the open toe Giuseppe heels I was wearing, then back up again. "Especially beautiful ones."

"So you're—"

"I'm whatever you need me to be," she said seductively.

I looked at her and smiled. "Grab your things, Lisette," I said.

"Why? Am I going somewhere?"

"Not if you keep me waiting," I said, then walked away. I stopped in front of Jonah. "She's getting her things. She'll be joining me at the villa."

He looked at me and shook his head. "Diamond, I don't think that's a good idea," he said firmly.

"It's not up for discussion," I stated.

"Gator would disapprove," he said.

"If my husband wanted to decide who I will entertain for our anniversary, his ass would be here with me," I said, flipping my hair over my shoulder. "I refuse to spend my anniversary alone."

Jonah really was just doing his job, following proper protocol. Gator would have raised hell if he had known I was planning to entertain a strange woman for the night. However, I was feeling defiant and buzzed. I figured if the shit hit the fan, which it inevitably would when I told Gator about my little escapade, I'd just blame it on the alcohol and his absence.

Jonah studied my expression for a brief moment then pulled out his cell phone. He pressed a number, then held the phone to his ear.

He's actually calling Gator? He's tattling on me? I could feel my anger slowly beginning to surface. I planned to tell my husband how I was going to spend my night, but I did not appreciate the fact that Jonah was taking it upon himself to beat me to it. Gator would be pissed anyway, but hearing the information from his soldier would only make things worse. I folded my arms across my breasts, then rolled my eyes while continuing to stare at him.

"Bring the car around," he spoke into the phone. "Diamond's on her way out."

I smiled victoriously.

He ended his call, then slipped his phone back into his belt clip.

"Thank you," I said sweetly.

"I still don't trust her," he said.

"You don't trust anybody." I laughed. "If you did, you wouldn't be so good at your job."

"You're right," he replied, staring at me.

"Ready!" Lisette said, walking up to us. Her bikini had been replaced with a fitted, yellow, above-the-knee, bra-top dress and matching sandals, and she was carrying an oversized bag on her shoulder.

"I need to check your bag and search you," Jonah said, sounding quite official.

"No problem," Lisette said.

We waited until Jonah finished searching through her belongings and patting her down. When he gave her the all-clear, the three of us exited the club.

* * * * *

The sounds of the ocean waves crashing against the shore echoed through my open window as the night wind whipped the silk, floor-length curtains back and forth whimsically. Inside my bedroom, I sat with my legs crossed, reclining against the small Italian leather loveseat while Lisette gave me my own private show. She stood in front of me wearing nothing but a purple lace bra, matching panties, and heels. She moved her hips slowly, looking at me with eyes dripping with seduction.

After we left the club, we'd returned to the villa Gator and I owned and had a drink while engaging in pleasant conversation. The conversation was simple and sweet, just fashion and current events and nothing too personal.

For the first hour of that conversation, Jonah had sat with his eyes locked on us, watching Lisette's every move. I swear, if I'd have had a dick, it would have gone limp under the power of his evil stare and unpleasant disposition.

I'd finally tired of Jonah's attitude and had led Lisette to the bedroom. I knew he was still posted on the other side of the door, but at least I wouldn't have to look at him.

"Dance with me," Lisette said, extending her hands to me.

"I don't dance," I lied playfully.

"I'll teach you," she said.

"We don't have music."

"We'll make our own," she said.

She stopped moving her hips, then reached down and took my hands in hers. I allowed her to assist me to my feet. Lisette then led me to the middle of the room, at the foot of the bed, and faced me. She held on to my left hand while cuffing my lower back with her right. "Follow my lead," she said. She rolled her pelvis slowly, moving against my body and causing my nipples to grow taut.

I smiled as her hand inched slowly down my back, over the curve of my ass, until she was gripping my cheek through my dress. I began to rotate my hips, matching her rotations. I could feel a warm, lustful sensation growing in the pit of my stomach as Lisette released my left hand and delicately traced her fingers down the curve of my side. She massaged my ass with both hands, pulling me closer, until our breasts were pressed together.

"The things I could do to you," she whispered, slowly inching my dress up, exposing my lace thong, "any man would envy."

The sound of her voice, combined with her soft touch, caused my already damp panties to become soaked. I could feel my heart rate increasing with every second, my body crying for relief with every breath. "Show me," I whispered, gazing in her eyes.

She grinned mischievously, then grabbed my hips with both hands and lifted me up. She was surprisingly strong and carried me to the bed, where she eased me down on top of the down-filled comforter. Lisette sat on her knees, positioned between my spread legs. "So sexy," she moaned. She traced her fingertips along the curve of my cheek, across my chin, then finally around the outline of my lips.

I opened my mouth slightly, sucking softly on her fingertip. I hadn't been with another woman in years, and from the way my kitten was jumping from Lisette's touch, I could tell I was long overdue for female attention. I loved my husband and was content with our lovemaking, but there were times when I needed something different, something softer, something forbidden.

Lisette pulled her finger from my mouth, then slowly pushed my dress up and over my breasts, then finally over my head. Her eyes remained locked with mine as she dropped the material on the carpeted floor. "Your husband is a lucky man," she stated, easing off the bed. I watched her in silence while she slowly removed her heels. "He's a fool for leaving you alone, but lucky nonetheless," she added.

I agreed with her but was not in the mood to talk about it. I needed action, and if Lisette planned to remain in my company for the rest of the night, she would have to start putting my kitty where her mouth was.

She climbed back on the bed and straddled my waist. She then trailed her luscious lips along the curve of my collarbone, up the curve of my neck to my ear.

I closed my eyes, enjoying the warm sensation of her lips.

"I'm gonna enjoy every moment of this," she whispered, flicking her tongue across my earlobe.

"That makes two of—"

I opened my eyes as my words were cut off, along with my air. The seductive gaze her eyes had held only seconds earlier had been replaced by a hate-filled glare. She stared at me while her hands gripped my neck tightly.

What the hell? I thought, clawing her fingers. *Is this some twisted sex game, or is the bitch actually trying to kill me?* I moved my head slightly back and forth, stuttering out, "I-I can't...I can't br-breathe!"

Her smile grew wide, and she pressed harder.

At that moment, I knew she was actually choking me, that Lisette really wanted me dead. I attempted to shift my hips in the hopes that I could knock her off of me, but I failed. She was strong as hell, and my resistance only made things worse. My windpipe felt like it was going to collapse from the hard pressure she was applying. I dug my nails into her wrist until I felt a warm liquid oozing out, liquid that had to be blood. My attacker didn't flinch and just continued to stare at me like a woman possessed.

But why? Who is she, really, and why is she doing this? I asked myself. My heart rate increased rapidly as fear started to set in.

"I wish Leon was here," she grunted through clenched teeth. "I'd rather this be him, but unfortunately, you'll have to do."

Lisette's mention of my husband's government name answered the question that was plaguing my mind: Her motive was revenge.

"He murdered one of the few men I've ever loved," she continued. "My brother, Tabious, was a good man who only wanted better for his family, but that piece of shit you call your man took him from us. Now I'm gonna take something of his."

I didn't recognize her brother's name, but it really didn't matter. I knew that if Gator or any of his associates had killed the man, they had good reason for it. Gator believed in raw justice, but he was not the kind of man to take a life simply for pleasure. I began to panic as my attempts to inhale became useless. Inside my chest, my lungs felt like they were going to rupture, and my throat began to burn unbearably. I extended my arms and managed to grab a handful of her hair. I tugged frantically on her silky strands, hoping to inflict enough pain to distract her so she would ease up, but my efforts failed. Even when I pulled my hand back and jerked a clump of hair from her head, she still didn't budge. I felt the salty tears trickling from my eyes as thoughts of death plagued my mind. I didn't want to give up, but trying to hold on to life, trying to breathe against all odds somehow felt worse. I closed my eyes; I was not about to give Lisette the pleasure of seeing the fear that I knew now loomed over my retinas. I wanted to ask God for forgiveness for the life I'd lived, but in that moment, I was too busy mentally celebrating. *When Jonah sees what this bitch has done, he'll inflict pain a thousand times worse upon her.*

Suddenly, a rush of air surrounded me, and the weight that had been crushing down on me suddenly lifted. For a moment, I thought I was dead, that death itself had released me from her bitter chokehold, but then I heard a loud *thud* and felt air filling my nostrils. I opened my eyes, then instantly rolled over onto my side. I gasped, then coughed, almost choking on my own saliva as I furiously breathed in and out, panting like a dog. I clutched the comforter tightly, inching myself over to the edge of the bed. I watched through my tears as Jonah punched Lisette with such force that her nose snapped like a Thanksgiving wishbone and shifted to the left side of her face. She laughed while blood spewed from her nostrils and across her lips, then dripped down her chin. I wiped the tears from my face with the back of my hand while continuing to catch my breath.

"Are you okay?" Jonah asked, walking over to the bed.

I nodded weakly.

Jonah assisted me off the bed and to my feet.

"Is that the best you got?" Lisette asked, catching our attention. She pulled herself up on her feet, then spat a sticky stream of saliva and blood on the floor, staining the plush carpet. "Piece of shit," she panted before rushing in our direction.

Jonah swung, but not before taking a blow to the center of his jaw from Lisette, a hit that caused him to stumble slightly. Lisette swung again, but she missed this time, when Jonah hit her with a brutal uppercut to the chin, followed by a left to the temple. Unconscious, she fell to the floor, ass first.

Once my breathing slowed, I explained to Jonah what had taken place before he entered the room. "But how did you know I was in trouble?" I questioned.

"She gave me a bad vibe right from the get-go," he explained. "When I didn't hear any noise in here, I decided to come to the door." He bent down and picked up my dress and handed it to me.

I quickly took the wrinkled garment from his hands and covered my naked body. I was thankful for his instincts and grateful he had saved my life.

"Take this." He reached behind him and pulled a .45 out the waistband of his pants, then handed the gun to me. "If she gets up or even moves, use it. I'll be back in a few minutes."

I nodded and held the weapon loosely in my palms. I sat on the edge of the bed, watching Lisette intently.

She moaned several times, then finally opened her eyes and stared at me. Her eyes traveled down to the gun, then back up again. "Do you even know how to use that?" She laughed hoarsely.

"Wanna try me and find out?"

"You talk hot shit for someone who's scared of the gun in her own damn hand." Lisette laughed again, then pulled herself upright against the wall. "Look at you shaking, Diamond. We both know you couldn't take a life if yours depended on it."

"You don't know anything about me or what I'm capable of," I snapped firmly.

She ran her hands through her disheveled hair, then smirked, rolling her eyes. "How'd you end up with someone like Leon anyway?" she questioned. "What was it? His charm? Security? The money?" She raised her eyebrows, then nodded her head. "That's it, isn't it? The money. *El dinero.*"

"I'm with Leon because of something you can't possibly understand. I *love* him," I said defensively.

"Do you love him enough to die for him? Hmm? Because that'll happen eventually, you know."

I sat silently, allowing her words to soak in and fuck with my head. Since my marriage to Gator, she was the first person who'd ever made a real attempt on my life, and I was worried that she might not be the last. *What if she's telling the truth? What if this is just the beginning? Were Mama and Daddy right?* I shook the thoughts from my mind; there was no way I was going to allow the woman to toy with my emotions. The broad had just attempted to kill me, and she was the last person on Earth I wanted any advice from. "I'll take my chances," I said.

"Stupid girl," she snapped.

"You claim your brother was murdered for crossing Gator, yet you come here and make an attempt on my life?" I asked sarcastically. "And I'm the one who's stupid?"

"My fate was sealed years ago. When death comes for me, I'll look it in the eyes. My only regret will be that I didn't finish what I started here today, that I didn't get the chance to avenge my brother's death."

"How do you know Gator was responsible?" I questioned, annoyed with her accusations. "What proof do you have?"

"Because I know Leon," she stated.

I listened as Lisette shared, detail for detail, the story of how she'd met my husband on one of his trips to New York. She'd been connected to a dealer who was fronting Gator his supply at the time. She and Gator had formed a special friendship, and eventually, she introduced him to her brother. "Your Gator and my brother Tabious formed a partnership that later led to Gator acquiring his connects in the Caribbean…"

I listened in silence as she explained that Gator had ordered the hit on Tabious when Tabious came up short with money he owed Gator after an unfortunate robbery.

"My brother was set up," she said. "Leon knew that, but he had his life taken anyway. He denies that he ordered the hit, but I know he did it. What happened to loyalty and *familia?*"

"*I'm* his family," I told her. "You and your brother were nothing more than employees."

"Employees?" she repeated, with a hint of anger and insult in her voice. "I took Leon to another level. Without me, those prissy-ass little American boys he calls an army wouldn't have made a dime outside of that country mark on the map that the two of you call home. Your husband was nothing but a nickel-bag hustler when I met him. I made him a boss."

I didn't know what bothered me more: the fact that the woman knew so much about Gator's organization or that she'd obviously had a personal relationship with him. I knew my husband was involved in illegal operations, but I had no idea how he ran things. I had never had any reason to ask about it, and Gator had instilled in me from day one that the less I knew about it, the better, but hearing Lisette ramble about his dealings touched a soft spot inside of me and ignited a bit of envy. There was nothing worse than feeling inadequate because another woman knew my man and his money better than I did.

Jonah returned to the villa carrying a black bag filled with plastic zip-ties and other items necessary to restrain Lisette. After securing her hands and feet, he covered Lisette's mouth tightly with a rag, then hoisted her up on his shoulders and carried her out through the balcony doors, where the limo was waiting. I watched as he dropped her on the floor of the trunk, then closed the door.

"I'll be back," he stated, walking around to the driver side door.

"I'm coming with you."

"Diamond—"

"I'm coming," I said firmly.

Jonah shook his head in disapproval while walking around to open the passenger side door for me.

"What are you gonna do with her?"

"I'll take her somewhere where no one will hear her or find her till I speak with Gator," Jonah answered, keeping his eyes on the road.

"What do you think he'll say?"

"I don't know."

"What do you think he'll do?" Gator had told me he would never hurt a woman, but I knew there was no way he would let Lisette walk away without consequences or repercussions either.

"Diamond, the less you—"

"I know, I know. The less I know, the better," I said, raising my hand to let him know I didn't want to hear it.

The two of us made the rest of the trip in silence to a secluded part of the island, where there was a boathouse. The shack looked unstable and appeared to have not been used in years. I stood outside searching the darkness with my eyes, looking for any possible onlookers while Jonah carried Lisette inside. A second later, I stepped in the doorway and watched Jonah as he tied Lisette to one of the dusty wooden beams. Lisette stared at me, clearly attempting to say something. "What is she trying to say?"

"Who cares?" Jonah said. "Let's go."

Lisette's muffled screams grew louder.

"Wait," I said, watching her. "Pull down the gag."

Jonah hesitated briefly, then finally did as I requested.

Lisette looked up at him and smiled. "I just wanted to tell you that you hit like a bitch," she said, grinning.

Jonah bent down to eye level with her, then whispered something in her ear.

"I look forward to it," Lisette taunted.

"Anything else?" he asked.

"Yes," she said, redirecting her attention to me. "My answer is yes, Diamond."

"Yes what?"

"Yes, I fucked your husband," she said.

"You're a liar," I said calmly.

"Diamond, do you really believe that?" she asked. "If you'd like, I can describe his dick, from the base right up to the r-shaped birth mark just below the head."

I could hear my heart beating in my ears as my pulse began to race. I knew she was telling the truth. There was no reason for her to lie, and her description of my man's penis was spot on. "And you're telling me this because?" I asked, attempting to mask my anger.

"Because I can," she laughed. "Because I know it'll will haunt the shit out of you, knowing that another woman was with your man."

"Burn in hell."

"I'll save you a seat," she answered smugly.

I turned and left out the door, then stepped down the ramp leading away from the house. I trudged through the warm sand toward the road, where Jonah had parked the car. With every step I took, Lisette's words replayed in my head. A loud *pop* sounded from behind me, and I turned in the sand, then stared at the rickety boathouse. Jonah stepped out the door, then jumped off the landing, into the sand. I noticed a light glowing behind the boathouse window, and in the next second, a burnt-orange flame burst through, shattering the glass, indicating that the boathouse was on fire. The flames spread rapidly, engulfing the structure. The thought that Lisette was inside the blazing inferno didn't affect me one bit.

"Let's go," Jonah demanded.

I caught the swift scent of gasoline as he walked by me. "I thought we were going to wait for Gator."

He looked at me under the glow of the moonlight, with an unreadable expression on his chocolate face. "I'll deal with the consequences later."

I followed behind him, gazing at the stars in the sky, as my lips curled up in a small smile.

Chapter 6

The next morning, I was awakened by the sound of my bedroom door slamming loudly. I hopped up, pushing my disheveled hair out of my face while focusing my eyes on the door.

Gator stood by the bedroom door, dressed in a light gray suit and a pair of matching alligator shoes. He was overdressed for our vacation, my first clue that something was wrong. "Shower and get your things," he ordered. "We're leaving." Although he didn't raise his voice, the stern look of disappointment in his eyes spoke volumes, telling me he knew what had taken place the night before.

I tossed the covers back, then climbed out of bed. I stood naked on the floor, my eyes locked with his. "She said you were lovers," I angrily spat. "Care to explain?"

"Shower and get dressed, Diamond...now," he barked. He gave my body a quick onceover, then walked out of the bedroom door, closing it behind him.

I had no doubt that Lisette had been speaking the truth; Gator's failure to respond was nothing more than an admission of his guilt. I decided I would address the subject at a later time. I showered, slipped on a fitted, above-the-knee tank-dress and a pair of open-toed pumps, then packed my bags as fast as I could before exiting the bedroom.

Jonah was sitting on the living room sofa, listening to Gator's instructions to stay behind and handle damage control.

"Find out who in the hell gave Lisette the heads up on Diamond's arrival. Start with the club manager. Make sure yours and Diamond's abrupt actions haven't put us under any scrutiny. The last thing I need is to be in the damn spotlight," Gator advised. "Rakeem will take you wherever you need to go. Once everything is clear, call me. I'll send the plane back for you, and all you'll have to do is load and take off."

"Sounds good," Jonah said, looking from Gator to me. "Sorry, Gator. I tried to tell her—"

"We'll discuss this later," Gator said, ignoring his apology and shaking his head in disgust. He turned and looked at me, then shook his head again and took the luggage from my hands.

I followed him out the front door of the villa and climbed into the car. The two of us rode in silence from the villa to the airport, where Gator had a private jet was waiting to whisk us away.

* * * * *

I stared out the window of the jet, cringing from the sight of the dark and gloomy clouds that were hanging in the sky. Splatters of rain hit the small window as the plane rocked and shook lightly.

When the pilot announced that we'd be arriving at Huntsville International Airport in approximately an hour, I looked out and noticed a distinct change in the appearance of the sky. I loved to fly, but I avoided doing so during inclement weather. *Birds were born with wings*, and *they don't fly in bad weather*, I thought. *Hell, if flying's in their nature and they stay their asses out of the air, then I should too.*

"Are you okay?" Gator asked, commanding my attention. He was sitting in the leather seat across the aisle from me, with one ankle resting on his knee; it was the first time he had spoken since we'd left the island.

"Yes," I said, looking at him.

He cocked his head slightly to the side and stared at me. "You lie," he said confidently.

"Why'd you even ask if you already know the answer?" I asked with attitude.

"Why would you bother lying when you know I already know the answers?" he retorted with raised eyebrows.

"Good question," I said. "I guess lying to each other is something we should both avoid." I sighed, then rolled my eyes.

"Come here, Diamond," he said, extending his arms to me.

"Why?"

"Because I asked you to," he said. "Now come here."

I hesitated, then finally eased out of my seat and walked over, welcoming his embrace while easing down on his lap. No matter how pissed I was with my husband, I always felt safe in his arms, and the stormy weather had me scared as hell, in desperate need of his comfort. *I can be pissed off again when we land,* I told myself. *But this feels damn good for now.*

"Is this better?" he asked, wrapping his arms around my waist.

"Yes," I answered, resting my head on his shoulder.

"Diamond, I'm not angry with you," he said, "but what were you thinking? You brought a woman you knew nothing about into our private circle."

"I was lonely," I confessed, "and since it was our anniversary, I wanted to—"

"To teach me a lesson?" he concluded. "Baby, that little temper tantrum and rebellion almost cost you your life."

"Is that why you're mad, or is it because Jonah killed her?" I asked sarcastically.

"I told you that I'm not mad at you. I'm just upset things had to take such a dramatic turn for the worst and that you were in the middle of it."

"I assume you're referring to the part when your disgruntled lover tried to kill me," I said, raising my head.

"You're right about the attempted killing part," he said, "but Lisette and I were not lovers."

"But she said you fu—"

"Yes, we slept together years ago, when we first met, but it was a onetime thing and nothing more."

I gave him a disbelieving smirk.

"Fine. You got me. I can't remember how many times we slept together," he confessed, "but the point is, it ended before I met you."

"It better have."

"You have my word."

"She also told me she put you in contact with your connects in the Caribbean," I said. "Was that true?"

"Yes."

"And her brother, Tabious, was once your partner?"

"I wouldn't call it a partnership," Gator said. "Yeah, he worked for me, but he wasn't my partner. There's a very big difference."

"Fine. So he worked for you," I said, annoyed. "Either way, you had a connection with her brother, too, didn't you?"

"Yes."

"Did you kill him?"

"No," Gator said firmly, "but I ordered it to be done."

"Why?"

"Because he crossed me," he said flatly, as if it was nothing at all. "He faked a robbery in an attempt to beat me out of what he owed me. I couldn't allow him to have a free pass, Diamond. In my line of work, it would have been a sign of weakness, and weakness is a death sentence. At the very least, it leads to hostile takeover."

I nodded my head in agreement and understanding. "Lisette knew a shitload about your business, much more than I've ever known. Do you know how that made me feel?"

"Yes, she knew some things," he said. "I won't deny that, but it was to be expected. The brunt of our communication was business. I've never disclosed much about my business to you because the less you know, the safer you are."

"I understand that, but do you know how it made me *feel* when I heard another woman telling me all about my man? Gator, we vowed to share our lives, all the ups, downs, and in betweens. When she told me that, I felt like an outsider."

"I apologize for that," he said, rubbing my back. "I've never wanted you to feel like anything other than number one in my life, because that's what you are. But, Diamond, baby, you've gotta remember that I vowed to protect you at all costs, and that means more to me than anything." He kissed my forehead softly, then tightened his grip around my waist. "It doesn't matter how the money comes or the methods I choose to deliver it, as long as your needs and wants are supplied."

I silently scolded myself for being so childish and silly. Gator had enough stress to deal with without me acting like a jealous teenage girl. Besides, no matter what Lisette had once meant to him, I was still winning, living and breathing and enjoying the fruits of my husband's labor. "You missed our anniversary," I reminded him, "but I guess that's okay. There's no telling what would have happened if Lisette had seen you there with me."

"I apologize again," he said. "If I'd have been there, she never would have gotten her grimy hands on you. I don't know what I would have done if something had happened to you."

"I'm fine," I said honestly.

"I've got a couple surprises waiting for you at home," he said with a twinkle in his eye.

"Make-up gifts?" I laughed.

"Yeah." He chuckled. "And we can plan another trip if you'd like, we can go anyplace you wanna go."

I pondered his offer, then shook my head. "I'd rather have a party," I said.

"Then a party you shall have," he said. "When?"

"Tomorrow night," I said.

"Hmm. That's pretty short notice."

"I know, but you'll make it happen," I said confidently. "Won't you?"

"Of course I will," he said. "No worries."

"Now, tell me…what had you so caught up that you missed our anniversary?" I questioned curiously.

"Not what," he said. "More like…who."

"Who then?"

"I located an old friend," he said, "one who incidentally owes me a bit of money, a gentleman by the name of Kelly. I paid him a visit, but then something else came up that I had to attend to."

"Did you get your money?"

"No." He sighed. "However, I'm sure it won't be long before I do." I wrapped my arms around his neck, then closed my eyes.

"I love you."

"I love you too," he said. "Get some rest now. I'll wake you when we land."

* * * * *

An hour later, Gator nudged me, gently letting me know we'd arrived in Huntsville. I stretched, then stood up and peeked out the window of the aircraft. Dark clouds were looming in the sky again, and heavy showers of rain were falling in sheets. Despite the nasty weather, I was truly grateful to be on Alabama soil again. It was always good to be home.

Gator had treated me to trips to some of the most beautiful and exotic lands in the world. From the beaches of Punta Cana, to the Swiss Alps, and even the crystal blue waters of the Maldives, since we'd been together, he'd whisked me away to paradises many only get the chance to read about. Still, there was no place closer to my heart than Huntsville, Alabama. I loved the clean streets, beautiful green landscape, and quiet atmosphere. My husband also appreciated those things about our fair city, as well as the fact that people often misinterpreted Southern charm and hospitality as a weakness; that often gave him an upper hand in the streets.

I stared out the window at AJ, Gator's driver, who was standing by Gator's SUV, holding a large black and white golf umbrella. I laughed, thinking to myself that he resembled Fonzworth Bentley, only with stacks of rippled chocolate muscle and a whole lot more intimidating than the musician and Puffy's valet.

AJ had become Gator's chauffeur a little over nine months ago, after a chance meeting at a local restaurant. When Gator and I were preparing to leave the restaurant one afternoon, we heard AJ speaking to the manager about an application he'd submitted for employment. I'll never forget the desperation in his voice as he explained that he was looking for a job and was willing to do whatever was necessary to earn a paycheck. The perky blonde he was pleading his case to smiled and told him she'd call if anything came up, but I could tell from the painted grin on the woman's face that she had no intention of calling him; she was only willing to keep his application on file because she was legally required to do so. AJ politely thanked her and exited the restaurant with his head hanging low.

The sad scene immediately grabbed Gator's attention. He followed AJ outside, then stopped him in the parking lot. It wasn't until the three of us were up close and personal that I realized I knew the man; the two of us had grown up in the same neighborhood. Without even knowing that, Gator had already made his mind up that he was going to offer the man some assistance.

"Thanks, but I don't take handouts," AJ said respectfully, turning down the bills Gator had attempted to give him. "I need a job so I can handle my own."

"What skills do you have?" Gator inquired.

"I worked at the carwash over on Pulaski Pike for about two years, till I caught a case and did a three-year bid. The real fucked-up part is that I took a fall for my family, and now they don't want shit to do with me. Man, I'm just trying to do the right thing out here. I just wanna eat, but doors keep gettin' slammed in my face."

The two of them went back and forth for a few minutes, until Gator gave AJ his business card and told him to call him.

AJ started out detailing our vehicles and the vehicles of Gator's employees, and Gator then began asking him to drive him here or there. He proved himself worthy over time, and he'd been Gator's on-call driver ever since.

"Go ahead, baby," Gator instructed. "I need to give the pilot some instructions."

"Okay, boo," I said, then stood and stretched. I grabbed my handbag and waited for the door to the plane to open.

Once the doors opened, AJ assisted me down the metal stairs with one hand while shielding me from the rain with the umbrella. "Welcome home," he said politely.

"Thank you, AJ," I said, holding on to his arm.

He escorted me to the car, under the shelter of his big umbrella. Once I was safely inside, he went to retrieve my luggage.

I settled against the leather seat and relaxed, then kicked off my heels. If Gator was going to go through with our party, which I knew he would, I wanted to change the color of my nails and also find me something cute and sexy to wear.

The car door opened, jerking me from my daydream.

"Everything all right?" I asked Gator as he climbed in.

"Everything is perfect," he said. He slipped his arm around my waist and pulled me against his body. "Have I told you how beautiful you are?"

"You just did," I said, smiling. I laid my head on his chest and looked out the window.

"What do you say we order in tonight?" Gator suggested. "How's lobster sound?"

"I'd like that."

"All right. Caviar for an appetizer," he continued, stroking my hair, "and you for dessert."

"Mmm. Now you're talking," I said sensually.

"Who knows?" he whispered in my ear. "Tonight may finally be the night."

I knew instantly, without further explanation, exactly what Gator meant. Without actually saying it, he'd made it clear that he was hoping it would be the night we'd conceive our first child. "Maybe it will," I said.

"I don't mean to sound overzealous, but I'm ready," he said, "if not a little concerned."

"I know, baby," I said, sitting upright. "We've only been trying for a few months though. It takes some people years." I stroked his cheek softly with my fingertips. "It'll happen. I promise."

"I know it will," he said. "I'm just not a patient man."

I pressed my lips against his, giving him a tender kiss and hoping to remove the doubt I saw in his eyes and heard in his voice.

We took the rest of the ride in silence, holding hands. AJ pulled up to the iron gate that protected our property, entered the code on the keypad, then pulled through when it creaked open.

In honor of our one-year anniversary, Gator had sold his bachelor pad and purchased the beautiful multi-level brick home we now shared. Our new home was located just outside the city, situated on seven acres of plush, green lawns, surrounded by an abundance of fully developed oak trees. Behind our property, just over the privacy fence, sat a quiet, fairly new development called Hidden Creek. I liked having my privacy and being able to walk around my lawn without having to worry about nosy neighbors on either side of me, but I also liked the security of knowing that others were only five minutes away. AJ shifted into park, then climbed out before coming around to open the car door for me.

"Home sweet home," I chanted, walking to the front door. I entered the foyer of our home and inhaled, taking in the fresh, clean scent of Pine-Sol, an indication that our maid, Vanessa, had been by and was on her job. I loved every inch of our 4,900-square-foot home, but keeping it clean was a task. I was just thankful Gator did not expect me to maintain the place on my own.

"I have to make a few phone calls," Gator advised. He stepped past me, then set my luggage down on the marble floor. "You wanna go up and take a nap until dinner?"

"I'm good. I slept on the plane," I said. "I think I'm gonna go get a mani-pedi. Plus, I need to look for a dress for tomorrow."

"You going with Venetta?" Gator questioned.

"Not today," I said. "I think I want some me time alone."

"Do we need to talk about what happened?" he asked. There was an instantaneous change in his demeanor, and he suddenly looked concerned.

"What do you mean?"

"With Lisette and...well, all that you witnessed."

It suddenly occurred to me that he was referring to the incident at the boathouse. Death wasn't something I was accustomed to, but considering the victim and the reason behind it, I hadn't taken the time to give the incident much thought. "No, I'm fine," I said, showing no remorse.

Gator frowned slightly.

"What?"

"I'm just...concerned."

"Don't be," I reassured him. "I'm fine. Trust me."

"I'll have AJ bring the car back around," he said. "He'll drive you."

"Baby, it's fine. I can drive myself," I said, knowing he'd never allow it.

"Until I'm confident that everything from the island is clear, I'd prefer that AJ accompany you. Once Jonah lets me know we're good, you can do as you please. Until then, AJ will take you wherever you need to go."

"Okay," I said; there was no point in arguing with him.

"Great," he said, then kissed me softly on the cheek.

* * * * *

AJ maneuvered through the slick streets, heading toward Bridge Street Town Centre, the place to go for upscale shopping, some of the city's finest dining, and the home of the Monaco Picture Studio. I normally did the majority of my shopping online or when I traveled, but whenever I spent money in my hometown, Bridge Street was where I laid it down.

AJ merged into the right lane, bypassing our destination and taking the Highway 233 exit.

"You missed our turn," I advised him.

He flashed his eyes up at me through the rearview mirror, then focused back on the road again. "I need to make a stop," he said flatly. "Is that okay?"

"It's fine," I said.

I watched as he took the Oakwood Road exit, then made an immediate right turn onto Rideout Drive before making a left into Willow Pointe, a small, secluded condominium community. AJ pulled directly to the back of the complex, then parked the car behind the brick building with a gold "6601" screwed into the side. He killed the engine, then climbed out of the driver side.

I watched the rain as it rolled down the windshield like a blurry curtain, obstructing the view from the outside.

A few seconds later, the left passenger door swung open, and AJ climbed into the car next to me. He stared at me with cold, dark eyes, a look I was all too familiar with and an indication that there was trouble to follow. He grabbed me before I could utter a sound, and in less than a second, he had my legs spread and my back pushed up against the car door. His weight bore down on me as he grabbed and squeezed my breast with one hand while pushing my panties aside with another. His full lips covered mine, muffling my objections as he saturated me with sloppy kisses. I felt a slight resistance and then cool air as he ripped my lace thong apart at the seams. He pulled back, staring at me with thirst and hunger swimming in his gaze. "You know how long I've been waiting to do this?" he asked roughly. He pushed his index finger inside me, making me jump slightly from the impact.

"Yes," I whispered. "One week and five days, since the last time." I cupped his warm, round face in my hands, then kissed him feverishly, forcing my tongue between his lips and claiming what was waiting for me. I fumbled with the belt of AJ's pants until the material finally hung open, revealing a large bulge pushing against his boxer briefs. AJ had the biggest dick I'd ever seen in my life, one of the best I'd ever felt. I tugged at the waist of his briefs, then pulled them down and freed the beast that was held captive behind the elastic band. I closed my eyes and elevated my hips as he positioned himself between my legs and penetrated my wetness with so much force he caused my shoulder to slam against the edge of the door.

* * * * *

I knew the game I was playing with AJ was a deadly one, but I couldn't possibly resist. The man brought me to multiple orgasms, and we shared an undeniable chemistry. Not only had we come up in the same neighborhood, but AJ, Alvin Staten Jr. to Uncle Sam, was an old friend. After we ran into him, I told Gator I knew him and that the two of us had once traveled in the same social circles. Of course I conveniently left out the fact that we'd hooked up a few times. I'd always been a firm believer that it wasn't necessary for a woman to know all her husband's previous conquests, nor was it necessary for him to know all hers. Besides, I felt there was nothing to tell; quite frankly, other than mind-blowing sex, I had no intention of anything serious developing between me and AJ.

The affair had started out as innocent flirting. While waiting for Gator, he'd always make a few slick comments: "You're working that dress, Mrs. Douglass," or, "What's a man to do with all that woman?" AJ's come-ons were lame, but I was turned on by the fact that he was bold enough to make them in the first place, and he always gave me some much-needed attention. Not to mention, the man was solid chocolate, a build that was obviously the reward of years of working out.

One day, Gator assigned him to accompany me on a shopping excursion to Atlanta. That time alone was all the two of us needed. As soon as we hit the Georgia state line, we found a rest stop and were all over each other, and we'd been stealing moments together ever since.

After AJ and I completed our sexual tryst, our sexy-ass chauffer drove me to Divaz for my mani-pedi and to cover my tracks and back up the story I'd told Gator earlier.

Back at home again, I entered my home and found Gator in the family room on his cell phone, immersed in heavy conversation. I was grateful his attention was elsewhere, as it allowed me to slip upstairs to our master bathroom, practically unnoticed. I quickly undressed then ran my bath water. Five minutes later, I eased myself down into our Jacuzzi tub and enjoyed the warm bubbles as I patted my skin gently with a soft sponge. I'd forgotten all about Gator's "dessert" comment and his plans for the two of us until he stepped through the bathroom door.

"Am I interrupting?" he questioned.

"Of course not," I said, smiling.

I watched as he stepped across the bathroom floor, removing his suit jacket along the way. He laid the jacket on the marble countertop in between the his and hers vanities, then stepped over to the tub and sat down on the edge. "Want me to wash your back?" he asked.

I wanted to say, *"Hell no!"* I wanted to continue washing off the scent of sex with AJ in private, but I knew asking for privacy would set Gator's radar in motion. "Sure baby," I said, handing him the sponge. I sat up in the tub, allowing him room to reach my back.

"How was your trip out?" he asked.

"Good," I said. "It was wet though," I said, secretly laughing inside at the double-meaning. "It's like a monsoon out there."

"Perfect lovemaking weather, if you ask me," he commented. Gator rubbed and massaged my back with the sponge in slow, circular motions, then worked his way to my breast.

"That it is," I agreed.

"Maybe we can have dinner on the terrace tonight," he suggested. "Candlelight and the moon will be nice, and afterward, we'll enjoy dessert... in bed." He slid the sponge down my stomach and into the water, then finally in between my legs.

"Mmm. I'd love that," I said, faking a yawn. "Sounds good, baby." I yawned again for dramatic effect.

"You tired, love?"

"I am," I lied.

"Why don't you climb out and lie down for a couple hours," he suggested. "I'll wake you when dinner arrives." He placed the sponge on the corner of the tub, then rose to his feet. I watched as he retrieved a towel from the linen closet and walked back over to the tub. "Here ya go," he said, holding the towel open for me.

I stood and gently stepped out onto the tile floor, allowing Gator to wrap the plush towel around me. "Thank you," I said. "You take such good care of me."

"It's my job," he said, "and my pleasure." He stared at me with s soul-quivering stare in his eyes, gently stroking my collarbone. "What happened here?" he asked, touching a spot on the back of my shoulder that was slightly tender.

"I-I don't know," I said, hurrying over to the mirror. I turned to the side, staring at the reddish-black bruise. "I didn't even notice it." Flashbacks of AJ fucking me in the back seat of Gator's vehicle replayed in my head. "No clue at all."

"Maybe it's left over from Lisette," Gator suggested.

"You're right." I sighed, looking at him. "She was one crazy, psycho bitch."

"Don't speak ill of the dead, sweetheart," Gator said sharply, "especially those you help to get rid of."

I laughed lightly, then yawned again.

"Lie down and get comfortable. I'll be back." He kissed my forehead, then exited the bathroom, leaving me alone.

I finished towel-drying my body, then climbed up on my king-sized bed and slipped under the covers. I closed my eyes, willing myself to sleep. After a few moments passed, my body finally obeyed.

Chapter 7

The next morning, Gator woke me up with a gentle tap on my shoulder. I was still attempting to recover from my little sneak-and-freak with AJ, and my body was crying for additional rest. Gator had allowed me to sleep through the night, even through the romantic dinner he had planned, but I knew there was no way I was going to get a pass again, so I put a smile on my face, rolled over to face my husband, then climbed on top of him. I arched my back, clenching the muscles of my southern lips tightly as I slid up and down on my husband's play pole. Squeezing my taut nipples tightly, I stared in his dark brown eyes, losing myself in their enchantment.

The pleasure he felt between my legs was obvious from the look of sheer ecstasy in his eyes. He grabbed my hips with both hands while I rocked and rolled on his man with precision and grace. "Right there," he groaned, closing his eyes.

I smiled victoriously, spreading my right leg out toward his shoulder until I was riding him in a partial split. I may have had my piece on the side, but I still took pleasure in knowing that my husband loved the way I made love to him. Yes, I was having my cake and eating it, too, but it didn't matter to me, as long as I took care of home. "Pull your legs up," I ordered.

Gator did as I requested, allowing me complete access to every inch of him.

"Yesss…" I groaned, biting my bottom lip. I rotated my wide hips seductively, serenading my husband's rock with my wetness. I strategically pulled my left leg up, then grabbed each of his forearms with my hands. I sat with my legs spread in a V, grinding up, down, and around, holding on to his arms for leverage and clasping his dick with the walls of my sopping-wet pussy.

"*Fick mich! Fick mich!*" he chanted over and over again. Gator spoke over six languages fluently, but nothing turned me on more than when he spoke to me in German.

I increased my speed, bucking wildly, granting his request.

"Fuck me, Diamond!" he repeated, this time in English.

Tiny droplets of sweat trickled from my skin down to his as I continued pounding my kitten against him. I felt a tingling sensation in the pit of my stomach as my cave became wetter and wetter with every second, until there was finally a wave of satisfaction coursing through my body. I leaned back until I was lying flat on my back between his spread legs.

Gator sat up, grabbed my ankles, then pushed my legs back until my toes were pointing above the crown of my head. He pulled himself up on his knees, using every muscle of his two hundred-pound physique as he assumed the position between my legs. The sound of him grunting, combined with his sac slapping against my ass and my gushing kitten, played in the air like a sweet melody. I felt his entire body shake as he pushed in and out before finally plunging as far as nature would allow. "Mmm…" He groaned savagely before collapsing beside me on the bed.

"Mmm is right," I said, trying to catch my breath.

"Come here, my love."

I rolled over on my side, then lay with my head on Gator's sweat-drenched chest.

He wrapped his strong arms around me, holding me tight, then kissed the top of my head lightly. "After five years, you still know how to bring out the beast in me," he said.

"Good," I said, tracing my fingertips over his pecks. "I plan to continue for many more."

A light *tweet* resounded from his phone, indicating he had a text message.

"I'm retiring tomorrow," he said, exhaling loudly.

"You always say that," I reminded him.

"What if I mean it this time?"

"Baby, we both know that in your line of work, it takes more preparation than a day to walk away," I said lovingly.

"But I'm the boss," he said with slight arrogance.

"True…and you're a damn good one," I said, stroking his ego, "and because you are, it makes it even harder to walk away."

The words I'd recited to him were not only to stroke his ego; they were also true. If my husband had been a regular white-collar worker with a respectable profession and a federally appreciated corporation, he could have announced his resignation, chosen a successor, cleaned off his desk, and walked away without a second look. However, the love of my life made his living on the opposite side of the law. Despite my lack of knowledge as to how, when, and what he did to keep his organization running smoothly, I knew he'd invested too much to simply walk away. Besides, no matter what Gator stated about retiring, we both knew and agreed that when a corporation was built on an illegal hustle or bloodshed, there were only two options out: prison or death.

When his phone tweeted again, I raised my head, allowing him to slide out from under me, then propped myself up on my elbows. I watched as he walked over to the dresser, where he kept his phone. As he moved, I admired the slope of his wide back that led down to his tight brown ass and finally introduced his long, well-crafted thighs and calves. I had seen my husband naked countless times before, but each time felt like the first.

"Interesting," he said, staring at his phone.

"What is it?" I asked, climbing out of bed.

"There's a situation I need to tend to," he said, turning to face me. His eyes scanned my naked body, from my lips to my breast, then down to my toes and back up again.

"Exactly how long is this 'situation' gonna take?" I questioned, making quotes in the air around it. "Do I need to remind you of the party we're supposed to have tonight?" I walked over to my armoire and removed my silk robe.

"No," he said, "but I know you're going to."

I slipped the material over my shoulders, then secured the belt around my waist. "Don't get cute," I said, looking at him with raised eyebrows.

He smiled, then laughed lightly. "I couldn't forget the party even if I wanted to," he said. "Last night, while you were sleeping peacefully, I was making it happen."

I smiled. "You always do, baby." I was pleased that Gator had pulled the strings to satisfy me, but I wasn't surprised; he always did what he had to do to make things happen, good or bad.

"I'll be there and on time, my love." He walked over to me and kissed my lips tenderly. "Thank you for being the best part of me."

"You're welcome, boo," I said, smiling brightly. "Thank you for recognizing."

"Sexy *and* conceited," he said, slapping me on the ass.

"Not conceited...convinced," I retorted, using his own words against him. "I only speak the truth."

"That you do," he said with a broad grin. "I'm gonna go shower so I can take care of my business before tonight. Care to join me?"

I knew if I accepted my husband's offer, it would lead to yet another round of lovemaking, this time up against the shower wall. I also had things I needed to tend to before the party, but that didn't stop me from slipping the robe off my shoulders and allowing it to fall to the bedroom floor. "Do you even have to ask?" I questioned, then sashayed toward our bathroom, with Gator following closely behind me like a little lost puppy, practically drooling.

* * * * *

An hour later, I stood at my bathroom vanity, applying a light layer of MAC conditioner to my lips while paying homage to my reflection. "You still got it," I said aloud.

I pulled out the bottom right drawer, far enough so I could feel around under the bottom of the right side of the metal rack. I pulled back the wide piece of duct tape, pulled out a round container, and set it on the counter. "The shit we do for love," I mumbled, flipping my birth control open.

I knew Gator wanted children, but I felt we weren't ready yet. I was still enjoying my freedom, like being able to pack up and go whenever I wanted. Besides, my husband's empire was making far too much money, and he had too many irons in the fire to be dealing with the stress of fatherhood at the moment. I chose not to be honest about my feelings when it came to having children because I believed in keeping my man happy, even if I had to do so by humoring him with a lie.

I took my last pill in the pack, turned off my bathroom light, grabbed my cell off my nightstand, and retrieved my handbag from my closet. I dropped the empty container into my purse and left the room. I descended the mahogany staircase while I speed-dialed Madison Drugs, my pharmacy of choice. I went through the automated system and confirmed my refill.

As I strolled through the foyer toward the kitchen, I heard something that sounded like music videos coming from the television. Vanessa never watched TV or listened to music while she was working, as she felt hard work left no time for distractions, so I knew someone other than Vanessa was in our kitchen. The sounds of laughter and chatter echoed in the air as I got closer. "Emerson," I said to myself.

At six-three, Emerson didn't carry an ounce over a hundred and thirty pounds and was slightly awkward looking. On the outside, he appeared to be the kid bullies would love to pick on. His eyes protruded out of his head like some kind of freaky fish, and he had big buck teeth; for the life of me, I couldn't understand why his parents had never had them fixed. In spite of his nerdy looks, though, Emerson was quick with his hands when it came to fighting and martial arts. It earned him a lot of respect from his classmates, and what he didn't earn with those skills was given without question when they discovered his family tree. Since his recent high school graduation, he'd been spending a lot more time at our home. I didn't mind because he was a smart kid who never caused any problems, and I liked having him around.

"Good morning," I said, entering the kitchen.

Emerson was seated at the marble kitchen island with a half-empty bowl of Fruit Loops in front of him and his eyes glued to the flat-screen TV mounted under the cabinet. "'Sup, Auntie," he said, looking over at me. His bulging eyes grew bigger while he stared at me. "Where you goin' in that dress? And does Uncle Gator know?"

I laughed, then continued my stroll to the refrigerator. I'd chosen to wear my blue, leopard print Cavalli dress for my errands. The figure-slimming dress stopped inches above my knees and had a plunging neckline that showed an abundance of skin. I set my ensemble off with a pair of black, peep-toe, six-inch heels. "Auntie is grown and sexy," I said over my shoulder. "She wears what she wants when she wants." I removed a strawberry parfait drink from the refrigerator door, then gave Emerson my undivided attention.

"I hear ya." Emerson chuckled. "Someday, I want to wife me a chick as bad as you."

I smiled while twisting off the cap on the bottle. "And one day you will," I said reassuringly. I took a sip of my smoothie while easing down on the high-backed chair next to him. "Just stay away from the ratchet hoes."

"I am," he said proudly, "especially now that I'm gettin' money." He looked at me with a goofy grin that stretched from one side of his dark chocolate skin to the other.

"You found a job?" I asked.

"Nope. . .a career." He grinned, standing. "Unc put me in the game."

"What!?" I asked, completely caught off guard. I'd always known there was a slight possibility of Emerson following in his uncle's risky footsteps, but I'd never anticipated it to be so soon. I watched as he carried his bowl to the sink, poured what was left of his breakfast down the garbage disposal, then set the bowl down.

"He didn't tell you?" he asked, looking at me. "I'm in collections now."

The sound of Emerson's cell phone ringing brought our conversation to a halt.

"Yeah," he said. "Umm. . .hmm. Okay, I can handle it. All right. Naw, trust me. I got this." He ended his call and placed his phone in his back pocket. "Gotta go, Auntie. Business calls." He smiled, then threw up two fingers, throwing me the deuces, then exited the kitchen.

"Emerson!" I called, following behind him.

"What's up?" he asked, turning around to face me.

"Be safe," I said.

"Always," he said.

* * * * *

I stepped out my front door and found AJ waiting for me, standing next to the passenger door of my Mercedes CLS, wearing dark slacks and a blue button-down shirt, looking like a chocolate gladiator. He gave me a cocky grin as he molested me with eyes. "Where to?" he asked.

"Madison Drugs," I said.

"Really?" he said, licking his lips seductively. "Who's home?"

"No one. Why?"

"You know why," he said.

There was one thing I'd never do, and that was screw another man in the home I shared with Gator. AJ knew that, so he grabbed me by the hand and led me around the back of the house to the deck. He pulled me up against his body and smiled, then slowly begin to push the hem of my dress up.

"Not now," I said, grabbing his hands.

"Come on, baby." He moaned, kissing my neck softly. "Just a little bit."

The feel of his lips against my skin, combined with the way his hands caressed my back then cupped my breast through the dress, sent my hormones soaring. I wanted to indulge in a little playtime with AJ, but I had things to do, not to mention I didn't want to risk getting caught. I also knew AJ would not stop begging and pressing me until I broke him off a little something. I eased down his body, squatting on my heels, then unbuckled his pants. "Make it quick," I ordered, pulling his dick out. I spat on the head of his soldier, then took him in my mouth, wasting no time in deep-throating every inch of him.

AJ grabbed my head, thrusting his hips forward. I sucked, licked, and sucked again, massaging his sac in the palm of my hand.

"Shit!" He grunted. "Right there, baby. Right there."

The sound of his heavy breathing made me jealous. I wanted to feel him, even if it was a quickie. "Ten minutes," I said, standing.

"Bend over," he ordered.

I looked up and thought I saw something moving in one of the second-story guestroom windows. "Oh shit," I blurted, pushing AJ away from me. I stepped back and looked up at the window again; the curtains were waving back and forth.

"What's wrong?"

"Someone's upstairs," I said frantically. "I-I think they saw us!"

"What!?" He quickly adjusted himself and zipped up his pants.

"I think I just saw someone staring out the window," I said through clenched teeth.

"I thought you said nobody's here?"

"I don't know! I thought they were all gone!" I snapped, walking over to the patio door. I was convinced my life as I knew it was about to change. *Emerson?* I thought. *No. I watched him leave.* I hurried through the kitchen, upstairs to the bedroom. Stepping inside, I found the room empty. The curtain continued to move back and forth with the air blowing from the overhead vent.

"The driveway is empty," AJ stated, entering the room.

I was partially relieved. It was possible that it was just the curtains, but the one thing I was sure of was that it was a sign. I needed to cut things off with AJ before something went wrong.

Chapter 8

The Huntsville Country Club was where the elite went to mingle and entertain. From the crystal chandeliers hanging from the ceiling to the round, glass tables adorned with lit candles and white and yellow roses, to the crystal dishes and sterling silver utensils, everything in the room screamed elegance and grace, including the tuxedo-clad servers. On any normal given day, harps and violins would serenade diners, but for my party, my hubby had hired a deejay and had given him specific instructions to play all my favorite songs. I had to commend the brother, because he was doing an excellent job.

"I'm living my life like it's golden, living my life like it's golden..." The sultry voice of Jill Scott flowed through the room like verbal seduction.

I swayed my hips under the sparkling, iridescent lights illuminating the dance floor, rocking and rolling my hips like no one was watching. I was engulfed in my own rhythm, lost in my own groove. I tossed my hair back and forth while raising my arms above my head and snapping my fingers. I felt like money, and there wasn't a shadow of doubt in my mind that in my designer gown and stilettos, I looked like money too. The diamond bracelet caressing my arm and the five-carat yellow diamond ring on my finger, make-up anniversary gifts from my husband, sparkled as I gripped my own waist. I puckered my lips seductively and blew a kiss to Gator, who was sitting with his sister, Venetta, and her husband, Terrance, at one of the many tables surrounding the dance floor. I smiled at Venetta and blew her a kiss as well. She shook her head then returned the gesture.

I winked, then focused on my husband; he looked distinguished and handsome in his dark suit and tie. The glimmering gold in his tie not only matched my golden gown but also accentuated his skin beautifully. His lips curved up in an appreciative smile as he nodded his head in my direction. There was a look of sincere admiration and pride in his eyes.

I casually glanced around the clubhouse ballroom. The room was filled with well-dressed gentleman and ladies, wearing only the finest designer gowns and custom-tailored suits, all business associates of my husband's. They were all living, breathing examples of how good life could be for people who had the cash flow to make things happen.

I briefly thought about my family. I wished my brother and mother could have been in attendance, but for Randall, it was physically impossible, and Mama just didn't give a damn. Not long after our family fallout, Randall had been busted on an array of charges, including theft of property and possession. He was sent down south, sentenced to four years. There were times when I wished I'd taken Gator's original offer to give him a job, but we couldn't turn back the hands of time; our cards had been dealt, and I wasn't about to get a new hand.

I recited the words of the song in my head while thinking they really didn't apply to me. I wasn't living my life like it was golden. Hell, my life was platinum, and there was absolutely nothing I would have changed about it. I exhaled as the song came to an end and strutted proudly on my heels as I approached the table where my husband sat.

"Enjoying yourself?" Gator asked, standing to greet me.

"Can't you tell?" I smiled, waiting for him to pull out my chair.

"I can," he said sweetly, "and I'm happy you're pleased."

I sat down, then waited for Gator to do the same before leaning in and pressing my lips against his cheek. "Thank you for this," I said.

"You're welcome, love," he said.

"I still can't believe you turned down a make-up vacation," Venetta said, shaking her head.

She was dressed in a simple but elegant red, one-shoulder gown that stopped just below her knees. She and Terrance had also decided to coordinate for the night. The bowtie on his dark tux complemented Venetta's dress and glowed against his dark skin. From his height to his physique, it was clear that Emerson had gotten his looks from his father.

"Believe it," I said. "Besides, I'm not always extravagant." I looked around the table as they erupted in laughter, one by one.

"Diamond, you're the most exquisite, expensive jewel in this room," Gator said. "You were born to be extravagant."

I pondered his words, then nodded my head in agreement. "I guess it's a good thing you can afford me," I teased.

"That it is," Gator agreed. "Terrance, care to join me on the terrace?" He pulled two cigars from inside his jacket and handed one across the table to his brother-in-law.

"I'm with you," Terrance said, standing.

Gator rose from the table, kissed me on the cheek, then walked off with Terrance following behind him.

"Do you know even half these people?" Venetta asked, looking around the room.

"Nope."

"We've come a long way."

"I know!" I said, smiling.

"Never take it for granted," she said seriously.

"Of course I won't," I said.

She looked like she wanted to say more but didn't. I'd never known Venetta not to speak her mind, so I assumed whatever it was it couldn't have been important.

"So…where's my nephew?" I asked, changing the subject.

"Working," she said, then took a sip from the glass sitting in front of her on the table.

"I've been meaning to ask how you feel about that. I always thought Emerson would go off to college and become an engineer or something."

"Emerson is doing what he knows," Venetta said. "Leon has built a family empire. It will someday be passed down, and…well, considering that you have no plans to have children—"

"What do you mean, no plans?" I asked. "You know we've been trying."

Venetta looked at me and shook her head. "Leon's trying," she said, staring at me, "but you and I both know it'll take a miracle for that to happen, considering that you're on birth control."

"Birth control!? Why would you think that?" I questioned, feigning innocence. "I want a baby just as bad as Gator does! I'd never—"

My dramatic performance was cut short when Venetta reached into her clutch and pulled out a peach-colored case that closely resembled the one I kept hidden under my bathroom vanity drawer.

"What's that?" I asked naïvely.

"You know exactly what these are," Venetta said, sliding the case across the table. "I stopped by Madison Drugs to pick up my allergy medication, and they asked me to give them to you. She said you called it in but missed your pickup."

Ain't that some shit? I thought, more than pissed that my privacy had been violated. "What ever happened to patient confidentiality?" I grumbled. I slipped the case off the table, opened my bag, and dropped the pills inside.

"Channel, the lead pharmacist, is a friend of the family," Venetta informed me. "The only concern she has with confidentiality is keeping others from finding out about her little cocaine habit. I normally don't patronize that location, but today I was in the area. I guess it's a good thing. I can only imagine what would have happened if Gator had been greeted with that little surprise."

I thought about that for a moment, and the image made me shiver. Gator would have been beyond pissed off. I knew he'd never lay a finger on me or do anything to harm me, but there would have been some form of consequence for my lying and deception, most likely in the form of my funding and allowance being cut off temporarily. For me, that would have been cruel and unusual punishment. "Listen, Venetta—"

"Don't worry," she said, cutting me off. "Your secret is safe with me."

"Thanks," I said, slightly relieved.

"But keep in mind that when my brother wants something, he'll do whatever it takes to get it," she warned. "Eventually, he's gonna get suspicious, and the truth will come out."

"I'll cross that bridge when we come to it," I said. "I just need a little more time." I looked up and saw Gator and Terrance walking toward the table. "Hey, baby," I said, nodding in their direction.

The look on both men's faces concerned me; clearly, something was wrong.

"What is it?" Venetta asked, noticing their expressions too.

"Have you heard from Emerson?" Terrance asked.

"No. Why?"

"He missed an appointment," Terrance stated.

"I'm sure there's a reasonable explanation," Venetta said calmly. "Did you try his cell?"

"Yes," Terrance responded. "Gator and I are gonna go look for him."

I shot a glance at Gator, silently letting him know that I did not appreciate his ass having to leave the make-up party he was throwing to make up for the damn vacation he'd missed. I knew he cared about his nephew, but he was supposed to care about my feelings too.

"It won't take long," he assured me, as if he'd read my mind. "Enjoy your guests. I'll be back shortly."

What the fuck ever, I thought to myself, but I said, "Okay, baby," and as soon as he and Terrance were out of earshot, I looked at Venetta. "See? This shit right here is why no one in this line of work needs children."

She gave me a look of disapproval.

"Sorry," I said, "but this is exactly why I've been taking those pills."

"I'm sure they'll be back in no time," she said calmly, "once they find Emerson."

I was so caught up in my own feelings that I'd forgotten that my best friend's son was missing. "I hope E.'s all right," I said sincerely.

"I'm sure he's fine," she said. "He's probably just running behind. That kid will be late to his own funeral."

Chapter 9

"Ashes to ashes, dust to dust," Minister Golston stated. There were tears forming behind my sunglasses-shaded eyes as I stood there in my fitted black dress and heels, watching as the clergyman opened his palm and allowed grains of dirt to sprinkle from his hand onto the casket that held Emerson's body. *"He's probably just running behind. That kid will be late to his own funeral."* Venetta's words echoed in my head.

I looked across the grave at Venetta. She was clothed in a simple black dress, and tears of a mother's sorrow were rolling down her brown cheeks. Terrance was beside her, dressed in a black suit, with a distant, pained gaze in his eyes.

As it turned out, E. was not just running behind; he was dead. An hour after Gator and Terrance left the party in search of Emerson, Venetta received a call from Terrance, informing her that he needed her to meet him at Huntsville Hospital. We left the country club immediately. When we arrived, the news was heart wrenching: Young Emerson had been murdered. The details of his death were sketchy, filled with so many holes that the news almost seemed like a cruel joke. If I hadn't been present when they identified his body, I wouldn't have believed it.

According to police, Emerson had been found in the streets with a man by the name of Victor Henson. Both had suffered multiple gunshot wounds.

Venetta had been an emotional wreck since that night, crying continually and barely eating. In a week's time, she'd lost at least twelve pounds. Terrance, a once happy and playful man, now mumbled words of hate and revenge. Emerson's death had shaken the two of them to their core, and it saddened me that they were suffering emotionally as well as physically.

I looked to my left, at my husband. His hands were clasped in front of him, and he was dressed in a tailored black suit and dark sunglasses. Gator had been extremely quiet since his nephew's death; mourning coupled with deep guilt and remorse. "He would never have been out there if I hadn't allowed it," he said, referring to the night of the murder.

I'd never heard my husband speak of any regrets for decisions he'd made, nor had I ever seen him so emotionally vulnerable, and I wasn't sure how to respond. So, I wrapped my arms around him, my nonverbal way of letting him know we would all get through our time of mourning together.

The minister recited a prayer, then offered Venetta and Terrance his condolences before walking off, leaving the four of us surrounding the casket. Outside of AJ, who stood waiting by Gator's truck with Jonah, and Darth, one of Gator's flunkies, we were the only ones in attendance at the memorial service for Emerson. One of the pros of being a part of the Douglass family was the money. One of the cons was that we had to mourn and bury our loved ones in private.

We stood by Emerson's grave until the sun began to set, until his casket was completely lowered in the ground and covered with dirt.

"Rest well, baby boy," I whispered, laying a single red rose on top of the grave.

I waited for my husband as he also laid a single red rose on top of the grave and whispered several inaudible words. Once he was finished paying his respects, he turned and extended his hand to me. I slipped my palm into Gator's and interlocked my fingers with his. We then walked, hand in hand, along the plush green grass, headed in the direction of his car, leaving Venetta and Terrance alone.

AJ opened the car door and stepped back to allow us room to climb inside the vehicle.

I settled against the cool leather seat, then turned to face Gator, who was staring out the window, loosening his tie. "Are you okay?"

"No," he said. "There are too many unanswered questions. I need answers, Diamond, and I plan to get them. That boy was my blood, and nobody fucks with that without justice being served."'

My husband's connections with the Huntsville Police Department had proven useless so far on Emerson's case. There were no leads, no witnesses, and no evidence linking Emerson to the other dead man. I'd never questioned or doubted Gator's pull in our city, from traffic tickets to gaining entrance to private city functions. All I ever had to do was mention my husband's name, and citations would turn to warnings and locked doors would fly open. We were considered local royalty and were treated as such. However, in one of our family's most trying and difficult moments, I was slowly beginning to wonder if there was someone of equal persuasion involved, pulling from the other side.

"How do you think you're gonna find those answers?" I asked.

"I have my ways," he said flatly.

"You have your ways, huh?" I said, slightly annoyed. "For once, can you actually share your ways with your wife?"

"The less you know," he said, looking at me intensely, "the better off—"

"Yeah, yeah," I snapped, cutting him off. "I'm your wife, Gator. What affects you concerns me, not to mention that I loved Emerson too. He was my best friend's son, for crying out loud, as well as my nephew. I loved that kid like he was my own blood."

Gator looked at me with eyes as bright as the stars in a night sky. "As your husband, it's my responsibility to protect you," he said.

"I don't need your protection. I knew what I was signing up for when I married you. I can handle anything thrown our way, and I think I've proven that." I looked at him and shook my head.

"Diamond, do you think for one moment I would've asked for your hand in marriage if I didn't see in you some of the same characteristics I possess? I knew within three seconds of speaking to you that you'd turn out to be the love of my life. I knew within thirty-six hours that you'd be my wife. I also knew you'll always do whatever is necessary to maintain the security of our family. Sweetheart, I know what you're capable of, but as your husband, it's still my responsibility to take care of you and prevent whatever I can before it becomes your problem."

"Your problems *are* my problems," I argued.

"Right now, my problem is that my wife refuses to honor my request," he said, raising his voice. "Do you think you can solve that one?"

I looked at him, slightly pissed at the rough tone in his voice. I was ready to render my response when the car door opened. I watched as Venetta climbed in, sliding into the second row of seating, followed by her husband.

"Where to, Boss?" AJ asked, climbing behind the wheel.

"Home," Gator answered.

Thirty minutes later, AJ pulled up in front of our home, with Darth and Jonah following behind. I decided to disregard my husband's earlier abrasiveness, reminding myself that he was emotional and going through a difficult time. After we all exited the vehicle, I led the way to our front door, relieved that the day's events were over and that our family could now attempt to get back to normal.

* * * * *

I lightly dabbed at the corners of my mouth with my linen napkin and looked around my dining room table. Venetta was sitting next to me, blankly staring down at her plate. Terrance was to her left, finishing off what I'd counted to be his third glass of brandy. My husband was at the head of the table, where he always sat, watching his sister closely.

After the members of Gator's team departed, Gator had called in a private chef to provide dinner for our family. Chef Javier had prepared a delicious spread consisting of steak, rice pilaf, green beans, and a Caesar salad. I usually did all the cooking, unless we ordered in or went out, but I was far too mentally exhausted to stand over a hot stove, and from the expressions on the faces around my table, it was clear that I was not the only one experiencing mental anguish.

I placed the napkin down on my plate and turned to my sister-in-law. "You should really try to eat something, hon'," I said gently.

"I'm not hungry," Venetta mumbled.

"I know," I said, "but you need to keep your strength up. Emerson would want you to." When she had no response for me, I added, "You know how he felt about bony women." I hoped the remark would lighten her mood.

"Yes, my boy always hated thin women." She sighed and looked up at me with tears in her eyes. "He always said, 'I need me some junk in the trunk.'"

"Or 'some goods under the hood,'" I said, smiling.

"Yes. That boy was a trip." She laughed lightly. "He liked curvaceous women, even though he was built like a pole."

I laughed, nodding my head in agreement. "We never knew what he was gonna say, did we?" I said. "He always found a way to make me laugh."

Venetta continued to smile as tears fell freely down her cheeks. I'd grown accustomed to seeing her cry, but these tears were happy ones, and I welcomed them. "My baby was somethin' else," she said, smiling brightly, "but I loved him."

"We all did, boo," I said sincerely.

"Yeah, we all loved him," Gator agreed.

I looked across the table at my husband and gave him a sweet smile.

"Right. We all loved the kid, but now he's gone," Terrance blurted, stating the obvious. "Why is that, hmm? Somebody tell me why my damn son is gone!"

The lighthearted feeling that had filled the room quickly dissipated, and we all fell silent.

"Right. Y'all got plenty of love for the dead boy, but ain't nobody got answers," Terrance ranted, slamming his glass down on the table. "My son is dead and no one has a fucking clue why, not even the damn police!"

"Terrance, honey, we can't change the fact that Emerson is gone," Venetta said, placing her hand on top of his. "If we could bring him back, we would, but all we can do now is talk about him and hold on to the memories and remember—"

"I don't want memories!" Terrance barked, snatching his hand away. "I want justice. I want whoever is responsible to look me in my eyes and tell me why they did it, and then I wanna see them suffer in such a way that the only relief they crave is death."

"Terrance, the police say Emerson and Victor died from gunshot wounds inflicted on each other," Venetta attempted to reason. "That's all we've got to go on now, baby, and—"

"It's not enough," Terrance raged, breathing heavily. "We deserve retribution for what we've lost. I want whoever did this, and I want them now."

"Vengeance isn't ours," Venetta said. "That's the problem with this family. We're all so…we take things into our own hands. Look where that's gotten us! We've lost my baby, one of our own."

"Venetta, we do what we have to in this family," Gator corrected her, "just as we always have and we always will."

"And just what are we gonna do now?" Terrance snapped. "Sit here and do nothing?"

"We'll pray," Venetta said.

I looked at her with raised eyebrows, as I'd never heard her mention prayer, faith, or anything even slightly religious.

"This is a sign of what's to come, a sign that we need to do things differently. We're reaping what we've sown, and—"

"Then we shouldn't be the only ones to reap," Terrance said.

"We won't be," Venetta debated. "Everything will come to light in due time."

"Due time? The time is already well overdue," Terrance spat angrily. He stood, threw his napkin down on the table in a huff, then quickly exited the dining room.

"I'll go talk to him," Gator said, rising slowly. He hurried out of the room, leaving Venetta and me alone.

"He sounds like a madman," Venetta said, shaking her head. "All this talk about vengeance and justice. It just…it scares me. I don't wanna lose Terrance too behind all this foolishness."

"He's hurting right now," I said. "Give him some time. I promise, it'll all work out."

"I know." she said lowly. "I just hope it works out in our favor."

Chapter 10

Two months had passed since Emerson's death, and Terrance was still volatile. He carried a gun wherever he went and seemed ready to snap at any moment. The change in his demeanor was scary sometimes, so much so that I attempted to keep my distance from him whenever he came around. He and Gator were spending more time together than ever before, and the two of them, along with Gator's team, were constantly on the go. Somewhere deep in my heart, in my soul, I knew they were working on something sinister, and there wasn't a doubt in my mind that it was a plot for revenge.

Venetta, on the other hand, had become an extremist of a whole different kind. She was now a scripture-quoting, Bible-toting, self-proclaimed Christian. The death of her son had led her to a spiritual 360. I questioned where the paths she and Terrance had chosen were going to lead and what it would mean for their marriage. The two of them were now living by two completely different principles, with far different priorities and goals in life and no child to knit them together, and they appeared to be growing farther and farther apart.

"They'll find their way back to one and another," Gator said when I mentioned my concerns.

As confident as he seemed, though, I wasn't at all convinced. I knew that in order for two people to share a life, they had to be on the same page or at least be willing to compromise. *How can you maintain a marriage if you aren't even reading the same damn book?* I wondered. I was as optimistic as could be about most things, but I knew my hubby was delusional or at least naïve or in denial about his sister's marriage. Their relationship was turning to shit, and mine wasn't faring much better.

Gator was keeping AJ busy, and that meant there was no time or opportunity for us to engage in any sexual activity. In the course of the last two months, we'd only managed to hook up once. I knew it was probably a good thing, because the less time AJ and I spent together, the less I thought about or lusted after him. Besides that, my hormones had been all over the place lately. I'd become a late-night junk-food junkie, and damn near everything had started to severely annoy me. There were times when my stomach felt incredibly weak and I couldn't so much as swallow without getting nauseous. I chalked my emotional instability up to the current chaos surrounding my family and my husband's lack of availability, knowing that stress could take quite a toll on a woman.

It was a beautiful Friday morning, and Venetta and I were spending some time together. Jonah was working with Gator, and since he'd given an all-clear upon his return from St. Maarten, we were allowed to venture out without a chauffeur. The two of us had a full itinerary that included getting our hair done, mani-pedis, and full-body massages. I originally had plans to go solo, but after seeing the atrocious condition of Venetta's cuticles and toes, I asked her to join me. I understood and supported her new lifestyle, but it was no excuse to let herself go. I was willing to bet that nowhere in her Bible did it state that in order to live holy, she had to walk around with her heels looking like she'd been out chipping bricks barefoot.

"Do you think you'll ever go back to your real hair?" Venetta asked, standing next to the styling chair, watching me closely.

I admired my reflection in the lighted mirror, feathering my fingers through my hair. My stylist, Nakita, had done yet another excellent job and hooked me up with a sexy sew-in with auburn highlights. It hung over my shoulders and stopped at the top of my ass. I swung all twenty-eight inches of the Brazilian Remy with pride and grace and said, "Sure I will, when they stop selling weaves or my husband goes broke." I laughed and stood. "But I wouldn't put my money on either of those happening anytime soon." I ran my hands over the front of my short dress, smoothing it out and cursing my slightly bloated belly. I looked fabulous regardless, but it was obvious that Aunt Flo was about to pay me a visit.

Diamond

After leaving the spa, we decided to have lunch at Beauregard's before heading back to my place. There were a few patrons in the restaurant, but it wasn't packed, which pleased me. I was starving and wasn't in the mood to wait around for our food. I sipped slowly from the glass of sweet tea sitting in front of me, hoping the cold beverage would calm my rumbling belly.

"Next time, we should check out this spot downtown that I heard Leon and Terrance talking about," Venetta suggested, looking across the table at me. "I think it's called Ambiance or something like that."

"Sounds good," I said, scanning the restaurant for our waitress. Originally, we'd declined the appetizers, but the loaded nachos I'd seen on the menu when we had placed the orders were still running across my mind. I saw the slim blonde weaving between tables and walking in our direction, her full breast bouncing inside her white shirt with every step she made. "Excuse me," I said, waving my hand in the air. "Excuse me!"

She nodded, acknowledging me, and walked over to our table. "What can I do for you?" she asked.

"Um…I think I'll have some nachos after all," I said.

She smiled. "Comin' right up," she said, then bounced away.

"Hungry?" Venetta asked, raising an eyebrow at me.

"Starving," I sighed.

"You shouldn't have skipped breakfast."

"I didn't," I confessed, "and it was a big one at that."

Venetta looked at me with both eyebrows raised this time, studying my facial expression. A second later, a small smile, almost a smirk, crept across her face.

"What?" I asked, slightly annoyed by her gawking.

"Maybe you're eating for two."

"What!? No way!"

"I'm just teasing." She giggled. "But you are looking a little, uh…full these days. I didn't wanna say anything, but that dress is a little snug."

"It's called water weight," I snapped defensively. I leaned over and whispered, "It's almost that time of the month, you know."

"Hmm. And a little snippy and emotional too," Venetta taunted. "I remember being like that when I was carrying Emerson."

"First of all, me being pregnant would be a miracle," I stated, rolling my eyes. "Second, my hormones are just all over the damn place with everything that's been going on. Gator's been coming and going at all hours of the night, and we can't have a decent conversation without his phone going off. "

"I understand that, girl," she said seriously. "If it wasn't for prayer and faith, I'd probably be locked in a padded room, chewing on my hair." She laughed lightly. "Terrance has been so distant and angry since…well, you know. I'm questioning his judgment more and more with every breath. Have I told you about his new friend?"

"No."

"His name is Z.," she said. "He's got no last name, just Z., the last letter in the alphabet."

"Z.? He sounds like a killer," I remarked. I smiled when I saw our waitress approaching with a plate of cheesy, messy nachos and two small saucers.

"Let me know if you need anything else." She smiled, flashing her green eyes. I waited impatiently as she sat our appetizer and the plates down on the table, then removed a stack of paper napkins from the apron secured around the waist of her pants. "Enjoy your appetizer, ladies. Your main course should be out shortly," she stated before walking away.

"Fabulous," I said. I wasted no time digging into the pile of cheese- and *jalapeño*-drenched tortilla chips in front of me.

"He's somethin'," Venetta said, eyeing me. "What he is, I don't know."

"I take it you don't like him." I covered my mouth while munching on my third chip.

"I don't trust him," she stated. "I don't know why, but I just don't."

"Have you talked to Terrance about this?"

"Heh. Right. Lately, we haven't talked about much of anything." Venetta shook her head. "We're growing apart, Diamond, and I feel like there's nothing I can do about it. It's as if Emerson was the glue that held us together, and now that he's gone…"

I paused and took a sip of my tea. My stomach was no longer growling, but it still felt empty. "Maybe you should go to counseling."

"I suggested that," she said, "but he refuses. All he wants, all he ever thinks about and talks about is—"

"Revenge?" I concluded.

"Yes," she said with a distant look in her eyes.

I paused, gathering my words in silence, as the waitress returned with our *entrées*. "I'm worried about him," I said honestly, as soon as our waitress was gone.

"So am I," Venetta grumbled, while picking over the chef salad in front of her, "but I've prayed about it, and whatever happens happens."

"Understandable," I said. I stared at the whiskey-jack burger in front of me. I didn't feel near full, but at the sight of the burger and cheese fries, I suddenly began to feel nauseous. "I-I'll be back," I said, quickly sliding my chair back from the table. I grabbed my purse, then quickly moved through the restaurant toward the ladies' room. *Maybe those nachos were a bad idea*, I thought. My tongue began to tingle as I pushed through the bathroom door. I hurried into the largest stall, the handicap one located the farthest from the bathroom entrance, and left the door open behind me. My stomach felt like it was on the Tilt-o-Whirl while I leaned over the toilet and allowed the contents of my belly to spill out into the porcelain bowl. I flushed the toilet, exited the stall, then looked at my reflection in the bathroom mirror while washing my hands.

"Impossible," I said aloud, drying my hands with a paper towel. I don't know if Venetta's words had me tripping or if I was actually beginning to second-guess my health. Turning sideways, I looked at my profile in the mirror, focusing on my stomach. "Diamond, stop trippin', girl," I said, shaking my head.

I turned on my heels, tossed the paper towel in the trash, and headed out of the restroom. I stepped across the wooden floor, digging though my bag in search of my breath mints. "Shit," I mumbled. My heart skipped a beat as I pulled out the small peach case containing my birth control pills. Flashbacks of the night of the party replayed in my head. After Emerson's passing, I'd completely forgotten about the pills. *Fuck!* I thought.

* * * * *

"I had a ball today," Venetta said as the two of us sat in my car, parked in front of her house.

"Me too," I said anxiously. "We'll have to do it again soon."

"Yeah. I needed some girl time."

"Me too," I said, tapping my nails against the steering wheel.

"Are you sure you don't wanna come in?"

"No. I'd better get home, just in case your brother's there. I like to catch some quality time with him while I can."

"I know that's right." Venetta exhaled. She had one hand on the door but still hadn't budged. On any normal occasion, I would have been happy to talk to her for a while, to give her some company, but the only thing on my mind at the moment was getting to the closest drugstore I could find.

"Well, hopefully the two of you will get some quality time in. Who knows? Maybe Terrance and I will as well." She gave me a quaint and unconvincing smile before finally opening the car door. She climbed out and turned to look at me. "Love you."

"Love you too," I said sincerely.

As soon as she was safely inside, I hauled ass pulling out of her driveway. Troubling thoughts flooded my head as I merged onto the interstate. *When was my last period?* I questioned. My stomach was still reeling, and I could feel the slow onset of a headache as I exited the interstate in the direction of the CVS Pharmacy.

* * * * *

I was perched on the edge of my bathtub, impatiently staring at my watch. My nerves felt like they would crawl out of my skin any second. I was experiencing what had to be the longest minutes of my life. I stared at the counter, looking at the little plastic stick I'd drizzled with my urine moments earlier. I wasn't a religious woman, as I'd strayed away from the church and my beliefs when my God-fearing mama had disowned me for marrying Gator, but I was now praying with everything in me that the test would prove my fears wrong. "Please let it be negative," I whispered aloud, with my heart thumping in my chest. "Please!" I darted my eyes back to my wrist, then stood slowly. "One line," I whispered, stepping over to the sink. "One line, one line, one...damn it!" I cursed when those two little horizontal blue lines stared back at me, as if they were mocking me.

"Diamond!" Gator called from our bedroom.

"Crap," I grumbled. I moved quickly to stuff the test, the box, and the brown plastic bag I'd carried them in into the bottom of the wastebasket, under a bunch of other trash. I slid the basket in the corner under the sink, then looked around, making sure I hadn't left any evidence. I made a mental note to take the trash out upon my first opportunity.

"Love, are you in there?" Gator called.

"Just a second," I sang, flushing the toilet. I quickly washed and dried my hands before opening the bathroom door and facing Gator. "Hey, baby."

"You all right?" he asked, instantly recognizing that something was off about me.

"I-I'm fine," I stuttered nervously, stepping past him. I could feel his eyes penetrating me from behind while I walked over to our bed and sat down. The look of concern and curiosity in my husband's eyes made me extremely nervous. I watched as he slipped his blazer off his shoulders and tossed the designer threads on the bed next to me. "When did you get in?" I asked.

"About five minutes ago," he stated. "Are you sure you're all right?"

Hell no! I thought, but I lied, "Yes, boo, I'm fine. Why?"

"Your face is flushed," he advised me, "and your eyes are red. Have you been crying?"

Not yet but I damn sure want to! Again I lied, "I was just thinking about the last time I saw Emerson. When Venetta and I hung out today, we were reminiscing, and…well, I guess it just hit me."

"I see." He walked over to the bed and eased down beside me.

I began to perspire nervously, fearful that he could see through my lies. The moment of silence between us made me even more uncomfortable. I pulled my eyes from Gator's, choosing to focus on the bedroom wall instead. Thoughts of the last time Gator and I had made love penetrated my mind. Just as fast as my thoughts of us in our bed appeared, they were quickly replaced with the vision of AJ and I screwing. The severity of my reality began to set it: I was pregnant with a child I didn't want and, even worse, a child who might not even be my husband's.

"So…did you have a good time?" Gator questioned.

"What?" I asked, looking at him.

"Today," he said with a frown. "Did you and my sister have a good time?"

"Yes," I said, shaking my thoughts from my mind. "Yes, we did."

"Good," he said, stroking my cheek with his fingertip.

I shuddered slightly from his touch, an involuntary reaction from the picture of what he would do to me if he found out about the baby and the possibility that the child might not be his. He would forgive me for lying about taking birth control, at least in time, but I was certain that carrying another man's child would be an unforgiveable offense. I was sure his idea of justice for me for that would be throwing me out in the streets. "You hungry?" I asked, standing, as I desperately needed to put some distance between the two of us. I needed air and a moment to get my plan together.

"No. I ate earlier. AJ's waiting for me outside. I just wanted to stop in and check on you."

"I'm fine. I was just about to tidy up a little bit," I said, remembering the test I'd buried in the wastebasket. "Are you going back out?"

"Tidy up?" Gator's tone matched his raised eyebrows and his look of bewilderment.

"Yeah." I laughed. "I need to do something to work off some of the food I ate earlier." I stood in front of him with my hands clasped in front of me, his questioning eyes making me feel naked, exposed, and guilty.

"The house is already spotless," he said.

"I know, but I wanna keep it that way." I gave him a weak smile, then turned toward the bathroom.

"Diamond…" Gator's voice resounded loudly, causing me to jump.

Get it together, Diamond, I told myself before turning around. "Yes?"

"Why do you continue to lie to me?"

"What?" I questioned innocently.

"I'm quite aware of your recent emotional and physical changes," he said, standing. "I've been busy, not blind. You've got a little extra weight around the middle, all that continuous munching on food, and the odd behavior."

"Are you calling me fat?" I probed, pretending to be offended.

"Don't do that. Don't insult me," he said smoothly. "We both know that whether you put on five pounds or fifty, insecurity is not a quality you possess."

He was right, for I was not the kind of woman to take insult when my weight or any other imperfection was mentioned. I was generally comfortable in my own skin, or at least I had been until I discovered I might be carrying another man's child inside it.

"Well? Are you gonna confess, or do I have to say it?"

"Yes," I whispered. I'd forgotten that Gator's eye for detail was as precise and sharp as his wardrobe. I'd paid my lack of a period no attention, but Gator probably had my shit stored in the events on his phone with a special alert. I knew I was busted, and there was no point in carrying on a façade. I told myself I could tell Gator about the baby and fake a miscarriage the next time he went out of town; it would be easy enough to get an abortion. *Hell, he'd probably feel guilty for not being there, and that'll only lead to him showing me even more gratitude and love. It might even keep him at home more.* "Gator, I—"

The sound of his cell ringing interrupted my confession.

"Excuse me, my love," he said, holding up his finger.

I nodded my head.

"You had me concerned," he said, speaking into the phone. "Any luck? I'm listening."

I listened quietly, watching Gator as he went back and forth with his caller.

"I'll be in touch." He ended the call and immediately made another one. "Meet me at the warehouse in forty minutes. Kelly just called me. He found the missing link." He ended the call, then reached for his jacket.

"What is it?" I questioned.

"Everything will be back to normal real soon, baby," he said, looking at me. "Diamond, I know the changes you've been experiencing are merely your body's way of crying out for attention and that the weight and overeating is due to stress."

Come again? "Stress?"

"Yes," Gator replied. "I love you, and I love you even more for being strong and keeping your emotions and feelings to yourself, but it's not fair to you. I know the last two months have been extremely stressful, and I've done little to nothing to show you that you are still the most important person in my life. That is all about to change."

I was relieved and slightly shocked that Gator was oblivious to the truth. "You're right." I sighed. "I'm just thankful that we had this moment to actually talk about it."

"Yes," he said, slipping his jacket on, "so am I." He leaned in and pressed his lips against mine. "I'll be back as soon as possible."

"Okay." I smiled, relieved.

"I love you."

"And I love you," I replied. I walked my husband downstairs to the foyer and gave him another kiss before he walked through the front door.

As soon as I heard the sound of his car engine revving up, I hurried into the kitchen, retrieving the Yellow Pages I kept in the top drawer. I flipped through the pages until I found the listings for clinics. I hurriedly memorized the number for the Alabama Women's Center, then hurried back upstairs and dialed it from my cell. I'd never terminated a pregnancy before, so I was utterly clueless as to the process. It had been my hope that I could get in, state my case, hop on a table, and have the problem taken care of with a few snip-snips and a casual, *"Take two aspirin and call me in the morning,"* but when I spoke to the receptionist over the phone, that hope was lost.

"In the State of Alabama, pregnancy termination requires two visits," the woman told me. "The first is for counseling. After your counseling session, you have to wait twenty-four hours before we can schedule an appointment for the procedure."

"I don't need counseling," I spoke with haste. "I just need it done."

"I understand that you feel you've made your decision," she said politely, "but we must abide by the law."

"Are there any exceptions?"

"No, ma'am."

"Okay." I exhaled heavily. "What time can I come in?"

"Our next opening is tomorrow at 1 p.m.," she said. "We only do the procedures on Wednesdays and Saturdays, so—"

"Are you telling me I'll have to wait until Wednesday to have it done?" I asked, cutting her off.

"Yes, ma'am."

"Listen, I can't wait that long. I need this done immediately."

"Sweetheart, we have policies and procedures we have to follow, and. . ."

I rolled my eyes while listening to the woman ramble on and on about the law and the procedures they were obligated to abide by.

"We could lose our license for noncompliance," she finally stated.

"Can you please pencil me in for a consultation today?" I begged. "Please?" After ten minutes of pleading and a few fake tears, I was convinced the woman would squeeze me in before they closed.

"Darling, I empathize with you completely," she said softly, "but again, the earliest appointment we have is tomorrow at 1:00. Would you like to schedule an appointment?"

I wanted to scream with frustration and defeat, but I knew that would be useless. "What do you think?" I asked sarcastically.

Chapter 11

The next morning, I woke up to an empty bed and morning sickness. I couldn't understand it. Now that I knew the kid existed, that he or she was growing in my belly, it was trying its damndest to make me as uncomfortable as possible. I'd barely gotten any sleep the night before due to indigestion, and dry-heaving had become my wake-up call. *Maybe it's your conscience,* I told myself. "Maybe," I replied. Regardless of the reason I was clenching my toilet with both hands, and I just wanted the entire experience to be over immediately.

I brushed my teeth, then washed my face before stepping into the shower. I stood in the shower until the water ran cold and my queasy stomach finally settled. I opened my bathroom door, allowing the steam to billow out into the bedroom, then reached for the Shea butter I kept in my vanity drawer. I sat on the edge of the bathtub, massaging the cream over my arms and breast, thinking about the mess I'd gotten myself into. *What in the hell was I thinking?* I had access to more money than I could have ever imagined and a husband who truly loved me and did everything in his power to keep me happy, and I'd chosen to risk it all. *For what? Good dick and a chocolate smile?* I made myself a promise that if I got out of my current situation without getting caught, I'd never cheat on Gator again. I looked at the empty jar of Shea butter and made a mental note to stop by Bridge Street after I left my consultation at the Women's Center. I screwed the top back on the jar and tossed it in the wastebasket.

After I got dressed, I headed downstairs. Joyful sounds of laughter and camaraderie greeted me as I stepped off the landing of the stairs into my foyer. I painted on my most gracious smile while walking toward the dining room. Gator was seated at the head of the table, and Terrance was to his left. There was a small table set up along the dining room wall, covered with trays of croissants, pastries, fruit, biscuits, eggs, bacon, and juice.

A chocolate-complexioned man I'd never seen before was sitting to Gator's right. The unfamiliar man had a clean-shaven, bald head, a full mustache, and a dark beard. He was the first to notice me and instantly stood when I entered the room. He was dressed in a basic black suit with a red shirt and black tie.

"Good morning," I spoke, looking from one man to the other.

"Good morning, ma'am," the stranger spoke in a deep, baritone voice.

"Morning, sis," Terrance said, smiling brightly and standing as well. Much like my husband's guest, he was dressed in a dark suit and tie. I was completely caught off guard by the cheerfulness in his voice, but although he looked and sounded somewhat normal for the first time in months, I was still leery that the crazy might come out of him at any moment.

"Beautiful," Gator stated, also standing. He stepped around the table, revealing that he was casually dressed in a navy button-down shirt, slacks, and loafers.

What the hell? I was caught off guard by his ensemble; my hubby never dressed down in front of company, and he was not one to be out done by his associates. For a minute, I thought the baby was messing with my head, making me hallucinate.

Gator opened his arms, embraced me, then kissed me tenderly on the lips. "How are you?" he asked, pulling back.

"I'm…well," I said, staring at him. "How are you?"

"Life is good," he said. He stared at me with a loving light in his pupils that made me want to melt. "Let me introduce you," he said, looking at his guest. "Diamond, this is Z. Z., this is my wife, Diamond."

"It's nice to meet you," Z. said, nodding his head in my direction.

"Thank you," I answered cordially. "It's nice to meet you as well." Z. was the man Venetta had told me about. From his appearance, he seemed harmless, almost boring. I wondered what it was about the man that had my friend on the fence. "Well, I'll leave you gentlemen alone," I said.

"No need," Terrance answered, standing. "Z. and I were just leaving."

"Thank you for breakfast, Boss," Z. said, pushing back from the table.

"Gentlemen, it was a pleasure," Gator said. "Z., I'll be contact."

"Sounds good," Z. said.

"Diamond, enjoy your day," Terrance said.

"You too," I replied.

"I'm gonna walk them out," Gator advised me. "I'll be right back."

"Okay." I watched as they exited, still in awe of the men's demeanor. I contemplated trying to eat something, but as I looked down at the table, I quickly decided against it. I grabbed one of the empty glasses sitting next to the small stack of plates and poured myself a glass of orange juice. I took one sip from my glass, and my taste buds were instantly on alert; there was champagne mixed with the juice. I didn't have an appetite, but I was definitely feeling the Mimosa. I grabbed the glass pitcher and sat down at the table with my glass in hand.

"Not hungry?" Gator asked, reentering the dining room. He walked over and sat down beside me.

"No, I'm still catching hell from the lunch I ate yesterday," I said.

"Didn't agree with you?"

"Not at all. I think it was the nachos."

"Well, maybe a little retail therapy will do you some good, baby," he suggested.

"You read my mind." I laughed. "I was just saying to myself that I need to stop by a couple stores at Bridge Street."

"I was thinking more along the lines of an overnight trip to New York," he said, leaning forward in his chair. "Just the two of us painting the city green, the color of money."

I smiled. "I would love that," I admitted. "Pick a day," I said, cutting my eyes at him while taking another sip of my drink. "I know you're busy, and I don't wanna be stood up again," I smiled, but I meant every word.

"I guess I deserve that," he said, "but the day is today. Our flight leaves in an hour."

"What!?" I hoped my shock was coming off as excitement rather than disappointment, but I was almost positive my tone had matched my thoughts.

"You're not happy," Gator stated, confirming my thoughts. "Why? I thought you said you'd love it."

I set my glass down on the table, then attempted to gather my words and regroup. I didn't have an excuse in my book of lies that would justify not wanting to spend the day in the city with the man I loved, spending the money we both loved. Hell, being Gator's wife was my profession, and spending money was part of my job. If I refused, he'd be on to me without a shadow of a doubt. "I-I am happy," I stated, attempting to reassure him. "It's just that it's been a while since we've gone anywhere, just the two of us. I guess I'm kinda surprised."

"I know," he said, reaching over and cupping my hand. "It's long overdue. It's time for the king to bring back the magic."

I was all for the king bringing back the magic, but I didn't know why he'd chosen that day of all days.

Gator continued to stare at me, searching my expression. The decision had been made, and unless something came up to change his mind, I was on the hook.

"I'll go pack," I said, forcing a smile.

"No need," he advised. "All you need to bring is you." He stood up, then leaned down and kissed me on the forehead. "I'm gonna make a few phone calls before AJ gets here."

The mere mention of AJ made me my skin crawl, but I wasn't about to say so. "Okay, baby," I purred.

Gator exited the dining room, humming lowly and walking with an extra spring in his step, leaving me silently sulking in my chair in secret disappointment.

* * * * *

The drive to the airport was one of the most uncomfortable I'd ever experienced in my life. I sat in the back of Gator's SUV, snuggled in my husband's arms, trying desperately to act normal and avoid the subtle eye contact AJ kept attempting to make with me in the rearview mirror. He was acting like a teenage boy, watching his girl crush with the high school football star. It was a good thing our affair had ended when it did, because I found myself suddenly questioning AJ's capability to maintain our façade.

I was thankful that the two-hour flight to LaGuardia Airport was a smooth one, with beautiful, sunny skies—a complete turnaround from the last time I'd flown. I was sure my nerves couldn't have taken foul weather, along with all the other changes my body was going through.

When we landed and arrived at our destination, I stood in the bedroom of the penthouse of The Waldorf Tower, admiring the stunning Italian mahogany canopy bed and all the accents and elegant décor throughout the suite. The entryway of the penthouse was flanked by marble pilasters. On the walls were murals depicting the beauty of Italy in vibrant colors. The adjacent living room featured ivory-painted trim, fabric-upholstered panels, and classic, fabric-covered furnishings that gave the room a royal ambiance fit for the queen of England. The suite was luxury at its best. "This is beautiful," I said appreciatively.

"Anything for my queen," Gator recited.

"Thank you."

"You'll have time to finish admiring our accommodations tonight, along with other things," he stated suggestively. "Stores are calling, and we have the funds to answer."

"You'll get no arguments here," I grinned, slipping my hand in his.

* * * * *

Gator had provided me more than retail therapy; he had given me a retail overdose, and I loved it. The two of us had graced boutique after boutique, stopping only for lunch before going right back at it. By the time we returned to the hotel that night, I had a complete wardrobe, and I was completely exhausted. The two of us now sat side by side in matching leather chairs, relaxing on the balcony of our room. It was a beautiful, warm, moonlit night, the perfect end to a perfect day.

"So…what did you think of Z.?" Gator questioned. "First impression."

"Polite, gentleman…boring."

"All in one, huh?" Gator chuckled.

"Yep."

"I just added him to our team," he informed me.

"Really?"

"Yeah. Terrance trusts him, and I trust Terrance's judgment."

"Do you think that's wise?"

"Terrance is normally on it," he said. "I know recent events have caused him to act somewhat erratically, but it's understandable. Soon, all that will turn around."

"I did notice a change in him today," I admitted. "He looked more like his old self."

"Trust me, my love, today's only the beginning."

I only hoped his words were true.

Chapter 12

Monday morning, I thought Gator would never leave the house. First, he awakened me with breakfast in bed, followed by a long, hot bath and a full-body massage. I was thankful for the time and the affection he was showing me, but I had one thing on my mind and one thing only: the clinic. Our little weekend getaway had set me back and forced me to cancel my appointment. Of course I enjoyed every minute of my trip, but it was now time for me to get back to the basics.

When he received a phone call and advised me he had to run an errand, it took everything inside me not to do a summersault. As soon as he kissed me goodbye, I became a woman on a mission.

The Alabama Women's Center was located in the medical district in downtown Huntsville. I was somewhat hesitant and fearful of being seen in the area, but I had to handle my business one way or the other, and going to see my own physician was not an option. I pushed through the glass door with my eyes covered by my sunglasses, then stepped right up to the receptionist's desk. "I have a 10:00 a.m. consultation," I said, staring at the pale, portly woman through the Plexiglas.

"Good morning." She smiled, revealing teeth covered by braces.

"Do I need to sign in?" I asked, dismissing her greeting.

She cut her brown eyes at me and slid me a clipboard full of forms through the slit at the bottom of the plexiglass. "Fill these out and bring them back to me."

I took the board, then turned on my heels and found an empty chair against the wall. I filled out the questionnaire, only answering certain questions, because as far as I was concerned, my family history was none of their damn business. I walked up to the receptionist and handed the clipboard to her, and she asked me to have a seat in the waiting room until my name was called.

I didn't have to wait too long, which was a relief. My consultation started with blood work and testing to confirm what I already knew, followed by an ultrasound. Dr. Blige, a pretty redhead with a curvaceous body, informed me that I was approximately four weeks along. After discussing all the alternatives, which included keeping the baby and adoption, she then spoke to me about the emotional repercussions some women experience and the effect that the decision to abort could have on me and my family. I listened quietly, not because I was having second thoughts, but simply because I liked to hear the woman talk. She was intelligent and sexy, so much so that under different circumstances, I might have attempted to take her home to play a little doctor of my own. When she was finished with her spiel, she asked if I had any questions. Since I didn't, she escorted me to the receptionist, where I finally got to schedule an appointment.

I slipped my sunglasses back on and exited the Women's Center with my handbag and keys in hand. I had chosen to park my car on the side of the building, in the hopes that it would be less noticeable to passersby. When I rounded the corner of the building and saw Gator's SUV parked beside me, I knew I was in trouble. I stopped midstride and stood there, motionless and staring at the car.

My heart raced uncontrollably, and my stomach felt like I was going to shit a brick as I watched the driver-side door open and saw AJ step out. He adjusted the lapel of his jacket, then shut the door. I waited nervously for him to open the back door for Gator, but he never did. "What are you doing here, Diamond?" he asked, cutting his eyes at me.

"Where's Gator?" I questioned nervously.

"With Jonah."

"He had me followed?" I questioned, walking toward him.

"No," AJ said, taking a step forward. "I just came from taking care of some business in New Projects. I was headed back to the spot when I noticed your car. What's going on with you? Why are you at the clinic? You sick or something?"

"I had a checkup," I said, slightly annoyed. "That's all…and it's really none of your business what I'm—"

"Cut the bullshit, Diamond," he barked.

"What?" I asked, attempting to walk past him.

"You know what," AJ snapped, blocking my path. "I've been here before with Charla, my ex. Women don't just come here for checkups." The glare coming from his eyes was more intense than sunrays on a summer day. "You're pregnant, aren't you?"

"Yes," I huffed in frustration.

"Is it mine?"

"I don't know who's it is," I said, slightly embarrassed. "The dates are too close together, but it doesn't matter either way. Even if it's not yours, I'm not keeping it."

"What!? Maybe you should think about this," he suggested. "I mean, we can work this out."

What the hell? It had become painfully evident that AJ had lost his damn mind. There was no way in hell the situation was going to work out in my favor. If the baby was my husband's, my freedom was over; if the baby was the chauffeur's, my life would be over. Either way, having that baby meant I was going to lose. "There's nothing to think about," I snapped. "I'm getting rid of it, period." I stepped past him again.

"Listen to me!" he barked, grabbing me by my arm, stinging my skin with pain. There was a savage look in his eyes that frightened me. "Diamond, I'll do whatever I have to. I wanna make this work. We can run away, or we could we can—"

"AJ, there is no 'we.' Whatever we had, it's over," I said. "I love my husband, and he's the only one I want to be with. If you don't stay away from me, I'll tell Gator about us, and we'll both suffer the consequences," I said, hoping he'd heed my warning.

"Diamond," he begged. "Baby, please just—"

"Let me go," I said, ignoring his pleas. "Now!"

AJ released his grip on me, then shook his head. "If you love him, why are you fucking me?" he asked, trying to call my bluff, except I wasn't bluffing.

I unlocked my car and opened the driver side door. "We aren't fucking anymore, AJ. I made a mistake," I said gently, "and it won't happen again."

"A mistake?" he repeated. "You weren't hollering that when you were sucking my dick."

"You were a good mistake," I said, "but a mistake nonetheless. Take the memories and cherish them."

"We can make more memories," he said.

"No we can't."

"Why? I can make you happy, Diamond. I know I can. I can give you what you need, baby," he stated tenderly.

"AJ you're the kind of man women come to for a good lay," I blurted out. I sighed, tired of the conversation. "Gator's the kind of man women marry. He's a boss, and you're just a worker. I'm not worker's wifey material."

He looked slightly hurt by my comment, but he maintained a strong disposition. I was thankful for that, because the last thing I needed was for his ass to start shedding tears or pop off. "Well, at least I know where I stand now."

"Good," I said. "Try not to forget again."

"The money has changed you, Diamond," he said, shaking his head.

"Are you serious?" I laughed. "Alvin, what do you expect? Money does that. It changes everything, even the way you eat, the way you dress." I studied his eyes and added, "It even changes who you fuck. I'll admit I've been screwing up on that last one lately, no pun intended, but I'm done with all that." With that, I climbed behind the wheel of my car, then shut and locked the door.

AJ stood outside and stared at me for a moment before he finally climbed inside the truck, started the engine, then sped off.

Chapter 13

I opened my eyes and tried to allow them to adjust to the darkness before pulling myself up against the wooden headboard. Stretching my legs out in front of me, I looked over at the small crystal clock on my nightstand; it was a little after 9:00 p.m. I'd slept for the majority of the afternoon, but I still felt like I could sleep for at least another three hours straight. I blamed my sluggishness on the sedatives the physician had prescribed. The day I'd been anxiously awaiting had finally come, and although I knew what I had to do, I had an unsettling feeling that something wasn't right.

That morning, Gator had appeared distant himself, as if he was also facing a major, life-altering decision. As always, he'd been loving and warm with me, but I still sensed that something was wrong. We'd had a quiet but delicious breakfast before going our separate ways.

I'd headed straight to the clinic. It only took eight minutes for the procedure itself, but I was in the clinic for almost four hours, going through all those last-minute tests and listening to doctors lecture me, giving me one last chance to change my mind. After I advised the doctor that if she didn't do it I would, the ball started rolling. Once I'd been cleared to leave the clinic, the doctor gave me some antibiotics and sedatives and sent me on my way.

I'd returned home to an empty house and a note from Gator, advising me that he would be home late. No matter how late it was when my hubby arrived, I planned to treat him to a rare surprise, a home-cooked meal. I settled into our family room and turned on the TV, ready to catch a couple movies on Netflix. An hour later, I was hit with cramps from hell. I took a quick shower, then retired to my bedroom, where I'd been ever since.

Reaching over to my right, I retrieved my phone from the nightstand. I'd missed a call from Venetta, two calls from an unknown number, and an *I love you* text from Gator. I smiled and replied, *Sorry, baby. I was sleep…but I love you too.*

I placed the phone on the bed next to me, then picked up the television remote. I stared at the flat screen on my bedroom wall and flipped aimlessly through the channels. "Umpteen channels, and nothing's on," I grumbled, shaking my head.

I flipped past Channel 19, CBS, then quickly went back when I noticed they were airing breaking news from Madison County. I watched as the cameraman zoomed in on the scene. There were marked squad cars with their lights flashing and news vans everywhere. "Who got shot this time?" I exhaled and turned the TV up.

I loved my city, but lately crime had been on the rise. It had only been a few weeks since the media had reported the story of a newlywed couple who had been shot on their wedding day during an alleged attempted robbery and car-jacking. There were no leads or suspects in the crimes, but something told me that whoever was responsible had motives other than robbery or stealing a damn car, especially considering that nothing was missing from the victims, including the car.

I listened closely while a brother with lightly toasted skin and a medium build stood in front of the camera, speaking into a handheld microphone, explaining that a hostage situation had taken place earlier. Two women were being held captive, and the situation ended with gunfire exchanged between the suspects and police.

As a previously recorded clip of the scene played, the reporter said, "So far, there have been five confirmed deaths. Among the dead are one of the female hostages and four men. We also have confirmation that the second female captive has been taken to the ER with minor injuries and is expected to be all right. Authorities have not yet released the names of the victims, but behind me, you can see that there is a suspect in custody, being held in connection with the events that unfolded here tonight."

The camera scanned to a patrol car, with a man sitting in the back, then back to the reporter.

"Sources say this man is Leon Douglass—"

"No," I whispered, sitting up straight in the bed. I grabbed my phone and speed-dialed Gator's number, hoping I'd heard the reporter wrong. The phone rang several times before finally going to voicemail. I tried again, only to get the same results. I hung up quickly, then dialed Jonah's number, only to receive an automated message stating that the number I'd dialed was no longer in service. My pulse raced as realty began to set in: *My husband is in trouble.*

I tossed back the covers and flinched slightly form the pain in my lower abdomen, then dialed Venetta's number. I slowly walked over to my armoire, removed a pair of yoga pants and a fitted t-shirt, and slipped them on while waiting for Venetta to answer.

"Hello?" she said, her voice low and scratchy, as if I'd interrupted her sleep.

"Venetta, they just said on the news that Gator's been arrested! I tried calling his phone and got his voicemail. I called Jonah, too, and his number is no longer in service." I was rambling a mile a minute, trying to explain. "Is Terrance there?" I asked, breathing heavily. "Can I speak to him?"

"He's not here right now," she said with a groan.

"Have you heard from him?" I probed, pacing back and forth across the carpet. "I mean, do you know if he was with Gator? "

"Yeah, he was," she said, "but he's not anymore."

"Well, where is he? Do you know when he'll be—"

"Terrance is dead, Diamond." She said the words so flatly that I almost thought I'd heard her wrong.

"What!?" I asked, stopping mid-pace.

"I said he's dead," she repeated, just as bluntly.

"Venetta, I…" I had no words to express to her what I felt at that moment. Of course I was still very concerned about my own husband, but according to the news, at least my man was still alive. I held the phone in silence, attempting to collect my thoughts. "Venetta, are you sure?" I finally questioned when I mustered the courage to speak again.

"It's him, Diamond," she stated. "The police showed up on my doorstep twenty minutes ago. My husband is dead."

Click.

Even though she'd hung up on me, I knew my friend needed me at that moment, but I was more worried about my husband's situation. I grabbed my purse and keys, then exited the bedroom, heading downstairs. As I approached the landing of the stairs, I heard our landline ringing. I moved as quickly as possible toward the cordless phone that was sitting in its cradle on the table in my foyer. "Hello?" I answered.

"Diamond?" a man replied.

"Who is this?"

"My name is Clint Harvey. I'm Leon's attorney," he said. "I've been trying to reach you for the last hour. I need you to meet me at my office immediately."

"How do I know you are who you say you are?" I asked, leery.

"Leon thought you'd ask me that," he advised me. "Inside your safe, there's a brown accordion file. Inside the file, you'll find three envelopes. One of those envelopes has my name on it."

"There's nothing in our bedroom safe that fit that's description," I informed him, keenly aware that he was lying. The only items we stored in the wall safe in our bedroom were my jewelry, a pistol, ten grand, and our marriage certificate.

"Not *that* safe," he said. "There's a wood panel beneath Gator's chair at the dining room table. The panel is slightly lighter than the others. Remove it, and you'll find the safe."

"Listen, I don't know who you are, mister, but—"

"Do it, Diamond," he ordered.

"Okay! Hold on." I exhaled and figured I may as well entertain the man. I walked into the dining room and pulled out Gator's chair at the head of the table. I eased down on my knees and pulled back the corner of the rug. I'd never noticed it before, but there was a panel there, a shade lighter than the rest. I played with the corners of the panel for a moment, and, much to my surprise, it popped open. I couldn't believe Gator had hidden the safe from me, and I wondered what else he'd been hiding right under my nose. "What's the combination?" I asked, staring at the safe door.

"Your birthday," Clint advised me.

I entered my birthday on the digital keypad, then pushed down on the handle. Once the safe was open, I reached in and pulled out the folder Clint had told me about. Inside were three thick envelopes, one with Clint's name, one with my name, and one with Venetta's.

"Do you believe me now?" Clint asked.

I'd forgotten all about the man on the other line, because I was too busy counting the cash inside the envelope with my name on it. There was over $30,000 in it, along with a note that read, "Emergencies only." I took the liberty of checking the other two envelopes as well; there was ten grand in Clint's and twenty in Venetta's. "What's the address?" I asked.

* * * * *

Clint was a slim, chocolate man with a baby face and low-cut hair. He was attractive and looked to be no older than I was. He was sitting behind a mahogany desk in his office, dressed in a soft pink shirt and gold tie. He made quick work of briefing me on everything that had taken place and what was to come.

As it turned out, the women who'd been held in the warehouse were allegedly tied to Emerson's death. According to Clint, Gator and Terrance had allegedly plotted to murder one of the women's husband for his presumed involvement. The plot had gone terribly wrong, however, when the police were tipped off.

"The news said there were five victims. Do you know all their names?" I asked softly. Venetta had already informed me that her husband was among the dead, but I was curious who else had gone down, besides Terrance and the one woman.

Clint flipped through the notes in front of him. "A female, Lena Jasper...Darwin 'Darth' McCulley, Alvin Staton Jr., Terrance Bailey, and a Zachery Crawley."

AJ? I fought the urge to shed tears in front of the man while attempting to digest the news he'd provided. I remembered the last words I'd spoken to AJ, and a cloud of regret hovered over me. Despite our argument and the way I'd dealt with him, I hated to hear that he was gone. I assumed Lena was one of the female hostages, and Zachery was the man we all knew as Z. "Was anyone else taken into custody other than Leon? What about Jonah?"

"Who?"

"No one," I said. I figured if Gator had never mentioned Jonah to Clint, there was a good reason. *Is it possible that Jonah tipped off the police?* I trusted the man with my life, and he had saved me from Lisette, but I could not rule out the possibility.

"So what happens next?" I asked, redirecting my attention to Clint.

"Tomorrow morning, the judge will decide whether or not bail should be set," he explained.

"So he'll have the opportunity to come home?" I said, relieved.

"Diamond, I'm on Leon's team because he appreciates my honesty," the lawyer stated. "That said, I think it'd be unfair of me to paint false hope for you. More than likely, the judge will deny bail, simply because of the severity of the situation. "

"No matter how severe the situation may look," I said, shaking my head, "my husband is an innocent, law-abiding man, and he deserves to come home."

Clint looked at me with an expression that said he knew I was lying. After several silent seconds, he leaned forward in his chair, clasping his hands together in front of him on the desk. "Do you know the other reason your husband hired me?" he asked.

"No. Why?"

"Because I know that eighty percent of my clients have committed ninety percent of the crimes they're accused of, not to mention a whole slew of other crimes no one knows about," he said. "To be frank, I know they're guilty, but I don't give a damn."

"That's real," I said, reaching down in my bag. I removed the envelope with his name on it, then handed it to him.

"Leon will call you in the morning," he advised, taking the envelope. "Until then, try and get some rest."

"Why didn't he call me tonight?" Even when his ass was in trouble, I had to hear everything from the hired help, and that ticked me off.

"There's really nothing you can do at this point," Clint said. "Besides, there's no need to worry you more than necessary. Go home and get some rest. I'll be in contact."

I wrapped up my meeting with Clint, then exited his office.

* * * * *

My thoughts ran rampant as I trekked through the parking lot toward my car. Lifting my head, I looked above me. If I had been a superstitious woman, I would have attributed the day's events on the fact that there was a full moon. I shook my head, wondering what could possibly happen next.

When I'd first arrived at Clint's office, the parking lot had been empty, with the exception of a red Mercedes that I assumed belonged to him. There was now a black Kawasaki Ninja sitting next to his vehicle. The engine was running, but there was no one in sight. I dismissed the owner's neglect as stupid; with all the crime that had taken place in our city lately, I wouldn't have left a rusty Huffy alone and exposed at night.

I unlocked my car and climbed in behind the wheel. I slipped the key in the ignition, then screamed lightly as my mouth was grabbed from behind. I darted my eyes up to my rearview mirror and stared at the intruder in the back seat. He was dressed entirely in black, everything from his t-shirt and sweats to the baseball cap he had pulled down over his eyes. "Jonah," I mumbled breathlessly.

"Are you okay?" he questioned, releasing his grip on me.

"You scared the hell outta me," I breathed, clutching my chest. I turned in my seat and glared at him. I took a deep breath then exhaled in an attempt to calm my nerves. "How'd you get in here…and how did you know where to find me?"

"Spare key," he said. He turned his head and looked out the left passenger-side window, then to the right. "And there's a tracker on your car."

I made a mental note to address the issue with the tracker later, for I had more important things to discuss with the man for the time being. "Jonah, what happened? What went wrong?"

"I don't know." He exhaled. "But I shoulda been there."

"Why weren't you?" I asked, as it didn't make sense to me that Gator's second-in-command would have been MIA during what had obviously been a major event.

"Gator sent me to Ambergris Caye last night," he said. "I just made it back a few hours ago. When I rolled up on the scene at the warehouse, I didn't stop, but I knew whatever had taken place there wasn't good. I sent Gator a text, asking if I should come through. When I received a *Yes*, I knew it wasn't him."

His mention of Ambegris Caye made me wonder if something had transpired involving Lisette. After we'd left the island and returned home, Gator had never much mentioned the incident again. "Is everything okay there?" I asked.

"Everything was fine," he said. "It was a wasted trip."

"Where'd you go after you left the warehouse? I called you, but it said your phone was disconnected."

"I went to my spot first," he said, looking around, "just to grab some essentials."

Jonah's absence and explanation seemed far too convenient to me. Clint had informed me that someone within my husband's circle had tipped off the police, and I was beginning to think that someone really was Jonah.

"Diamond, I'm many things, but disloyal isn't one of them," he said, reading my mind.

"I know Jonah. I'm just worried about Gator," I lied.

"Have you heard from him?"

"No, but he had his attorney call me. That's why I'm here. He said Gator will call me in the morning."

"Okay. Look, I'ma go to a partner's house and lie low for a few days," he advised, reaching into his pants pocket. He pulled a piece of paper out and handed it to me. "If you need anything, hit me up. You can reach me at this number. Don't mention my name when you talk to Gator, but tell him the exterminator stopped by." With that, he opened the passenger door and scooted out.

"What? No, wait! I—" I said, confused.

"Just do it, Diamond," he ordered. "I'll be in touch soon." He closed the car door, then ran over and hopped on the motorcycle and took off.

Chapter 14

The next morning, I called to check in with Clint, and he informed me that Gator had, in fact, been denied bail. "They think he's a flight risk," Clint said matter-of-factly, "but we knew this would happen. Don't worry, Diamond. This is just a stumbling block and only the beginning of our battle, but in the end, we'll win."

I heard every word the man said, but I wanted my husband home with me, and there was nothing anyone could say to make me feel better at that moment. When I asked if I could visit Gator, Clint advised me that I'd have to wait thirty days, and that only made me more miserable.

An hour after I ended my call with Clint, I received a collect call from Gator. It took every fiber of my being not to erupt in tears when I heard his voice.

"How's my baby?" he asked, as if I was the one who was in trouble.

"I'd be doing much better if you were here with me."

"No worries, my love. I *will* come home to you soon," he said confidently. "You've got my word on that."

"I know," I said.

"How's Venetta?"

"As well as can be expected," I said sadly. "I'm gonna see her today. I was just waiting for your call."

"That's my girl," he said. "Give her my love."

"I will," I promised. "Gator, baby, I miss you so much"

"I miss you too," he said gently. "Just try not to worry."

"Gator, are we okay? Do I need to do anything?" I questioned. I was not only worried about my husband's freedom but also what his time in jail would mean for his business. In more ways than one, his absence was not a good thing.

"We're fine," he said abruptly. "I just need you not to worry."

"But you—"

"Diamond, trust me. This, too, shall pass," he said strongly.

I hope so, I thought. "Oh…the exterminator stopped by," I said, remembering Jonah's instructions.

"Good. Tell him to keep up the good work."

"I will."

"I've gotta go. I'll call you tonight around 8:00," he said. "I love you."

"I love you too."

After ending my call with Gator, I got dressed and headed out to go visit his sister. As I pulled out of my driveway, a million thoughts ran through my mind, mostly about Gator being in jail. All the times I complained about him being late suddenly appeared irrelevant and ridiculous. Now he wasn't coming home at all, at least not anytime soon. I told myself I had to stay positive for Venetta's and Gator's sake as well as my own. I could only imagine the pain and sorrow she was experiencing, having lost her son and husband in less than twelve months, a hard pill to swallow. I didn't believe we would ever be given more than we could bear, but I wondered how much more weight my friend would be able to carry.

The drive to Venetta's home was only thirty minutes, but because I was dreading the visit, it seemed twice as long. I had traveled the winding, curvy road several times throughout the years, but for the first time, it seemed intimidating and dangerous. It was amazing that my mind was making every possible excuse for me to get out of visiting the broken-hearted woman.

I finally pulled off the road and into Venetta's driveway and up to her house, where I parked behind the white Mercedes-Benz that had once belonged to Emerson. Venetta's Ferrari was also parked in the driveway, right beside the midnight-blue Escalade that belonged to Terrance. I killed my car engine and sat behind the steering wheel for a moment, just staring at the house. Memories of the days when Venetta, Terrance, Gator, Emerson, and I had sat on that wooden porch for hours, laughing about nothing, flooded my mind. I laughed while looking at the eggshell-colored frame and green shutters, remembering the holiday barbeques and Emerson running across the driveway with sparklers. It all seemed like yesterday, a far cry different from the madness and turmoil we were now facing.

I shook my head, tossed my cell phone inside my handbag, removed my keys from the ignition, then climbed out of my car. I stepped onto the porch and pressed the button to ring the doorbell. After several rings and a few knocks garnered no answer, I finally decided to let myself in using the spare key Venetta had given me. "V.!" I called, poking my head inside the door. "Hellooo?"

I gingerly stepped across the living room floor, scanning the room with my eyes. Venetta's normally spotless home was in complete disarray. There were pictures and newspapers scattered everywhere, along with empty wine bottles and sticky, dirty wine glasses.

"V., baby!" I called, entering the kitchen.

There was a strange stench floating in the room, and it caused my stomach to churn slightly. "What the hell is that?" I questioned, covering my mouth and nose with my hand. The disgusting aroma grew stronger and fouler as I approached the kitchen sink. There, lying in the steel sink, was a large, defrosted, raw salmon, more brown than pink. "Shit." I grunted, then took in a quick breath that I instantly regretted.

I set my bag down on the kitchen counter, then walked over to the pantry and retrieved a garbage bag. I tossed the fish in the bag, pulled the plastic handles together tightly, and placed the bag on the floor. I washed my hands and made a mental note to take out the trash before I left.

Since there was no sign of life downstairs, I headed upstairs to find Venetta. As I strolled down the hallway toward their master bedroom, I noticed that the door leading to Emerson's bedroom was now secured with a padlock. *How does she expect to heal if she keeps the memories of her boy locked away?* I wondered. I concluded the behavior couldn't have been healthy and was probably Terrance's idea.

"Venetta!" I called, knocking on her bedroom door. "V., are you in here, hon?" I turned the door handle and slowly pushed the door open, not wanting to startle her since I was sure her nerves were probably already on edge.

Unlike the living room and the funk that was festering in her kitchen, Venetta's bedroom was clean and odor free. I strutted across the carpeted floor and stopped a few feet from the bathroom door. I could hear water running and the soothing sounds of Miles Davis on the other side of the door. Rather than knocking on the door and scaring the hell out of my bestie, I decided to go back downstairs and wait for her. As I turned on my heels, I felt the carpet shift slightly under my feet. Stepping back, I stared at the indentation caused from my shoes; the carpet was clearly wet. "What the hell?" I whispered aloud.

I rushed toward the door, practically holding my breath as I turned the handle and pushed it open. Venetta was lying next to the bathtub, wearing only her bra and panties. Her hair and skin were soaked from the water overflowing from the tub, and there was an empty prescription pill bottle on the floor beside her, along with a spilled bottle of red wine.

"Venetta!" I screamed, rushing toward her motionless body.

* * * * *

The shrill beeping and wheezing of the heart monitor connected to Venetta pushed my already frazzled nerves closer to the edge. I was thankful I'd gotten to her in time to call 911 so permanent damage and death could be prevented, but I was still slightly in shock that she'd attempted to take her own life. Staring at her with empathy and sorrow, I observed the changes in her appearance. Her once-rich chocolate complexion was now shockingly pale, with several tiny lines creasing the area below her eyes. Her usually smooth lips were now chaffed and dry.

I continued to stare at her until she slowly began to open her eyes. "Hey," I said softly, stroking her head with my fingertips.

"Hi," she said quietly. A single tear trickled from her eye, then ran down her cheek.

"How are you feeling?"

"Hoarse…and sore."

"Understandable. They pumped your stomach," I advised her.

"I'm sorry, Diamond," she cried. "I just…"

"V., it's okay," I said tenderly. "I'm just glad you're all right. Baby, what were you thinking?"

"That I-I just wanted the pain to be over," she stuttered.

"Venetta, suicide isn't the way. You still have so much more left to give in this world. Emerson and Terrance wouldn't want you to give up."

Diamond

She nodded her head, then dabbed at the tears that coated her cheeks. "The night it all happened, I was gonna make grilled salmon for dinner," she said. "I was in the kitchen, and this uneasy feeling came over me, telling me something wasn't right. I could just feel it. I remember going in the living room and falling to my knees. I prayed that the feeling would go away, that I was wrong, but an hour later, the officers came and confirmed what I already knew."

"Did you know what they had planned?" I asked.

"No, but Terrance told me before he left that we were finally gonna get our justice, that we'd finally have closure and peace. That man's last words to me were a lie." She began to sob uncontrollably. "I don't have peace or justice. I-I have nothing."

"You have me," I said sincerely, "and you still have your brother. V., things will get better. I promise."

"When? When will anything be better ever again, Diamond?"

I wanted to respond with a brilliant answer, something that would wash away all her worries and woes, but I'd been asking myself the same damn question, and I didn't have a clue. All I could do was give her the only response I felt was suitable for the moment. "Soon," I said. "Soon."

G STREET CHRONICLES
A LITERARY POWERHOUSE
WWW.GSTREETCHRONICLES.COM

Chapter 15

*G*ator decided, and I agreed, that it was best if Venetta stayed with me at our home for a while, at least until she was emotionally stable. I had no objections or complaints. We had plenty of room, and I was extremely lonely in that big house without Gator anyway.

When it came time to bury her husband, Venetta and I stood, hand in hand, paying our final respects in the same memorial garden where we'd put her son to rest months before. The graveside service was short and bittersweet, and the minister was the only other person in attendance. Despite her attempted suicide, Venetta still professed her faith and proclaimed that we would survive through prayer. I had to commend her on her optimism and applaud her faith; even I was beginning to believe her. However, as we soon discovered, the truth was that our family was falling apart at the seams.

Venetta and I were sitting in the family room, trying to relax, when Clint called to inform me that Gator was being investigated on charges of extortion and racketeering.

"How is that possible?" I asked, stunned.

"The prosecution claims to have viable evidence and witnesses to support the charges against Leon," Clint explained.

In layman's terms, there were snitches who were able to sell my husband out. I was concerned but not worried. Being able was one thing, but being ready and willing was something else. *Who, in their right mind, would go against Gator?* I was convinced that my husband's reputation was more than enough to keep anyone from betraying him.

Clint went on to explain that the prosecutor planned to offer Gator a plea bargain. "I've advised Leon of this," Clint stated, "but it would help if you could talk to him before he gives them his decision."

"And what did Leon say when you advised him to take the deal?"

"He laughed," Clint said flatly.

I could easily envision Gator doing just that. No matter how bad things seemed, there was no way my love would compromise or admit any guilt. "I think we both know his mind is made up. Thanks for calling Clint," I said. "Keep me posted."

Venetta was sitting on my sofa, watching me intently, hanging on my every word.

I placed my phone down on the coffee table, then sighed.

"Is everything all right?" she asked.

"Yes, everything's fine."

"I'm not gonna have an emotional meltdown, as long as you tell me the truth," she stated. "What's going on?"

I broke down and told her, detail for detail, what Clint and I had discussed.

"Ungrateful-ass snakes," she said angrily, cursing for the first time in a long time. "I guarantee that whoever is running their damn mouths also reaped the benefits of Leon's hustling."

"I'm sure," I said.

"I will not allow my brother to be torn down," she whispered, standing, "I refuse." There was a venom in her voice I'd never heard before, a look in her eyes that seemed strangely familiar; it was the same look I'd seen in Terrance's face the day we'd buried Emerson.

"Just keep praying—"

"Pssh, I've tried that," she said, turning to look at me. "I'm through praying. Now it's time for something else!" She cut her eyes at me, then stomped out of the room.

"Okay," I whispered.

I contemplated on whether or not I should follow Venetta and attempt to calm her down, but I thought it best to let her have her moment. I decided I needed to tell Gator to hurry up and get his ass home before his sister jumped off the bridge into the river of "crazy".

Diamond

* * * * *

Since Gator's arrest, I'd only left my home to go to the cemetery with Venetta and for the occasional trip to the store. I was keeping a very low profile, including keeping a tight leash on my speeding habits, I'd even let Vanessa go. Being frugal was Venetta's idea, but I thought it was a good one, in the event that the Feds were watching. After the news Clint had provided me, I knew I'd made the right choice.

After a while, I decided for my good behavior, I deserved a little reward and something to relax my mind. I got dressed, ready to go out and treat myself to a drink or two. I'd received a couple postcards in the mail, advertising the Presidential Bar and Grille, a new establishment off Sparkman Drive and figured it was the perfect time to try it out.

* * * * *

Shifting in my seat, I stared at the glass sitting on the bar in front of me. Rotating the small straw in a circular motion, I watched as the light yellow liquid swirled around and around.

"You okay, mami?" the petite bartender asked, staring at me.

"Yes." I smiled up at her.

"A'ight. Let me know if you need anything."

I nodded my head, then took a long sip of the vodka and pineapple juice. I turned around on the barstool and scanned the crowd, until I spotted a tall, bowlegged brother with chocolate skin. He was wearing dark jeans and a white and red I AM HuntzVegas t-shirt and bright white sneakers. I blinked quickly, thinking I'd seen a ghost. He looked up, locked eyes with me, then smiled, providing me assurance that he was real. I watched as he weaved through the crowd until the two of us were standing toe to toe.

"Baby girl," Randall chimed, engulfing me in a hug.

I closed my eyes, allowing myself to get lost in my brother's embrace. "When did you touch down?"

"A couple weeks ago," he said, "but I just got in town last night. I woulda called you, but…"

"Yeah, I know," I said, feeling extremely guilty. I'd changed my number as soon as Gator and I had exchanged our "I do's," and I'd left behind everything associated with my past life, including my family. My mother wanted nothing to do with me or my new lifestyle, but I knew that didn't justify me turning my back on my brother. I sat down and took another sip from my glass.

"Diamond, I forgive you," Randall said, sitting down beside me. "I mean, I was fucked up back then, and to tell you the truth, I woulda been fed up with my bullshit, too, if I were you." He waved down the bartender and ordered a double-shot of Grey Goose.

"You look good," I said honestly. I patted the tiny twist that now grazed the top of his head.

"Not half as good as the kid." He laughed. "Gator's been good to you."

The mere mention of my husband evoked my desire to smile and cry at the same damn time. I turned my head to keep Randall from seeing my mood swings.

"What's wrong?" he asked seriously. "Dude been treating you all right?"

"Yes," I said, giving my brother my undivided attention, "even better than I expected."

"So…what's up? Come on, sis. I know you. No matter how long it's been, you're still my baby sis, and I can tell when something ain't right."

"You haven't heard?"

"Heard what?"

"They got him."

"Who?" Randall asked, shocked. "Dem boys?"

"Yes."

"Hell naw!" He frowned. "What happened?"

I brought him up to speed, from Emerson's murder to Gator's arrest.

"Damn. I hate hear that," he said. "Shit got too real."

"That it did," I said.

"And who's holdin' it down while your man's outta commission?"

I hesitated momentarily, wondering exactly how much I should confide in Randall. Granted, he was my blood, but it had been nearly six years since the two of us had seen each other.

"Diamond, you know I ain't no snitch," he said, "I served four years for holding my tongue."

I needed someone to talk to candidly, someone I loved, someone who loved me. I knew that no matter what, Randall would be by my side, so I opened up to him, disclosing what I knew, which wasn't much, other than that Jonah was still working the streets, handling Gator's business.

"I'm sure he's got the right man on the job," he said, "and if your man told you it's gonna be all right, I'm sure it will. Gator's been in the game for a minute. If anybody can make it happen, it's him."

I nodded my head in agreement. "So, uh…how's Mama doing?"

"Hell, your guess is good as mine." He laughed and took a gulp from his glass. "She stopped claimin' me as her blood soon as I caught my case. I'm talking no phone calls, no letters, no puttin' money on a brother's books, no love whatsoeva. That woman can hold a grudge like nobody's business."

"So you did your entire bid solo?"

"For the most part," he said proudly. "I mean, I met a couple broads on the Internet, and they looked out for your boy toward the end."

"So you've got a girl now?"

He chuckled. "No. I *had* a girl till about a week after I was released. Then I had nothin' but memories."

We both laughed.

"You wrong, boy. You know that?"

"Meh, you gotta use what you got access to," he said.

We laughed and talked for a few more minutes, until I decided it was time for me to go.

"Where are you staying?"

"At the Extended Stay America, over on Governor's House Drive."

"Are you working?"

Randall smirked, then shook his head. "You know how I do, just odds and ends here and there."

"You'd better not be stealing!"

"I'm not," he said. "I swear."

"Lemme give you my number and a little something," I said, digging in my bag.

"Naw, sis. I'm straight," he said, waving his hand. "Just give me your number and promise that we can stay in touch. I got the rest."

"Randall it's not an issue," I said, slipping $300 out of my wallet.

"Diamond," he said strongly, "I'm good, okay?"

It was funny; there was a time when I'd argued with my brother because I didn't want to give him money, but now I was practically having to beg him to take it. "You sure?"

"Positive," he said, "but I appreciate the offer."

"Well, at least let me buy you another drink."

"Now *that's* a deal your big brother'll take ya up on, sis," he said with a grin.

Chapter 16

$\mathcal{I}$'d never dreamt I'd be visiting Gator in jail; however, when the thirty-day waiting period was up, I did just that. The two of us sat, face to face, at a small plastic table among a roomful of conversing strangers. I'd chosen to wear a sexy V-neck, fitted dress and pumps. I was pushing the dress code, a bit overdressed compared to the other women in the room, but I didn't care. I wanted everyone to know that although my husband was wearing the same baggy, unflattering orange jumpsuit as the others, we were royalty. Our money was still very long. When heads began to turn, I knew my mission was accomplished.

I stared into Gator's face, smiling brightly, admiring every beautiful detail.

"Oh how I've missed that smile," he said.

"And I yours."

"You look beautiful, love," he said, leaning forward in his chair.

"Nothing but the best for my baby."

We made small talk for a few minutes, until I finally decided to address some things that were weighing on my mind.

"Clint said an insider tipped the authorities off," I whispered, leaning forward. "Do you think it was Jonah?"

"No."

"Then why wasn't he with you that night?"

"'Cause I sent him on an assignment before it all went down," he said lowly, confirming what Jonah had told me the night before.

"Clint says there are people willing to turn State's evidence against you, baby," I said. "What if Jonah's one of the them?"

"People might be willing," he said, "but willingness also requires opportunity. I still have faith that my name rings more than a few bells, and so do the consequences of betraying me." He looked at me with a straight face that required no further explanation. "When it comes to Jonah, he's always been one of my most loyal associates. He's proven that, and I hope he still is."

"I understand," I lied.

"Is there anything you need?"

"I'm good," I said. "Just come home."

"I will, baby. I promise. Did you put the cash I gave you back in case of an emergency?"

"Of course," I said, "and I've been carefully watching my spending."

He looked at me with both of his eyebrows raised.

"What?"

"Nothing," he said, nodding.

"Gator, I know when and how to cut back when necessary, and right now I know I have to be careful," I said seriously. "But as soon as you're free, baby, it's on! It'll be registers ringin' back to back."

"I have no doubt in my mind about that." He laughed lightly.

"Guess who's home," I said happily.

"Who?"

"My big brother, Randall." I'd reconnected with Randall some time ago, but I wanted to tell Gator about our happy reunion face to face so I could gauge his reaction. Gator had never tried to keep me from my family but I also knew how protective and cautious he was.

"That's wonderful, sweetheart."

"I know, and he's changed so much," I said proudly. "It's like he's a completely different man."

"I'm glad he's there for you."

"Really?"

"Yeah," he said.

"Good, because I let him move in two days ago," I quickly tried to explain. "I mean, he's been working when he can, layin' his head at the Extended Stay, but you know how expensive that is, and it's hard for brothers who've done time to get jobs, so—"

"It's fine," he said, cutting me off.

"Really?"

"It's good that there's a man around to look after you and Venetta. It puts my mind at ease a bit while I'm locked up in here. I know your brother's had issues in the past, but he's family. You should never turn your back on family."

"That's one of the reasons I love you," I said sweetly. "You have such a giving and a forgiving heart."

"I promised myself a long time ago that I'd help as many people as I can in this life," he said, "no matter how much wrong I do in between."

"I don't even see the wrongs," I said truthfully. "All I see in you is love, Gator."

He gave me a small smile, then stared at me with an unreadable expression etched on his face. I was familiar with the look, one he often gave me when he was in deep thought.

"What's wrong?" I asked, concerned.

"Nothing," he said, rubbing his hands together. "I just expected you to look...well, somewhat different."

"You don't approve of my outfit?"

"You're killing that dress," he said. "I only wish I could show you just how appreciative I am that you wore it."

"Then what were you expecting?"

"Well...for you to be showing."

If there had been an Olympic medal awarded for awkward moments, mine would have been gold. I was caught off guard by Gator's words, but there was no doubt in my mind that I'd heard him correctly. I pulled my eyes from his in an attempt to hide the guilt that I was certain was flashing in my gaze.

"The morning we flew to New York, I found the home pregnancy test in the garbage can," he said.

Flashbacks of the trash being empty surfaced before me. I hadn't given the empty can a second thought, for I was too focused on getting to the clinic. "Why didn't you say anything?" I finally asked, looking at him in disbelief.

"I planned to," he said. "I assumed you had something elaborate planned to let me know the wonderful news. I figured that was why you hadn't said anything, that you wanted to surprise me or—"

"I-I did," I stuttered. "First, though, I wanted to make sure the test was accurate, because those home tests aren't always the best. The day you were arrested, I went to the doctor, and she confirmed that I was pregnant, but... oh, Gator. When I let the office, I started bleeding. I drove myself to the ER in a panic, only to discover that I'd had a miscarriage. I-I'm so sorry I lost our baby, Gator. I know how bad you wanna be a daddy." I continued spinning my web of lies as I went along, putting on a Broadway performance of grief, silently hoping I wouldn't get caught slipping in the details.

Gator's eyes lowered to the table. "Why didn't you call me? I woulda gone with you. You shouldn't have had to go through that alone."

"I was so heartbroken, and I felt like I'd failed you. I planned to tell you when I got home, but when I got there and saw your note that you were gonna be out late, I lay down to take a nap. Then, when I woke up, I saw you on the news, and...well, here we are."

Gator stared at me in silence, making me feel like I was on trial.

"Now I wish I had called you," I said quickly. "Then maybe you wouldn't be here now."

Damn right I took the blame for him getting apprehended. I hoped if my deceitful explanation didn't save my ass, sympathy and regret would.

"None of this is your fault, Diamond," he said. "I shoulda been there for you. Yes, I'm disappointed, but everything happens for a reason."

"We can try again," I volunteered. "As soon as your home, I'm gonna give you a houseful of babies. I promise."

I was exaggerating my ass off, but the smile on Gator's face told me my lies were working as intended. "I'll hold you to that," he said sweetly.

The overweight guard standing watch over the visitation room made the announcement that it was time for us to say our goodbyes.

Gator stood and extended his arms to me.

"I love you," I said, wrapping my arms around his neck.

"I love you too."

He gave me an innocent kiss on the lips, followed by a big squeeze. I was disappointed by the wimpy peck, but I understood that public displays of affection were not welcome there. Next, Gator pulled away, looking at me, and he kissed me again, this time with so much passion that he left my legs shaking and my panties moist.

Chapter 17

Throughout my husband's incarceration, I spent a great deal of my time working out and kept my nose buried in books, just the distractions I needed to keep my hormones under control and my focus off my need for sexual gratification. I'd made a promise that I would never cheat on Gator again, and I'd managed to keep that promise, but I was tired of sleeping alone and anxiously awaiting my man's return.

I had just completed a four-mile run on my treadmill and had worked up a thirst when I entered the kitchen and found Venetta leaning against the kitchen island, holding a broom in her hands, staring at the TV. "Good morning," I greeted.

"Hey," she said. She immediately pressed mute on the remote and redirected her attention to me.

"What is it?" I asked, concerned by the blank look on her face.

"Have you seen the news?"

"No," I said, shaking my head. "You know I try to avoid depression and death at all costs, and lately that's all that's ever on TV." Sure, I loved to be as informed as the next individual, but it seemed the whole world had lost its damn mind as of late. From murders to robberies and constant stories of missing or violated children, it was enough to depress even the strongest of hearts. Considering everything my family was going through, I didn't need to wallow in other people's sorrows; we'd had enough of our own.

I walked over to the refrigerator, pulled the door open, and removed the glass pitcher of orange juice. As I set it down on the kitchen island, the volume on the TV slowly rose. I attempted to tune it out as I retrieved a glass from the cabinet and began filling it with juice.

"We now return to Lois Whitaker…"

"Tom, I'm standing outside the Madison County Courthouse, where sheriff's deputies have announced one of the largest local drug busts in ten years. Detectives and the Tactical Response Unit have arrested twenty-five-year-old Jonah Washington of Huntsville on charges of manufacturing and intent to distribute a controlled substance. Washington is also charged with unlawful possession of a firearm, and sources tell us…"

I listened in horror as the reporter continued explaining that drug task force officers had also raided an apartment and storage facility in other parts of the city, confiscating a total approximately $550,000 in cash and thirty kilograms of cocaine.

"Do you know what this means?" Venetta asked, turning off the TV. "We're screwed, Diamond. Those spots were Leon's, every last one of them."

I grabbed the cordless phone, jerking it from its cradle on the counter.

"Who are you calling?"

"Clint," I said. "He needs to represent Jonah to see if they set bail."

"Are you fucking crazy?" Venetta blurted, snatching the phone from my hand. "If you post Jonah's bail, it'll scream that he was working for Leon."

"He was!"

"Yeah, but at this moment, they don't know that," she disputed, "and the only way they'll find out is if Jonah runs his mouth or if *you* screw up."

"He won't do that…and how is my helping someone who's a part of this family screwing up?"

"*Maybe* he won't talk," she said. "We don't know what he'll say to the cops if they threaten him with jail time, but I do know you can't be associated with him right now. They're looking for anything and everything they can find to keep Leon locked down. You go bouncing your ass down there posting bail, things are gonna get real ugly for Gator and for us. Jonah's got plenty of friends and blood to handle his case. Right now, we have to handle ours."

I didn't want to argue with her, but every word she was saying was complete bullshit. Jonah had protected and saved my life, and now she expected me not to give a shit, not to return the favor when he needed help. *No way!* I would let Venetta have her moment, but I planned to address the subject with my husband at my earliest opportunity.

Chapter 18

An entire year and a half passed before Gator had his day in court. The first case on the docket for him involved the extortion and racketeering charges. The solid case the prosecution had attempted to build against him came tumbling down when evidence and witnesses mysteriously began to disappear. Even though it appeared my husband was a man standing alone, he was still feared. When it came to actually putting their asses on the line and looking eye to eye with Gator, those who'd so quickly flipped to State's evidence were nowhere to be found . The charges were dismissed, and that gave me confidence that the kidnapping and conspiracy to commit murder charges would also be dropped.

Less than a month after the first case was thrown out, we were back in court to listen to the testimony of the kidnapped woman and other witnesses. Octavia, who looked to be at least six months pregnant, was an enticing female with a brown-sugar complexion, jet-black, wavy hair, and pretty fuck-me, honey-brown eyes. She was clearly intelligent and articulate, but she could also let the ghetto flow when she needed to. Under different circumstances, and if she hadn't been knocked up, we probably could have been lovers or friends, but my husband had fucked that up by abducting the woman in the first place on his quest for vengeance.

When Octavia gave her testimony, something about the details made my heart ache a little for her. I knew who I was there for and whose side I was on, but I still felt remorse for the things she'd endured. She told the jury that Gator's boys had snatched her right in front of her daughter, leaving her baby girl alone in her vehicle in a parking lot. Her voice grew shaky when she described how she felt when she thought she'd never be able to kiss or touch her baby again. "My heart ached when I learned that they planned to murder my husband," she said in a near whimper.

Her husband, Damon, was a caramel-skinned brother with sculptured facial features, just as sexy as his wife and dressed to a tee in a designer suit. He walked with a swagger that screamed that he had money. When he took the stand, his eyes immediately fell on Gator, where they stayed throughout his testimony.

The reaction I saw on the juror's faces when the couple testified made me nervous and had me wondering if Clint really had the case in the bag like he claimed he did. Clint's defense was simple and sweet: Gator had simply been in the wrong place at the wrong time. The attorney placed all the blame on Terrance for the crimes that had taken place. Several character witnesses, including Erica from Divaz and Big Boy from Brother's Groceries, spoke eloquently about how Gator had helped save their nearly drowning businesses and would do anything to help his fellow man. The defense presented on behalf of my husband made him look and sound like a saint on Earth, awaiting his crown and place amongst the gods.

After three days of proceedings and only six hours of jury deliberations, I sat behind my husband with my hands folded together and my heart thumping loudly in my chest, listening as the judge asked the jury forewoman if they had reached a verdict.

"We have, Your Honor," the forewoman spoke.

I nonchalantly looked across the room at Damon and Octavia. He was sitting with his arms wrapped around his wife's shoulders in a public display of affection and support; I envied them. Octavia's father was with them, as well as a woman I assumed to be her mother. In that brief moment, I wished my own family was there to support me. Even after my husband's very public arrest, my mother still hadn't reached out to me, and I didn't see any point in bothering a woman who didn't want to be bothered. Still, I wondered, *Isn't there something in the Mommy Handbook that even if you disapprove of their decisions, you're supposed to stand by your children until death? If not, there damn well should be.*

Randall had offered to accompany me at the trial. I refused his offer, but I appreciated the fact that he'd actually made an effort.

Venetta chose to avoid the trial because she didn't want to hear the ugly details of our husbands' dirty deeds. "I wanna remember Terrance how he was those last few days," she said, "happy…and good."

I respected her decision, but deep down, I thought it was bullshit, that she was being a coward. She didn't want to hear the truth that, although her husband had not acted alone, he'd clearly lost his damn mind in the process and snapped.

I pulled my eyes from the Whitmores and focused on my husband, who was standing with his back straight and his head held high, like the king I knew he was.

"On the charge of kidnapping," the jury forewoman began, "we, the jury, find the defendant guilty."

I cut my eyes at the woman, hoping I'd heard her incorrectly.

She continued, "On the charge of conspiracy to commit murder, guilty."

I felt a knot rising in the center of my throat and tears forming in the wells of my eyes. I stared at Gator in utter shock as the Whitmores erupted in a celebratory uproar while my heart slowly sank to my toes.

* * * * *

"There's still more than enough money in the account for you to start over," Gator stated.

I was sitting on the patio of our home, barefoot, with the phone pressed to my ear, stretched out on one of the chaise lounges surrounding our pool. I stared at the sun and watched as it slowly began to sink into the horizon. I was still wearing the fitted white pantsuit I'd worn to his hearing hours earlier; since leaving the courthouse, I'd only summoned up enough energy to tell Venetta and Randall the verdict and to have a good cry for myself. Five hours later, my tears had subsided, but I was still trying to grasp the reality of the harsh verdict. "Start over?" I said in disbelief.

"Yes. You can leave town and start fresh."

I'd never considered leaving town. I had, on the other hand, considered cleaning our bank accounts out on more than one occasion, but I'd quickly abandoned those thoughts. "This is my home," I said, running my fingers through my hair. "I'm not going anywhere without you. Besides, we're gonna appeal. You promised me you'd come home to me, Gator, and I'm gonna hold you to it."

"I always keep my promises," he assured me.

"You better," I said softly.

"Until next time, my love."

"I love you."

"I love you too," he said, then hung up.

I continued to sit on the patio until nightfall, replaying our conversation over and over in my head. I didn't want to start over without him, and I refused to run out on my husband. I refused to abandon him, especially when he needed me most, but the possibility of what could come terrified me. *What kind of life will we have with him behind bars?* I'd heard about plenty of honorable, ride-or-die females who waited patiently, day by day, for their loves to return home, and I could salute every one of them, but I had to be real with myself. Loneliness was a motherfucker for me, and I needed another's legs, arms, and hands wrapped around mine from time to time. Being alone for two or three years was one thing, but twenty years or, worse, the rest of my life was a whole different ballgame.

"You okay, sis?" Randall asked, stepping out onto the patio, holding a six-pack of Heineken and a bottle opener.

"I will be," I said, watching him as he sat down beside me.

He set the six-pack down on the concrete and offered me an icy bottle.

"No thank you," I said politely. "I'm not big on beer."

"Never insult a man by turning down his drink," he said.

"I'm good...really."

"Take it, Diamond," he said firmly.

After several seconds of going back and forth, I honored his request, and Randall smiled victoriously while popping the top on the bottle with the opener. I took a quick sip of the beer, frowned, and set the bottle on the ground next to the chaise.

Randall looked at me, then turned the corner of his lips up.

"What?"

"I know we ain't got that damn bougie."

"I told you, I'm not big on beer."

"Anymore," he laughed, popping another bottle open. "Back in the day, you always sneaked swigs of my Icehouse."

"I was twelve." I laughed. "And if I remember correctly, they tasted like watered-down piss."

"They do now because you're used to that high shit," he said. He turned the bottle up, guzzled down half the beer, then exhaled. "Ah..." He belched. "But back in the day, you thought that watered-down piss was the bomb."

"That was only because I didn't know any better." I giggled. "Not to mention, I was doing somethin' I wasn't supposed to be doing. Things always taste and feel better when you're not supposed to do them."

"True," he agreed, and we both took another drink. "You were bad as hell, too, twelve years old and at the party gettin' tipsy."

"Says the sixteen-year-old who took me," I reminded him.

He laughed. "Mama and Daddy woulda beat both our asses if they'da known."

"Hell yeah, they woulda. Those were good times though. Life was simple and easy," I stated sadly.

"That's because we took what we had and made the best out of it," Randall said seriously. "We didn't have much, but we had each other, and we were happy as hell."

"How do we get that back?" I questioned.

"What?"

"That simple, easy happiness."

"We can't, but we can start over. I know because I've done it."

"What am I gonna do without him?" I questioned, referring to Gator. "Clint says he might get life, Randall."

"What were you doing before you met him?"

I shrugged. "Just living, I guess."

"So that's it. You'll keep on livin', sis. That's all you can do."

The sound of the patio door opening captured our attentions. I turned slightly and saw Venetta standing in the doorway. Her eyes were bloodshot and swollen from tears. Earlier, when I'd confirmed the verdict, she'd suffered an emotional breakdown, and Randall had had to carry her upstairs to her bedroom. She cut her eyes from me to Randall erratically. "Are we celebrating?" she asked lowly.

"No. Randall's just trying to help me keep my mind off things."

"Keep your mind off things?" she repeated, stepping out onto the patio. "Who's gonna keep Leon's mind off things? You do realize my brother is going to prison, right? Do you even care?"

I understood that Venetta was dealing with yet another heartbreak and that she had no idea how to channel her anger, but I was not in the mood for her bullshit. "Of course I care," I said calmly. "I love him."

"Venetta, there's nothing Diamond can do," Randall advised her.

"Nothin' we can do? Pssh! Am I the only one who thinks *they* deserve to be punished?"

"Who?"

"That family," she snapped. "*They* did this. *They* killed my baby, got my husband killed...and now *they've* basically destroyed my brother."

"V., the Whitmores are not the problem."

She looked at me with rage and hatred blazing in her eyes. "You've never been truly dedicated to this family, Diamond," she spat. "Leon shoulda left your ass in the streets where he found you. He never should have talked to you at that damn gas station."

"Don't you dare question my dedication! I was there for every second of that trial. I sat there in that courtroom alone when they announced the verdict. You didn't even have the courage to show up. Secondly, I wasn't in the damn streets when he met me. I was handling my own, without a problem," I said, standing. "I know you're hurting right now, Venetta, but don't forget that this is *my* house." I studied her expression, waiting for her next move or word. I loved Venetta like my own flesh and blood, but I knew I wouldn't have any problem whooping her ass if I had to.

"I think I've overstayed my welcome in *your* house," she said, glaring at me. "It's time for me to return to my own home." She rolled her eyes and marched off through the patio doors, letting them slam behind her.

"She's crazy," Randall said, shaking his head. "Certifiably crazy."

"Nah, she's just dealing with too much at one time. She's actually a really good person."

"I understand she's going through some shit," he said, "but somethin' isn't clickin' right in her head. It's good that she's going home, Diamond. She sticks around here, and I'm afraid she'll start something she won't be able to finish with that whacked-out mind and that nasty mouth of hers."

Chapter 19

ator's sentencing came swiftly, but the weight was unbearable. Two weeks after the jury found him guilty, he was sentenced to life in prison. I'd tried to prepare myself for any outcome, but the truth was that I'd been naïvely deluding myself, hoping that somehow or someway, my husband would receive mercy from the court.

After Gator's official conviction and sentencing, the government stepped in, freezing our bank account and ordering seizure of all properties held in his name. That left me with only our primary residence and $42,000 in cash.

I couldn't understand how it was possible. Jonah had taken complete responsibility for their business and hadn't so much as whispered Gator's name. He'd stood firm on his word, commitment, and loyalty to my husband, so there was nothing tying Gator to their illegal activities but word-of-mouth, a whole bunch of he-said, she-said, circumstantial bullshit. The properties that had been raided were even in someone else's name, but even that didn't stop Uncle Sam from breaking me.

I immediately turned to Clint for answers. "How is this happening?" I snapped. "How are the Feds allowed to do this?"

"It's call forfeiture," he explained. "If the police have suspicion that your property was purchased using monies earned from illegal activities, they can seize it."

"Suspicion? What ever happened to proof?"

"In this situation, Diamond, you'll have to prove your own innocence.

You can fight it, but you'll have to prove, without a doubt, that your money and property were earned from legitimate business."

"This isn't right! What am I supposed to do?" I felt tears of anger surfacing in the wells of my eyes, but I bravely fought them back.

Clint sat behind his desk with an expression of remorse and regret plastered on his face. I was on the verge of broke, without a clue of how or what I was going to do next, and all my husband's high-priced attorney could do was give me a pitiful expression and a sorry excuse. I didn't know what pissed me off more: his lack of success with Gator's case or the fact that Gator actually trusted him.

"Diamond, do you realize how lucky you are ?" he asked firmly. "You still have a roof over your head, and—"

"What good is the damn roof if I can't keep the lights on under it?"

"Maybe you should find a house you can afford to light," he suggested, sounding almost cynical.

"Don't get grand, Clint."

"Then stop acting like a damn victim. What do you do next? You get a job, sell the house, and move in with your sister-in-law till you can get back on your feet. You build a respectable name for yourself." He stood and adjusted his jacket. "Any one of those just might work."

I stared at him like he'd lost his mind. "As of today, my husband is no longer your client," I stated. "I'll hire someone else to handle his appeal, someone who can handle the job."

"Hire someone with what?" he questioned sarcastically. "You can't even afford the retainer for one of those rent-a-lawyers on the daytime TV commercials."

I suppressed my desire to tell the man to kiss my ass and instead turned on my heels, swung the office door open, and left. I stomped down the carpeted corridor toward the elevator, with tears streaming down my face. My stride came to a halt as memories and flashbacks of how far I had fallen plagued my mind like a bitter disease. I leaned against the wall, covering my face with my hands. The weight of my emotional anguish came crashing down upon me in a wave of breathless tears as I broke down, overcome with defeat. I cried for my husband. I cried for myself. I cried for what we had become.

Diamond

* * * * *

The home I'd once shared with my parents was located in a small subdivision, Ebony Heights. It was at the at the end of a cul-de-sac, surrounded by rows of hedges that my father had spent hours meticulously trimming when he was still alive; Daddy had always taken the same pride in his lawn that most women took in their hair. My mother, Anna, took the same pride in maintaining the interior of our home.

I sat in my car, parked against the curb, staring at the house, the same red bricks and green shutters I remembered. In the driveway sat my mother's white, four-door Toyota Camry; she'd been driving the same car for years, but it still looked almost showroom new on the outside. I wondered why she hadn't upgraded and traded the car in, but then I reminded myself that some women were content with the basics, even if I wasn't.

I grabbed my handbag and climbed out of my car. As I walked up the cement driveway, I realized I had no idea what I was going to say or even how to say it. I stood in front of the door, attempting to get my nerves together. I considered returning to my vehicle and leaving, but inside of me burned a deep desire to see her face, hear her voice, and hopefully see her smile. I hesitated while staring at the doorbell, contemplating whether or not I was making the right decision.

The door opened before I made up my mind, and I found myself standing face to face with my mother. Her light brown skin and penetrating, dark brown eyes were exactly as I remembered them. A few laugh lines creased the area around her full lips, but she was still one of the prettiest women I'd ever seen. She was wearing a plain denim dress that stopped just below her knees and black sandals. Her head was covered in cornrows, secured neatly in a bun. She looked at me intensely for a moment, allowing her eyes to travel from mine down to my open-toed pumps and then back up again. "Hello, Diamond," she said. "I'm sorry if I startled you, but I saw you drive up."

"Hello, Mama," I said softly.

"It's been a long time," she said, staring at me.

"I know."

"Come on in," she said.

I followed my mother inside her home and shut the door behind me. I looked around the small living room and noticed that not much had changed since the last time I'd been there. The walls were still painted the color of eggshells, and there was still a shrine of family pictures covering all the walls. The only difference was that the drab, floral-print sofa and matching chair I remembered had been replaced with a nice, plush tan sofa and loveseat.

"Sit down," Mama ordered, situating herself on the loveseat.

I sat on the edge of the sofa closest to where she was sitting and placed my bag down on the wooden coffee table in front of me.

Mama shot a glance at my bag, then looked at me; I was positive she was calculating the cost of the bag in her head. The tension in the room was so thick that it was almost suffocating.

"How have you been?" I questioned.

"All right," she said casually, "just livin' by the grace of God."

"That's good," I said.

A long silence ensued before she said, "I knew you'd come a-callin' eventually."

"How did you know?"

"Diamond, don't pretend this visit is a friendly one," she said. "I been watchin' the news, readin' the papers." She shook her head. "I warned you that he'd drag you down. I just knew that man would lead to your destruction."

"*That man* is my husband," I corrected her, "and I'm not destroyed. I'm still here, so I guess you were wrong."

"Why are you here?" she asked coldly.

"Because I wanted to see you."

"Because you're in trouble." She huffed. "Just like the prodigal son, you wanna return home after you been out there whinin' and dinin' and swinin'."

I had no intention of asking my mother to let me back into her home. My only wish was that I could sit down with her and have a decent conversation.

"I haven't laid eyes on you in years, child," she continued. "You haven't even called me. Just checks in the mail, with no return address."

Wait...checks? I'd never sent her a check in my life, and I knew there could be only one person responsible; Gator. "I thought you were mad at me," I confessed, "and I didn't know how to reach out to you."

"You've always known where I live," Mama disputed.

"Well, I guess I'm reaching out now."

"For the record, Diamond, I wasn't mad," she said, leaning forward on the sofa. "I was disappointed. Between you and that brother of yours, you were the one I thought I'd never have to worry about. You didn't mind working, and you were smart enough to want more out of life than just a title or fancy things. You wanted to be successful, and you could have. It's in your genes, somethin' you got from your daddy," she said, clutching her chest.

"Was Daddy really all that successful, Mama?" I asked. "He died struggling to make ends meet, ends that never came together. What kind of life is that?"

"My Oscar did what he could," she said. "He was kindhearted and maybe a little naïve sometimes, but he was a good man."

"Leon is a good man, too, Mama."

"Humph." She grunted. "You coulda done much better. You deserve more than a killer and a thug, and that's why I'm so disappointed."

"So I let you down. I screwed up. Okay, but what ever happened to forgiveness?" I asked solemnly.

"You don't want my forgiveness, Diamond," she stated. "You want me to tell you everything is gonna be all right, that this, too, shall pass. You want me to say that despite all the wrong you've done, it'll all come together for good, that it'll all work out in your favor."

I couldn't argue with her, because that was exactly what I wanted to hear. I wanted my mother to wrap her arms around me and repeat those very words, and I wanted her to mean them. "You're right," I said, swallowing the small lump in my throat. "I need you to tell me that." I dropped my head, allowing my tears to fall freely.

"I can't do that, Diamond." She sighed. "I've never lied to you, and I don't plan on startin' now. You made your bed, and now you've gotta lie in it. I love you. Lord knows I do, but I won't lie to spare your feelings."

I nodded me head. "Thank you for your honesty," I whispered, echoing what Gator had said to her so long ago. "I should have known better. You have more care and concern for a stranger on the street than you have for your own flesh and blood. How is that possible, Mama? Isn't love supposed to start at home?"

"My home has always been filled with love," she said defensively. "You walked away from the love. You wanted the money and all the flash and glitz instead. You got what you wanted, and now you have to deal with the repercussions."

I decided it was time for me to go while I still had a thread of pride. I loved my mother, in spite of everything, and even though her callous words had me feeling completely alone, I refused to grovel or beg. I grabbed my purse and stood. "Take care of yourself," I said, with my head held high. I could feel her eyes on me as I walked to the front door. I turned the knob and prepared to step outside.

"Diamond!" Mama called.

"Yes?" I asked, turning to face her.

"Please cut your losses while you still can, baby, before anything else happens. He's in prison now. This is your chance to break free."

"To just walk away and leave him alone?"

"Yes."

"I can't do that, Mama. Gator is my husband. I took a vow, for better or worse, and I mean to keep it."

"Some vows are meant to be broken," she said sarcastically, "especially when they never shoulda been made in the first place."

"I'll take my chances," I said firmly.

"Goodbye, Diamond...and thank you for the money."

"You're welcome, but I think you should know those checks weren't from me."

She stared at me with her eyebrows raised.

"Just so you know, they were from the son-in-law you hate so much. Matter fact, I knew nothing about them until now."

She parted her lips as if to say something, then just shook her head.

"Goodbye, Mama."

With that, I hurried out the door and down the driveway to my car. Once I was safely inside, I started the engine, gave the house one last look, then pulled off.

Thirty minutes later, my cell phone vibrated loudly in my center console. "Hello?" I answered, clearing my throat.

"You okay, baby girl?" Randall asked.

"Yeah, yeah. I'm good."

"You sure?"

"Yes. I just need some time to myself."

"A'ight. I understand that. Look, I gotta make a run up to Nashville to check on some business. I'll be back first thing in the morning. Are you gonna be all right on your own till then?"

"Yes, I'll be fine."

"Don't worry, Diamond. We're in this together. Love you, baby girl."

"Love you too."

* * * * *

During my drive home, countless thoughts ran through my head: *How did I allow myself to get in this situation? How am I gonna get out of it?* I decided to drown my sorrows instead of dwelling on my current issues, so I stopped by ABC and purchased myself a bottle of cognac.

Back at home again, I sat in my living room, staring into the darkness, sulking and wallowing in self-pity. My cell phone had been ringing nonstop for the last hour with back-to-back calls from Venetta. I'd let them all go to voicemail and had finally gotten sick of the ringing and had just turned off the phone. When my landline rang, I knew it was Gator calling, but I chose to ignore his call too. I was not in the mood to hear Venetta's psychotic venting, nor was I in the mood to hear my husband's apologies.

I turned the small crystal glass and held it up to my lips, consumed the last of the liquid in it, then set the glass down on the end table next to the sofa.

My doorbell chimed, piercing my silence and rattling my nerves.

"Go away," I whispered aloud. I picked up the glass and bottle and poured myself another shot.

The bell chimed again and again and continued to do so until I could take no more. I marched to the front door, unsecured the locks, and swung the door open, prepared to curse Venetta's ass out. "Clint?" I said, annoyed.

He stood in front of me wearing casual slacks and a button-down shirt, a dramatic difference from the suit he'd been wearing earlier.

"How'd you get through the gate?"

"You left it open," he said, stepping past me.

Did I invite him in?

He looked around until he spotted the light switch on the wall, then flipped on the lights. "I was concerned when I called you and you didn't answer," he continued, looking at me. "I reached out to Venetta, and she said you've been ignoring her calls as well."

"What do you want?"

"Well, I spoke with Gator and told him about our disagreement earlier. He asked me to come by and check on you."

"I'm fine," I lied, "so you can go now."

He ignored my fib and walked over to the sofa and sat down instead. It was obvious that Gator had allowed the man to get too comfortable in our business. He knew the combination to our safe, and now the motherfucker was making himself at home in our house without even being invited inside. It was Gator's stupidity and decision to trust the man that had me in my current situation, and I realized I should have followed my gut and drained every dime out of our accounts when I'd had the chance. I slammed the door shut, then stood with my arms crossed across my breast, glaring at Clint.

"I can tell you're fine," he said, holding up the bottle of liquor. "Rather than coming up with a plan for your next move, you're wasting money on things you can't afford? Smart move."

"I don't need a lecture right now," I snarled, rolling my eyes. I tossed the shot back, flinching slightly as the liquid made a warm and slightly bitter trail down my throat.

"No, what you need is to get your shit together," he stated coldly.

"Fuck you."

"I don't do depressed and pathetic," he said with a snort, then laughed lightly.

I pulled my arm back, then threw the glass, barely missing his head, shattering the glass on the wall behind him.

Clint jumped to his feet, looking in awe at the shards on the floor.

"Get out!" I screamed, swinging the door open.

My chest rose and fell rapidly with every breath I took while I watched Clint take his sweet time to approach me. He stopped in front of me so the two of us were standing toe to toe. His eyes became small slits, and the corners of his mouth turned up into a smirk. I wanted to slap the expression off his face, rip the arrogant half-smile from his lips. He put one hand on the edge of the door and pushed it closed.

"Leave!" I demanded, breathing heavily. "Now!" My entire body begin to shake with hatred and disdain.

Clint just watched me, remaining unnervingly silent.

"Get out!" I screamed. "Now!" My heart raced erratically. My knees wobbled until they finally gave out, and I dropped to the floor. I lay at his feet, sobbing at the top of my lungs. The pride I'd attempted to maintain hours earlier was now gone, along with all my strength. I lay with my face down and my hands pushing against the floor.

"Diamond..." he said gently, pressing his hand to my back, stroking the curve gently.

"Don't touch me," I mumbled.

Clint ignored my request with the same stubbornness with which he'd ignored my request for him to leave.

I fought, pushing against his chest as he pulled me into his arms. I told myself I didn't want him to console me, but truthfully, I *needed* him—needed someone—to console me. When Clint tightened his grip around me, in one of my darkest moments, I succumbed to the one thing I didn't need money for: the comfort of a man. I settled into Clint's arms, burying my face against his chest.

"It's gonna be all right," he whispered. "Don't cry, Diamond," he said, providing me with the comfort I'd sought from my mother.

I raised my head, searching his eyes with mine, and found something that reassured me that everything really would be okay in the end, even if I couldn't see how. "Thank you," I whispered, kissing him softly on the lips. I pulled away, gauging his expression and suddenly coming to the realization of what I was doing with a man who was practically a stranger. "Clint, I'm so sorry," I said. I quickly pulled myself from his arms and stood, covering my mouth with my hand. "I'm so sorry. I-I just miss Gator, and it's been so long since...well, since anyone has made me feel safe," I rambled, trying to explain my actions and shaking my head. "I'm just so sorry. You're just being nice, and I-I..." I gazed at him through low, shameful eyes. "I shouldn't have done that," I whispered. "I'm sorry."

There was understanding and tenderness in his eyes as he rose to his feet. He looked like he was trying to find the right words to express himself, as if he was torn. That confusing moment quickly came to an end, and he moved in, closing the distance between the two of us, leaving room for nothing but air between us. He cupped my face with his hands before leaning in and capturing my lips with a kiss.

I pressed my breast into his chest, and our tongues introduced themselves. The initial connection was awkward, until we found our groove and began to match each other's rhythm. Clint pulled me back down to the floor, easing me onto my back. I gasped softly while he trailed kisses down my neck and back up to my ear. The sensation of his warm breath and moist tongue on my earlobe, caused my pussy to throb in wanton agony. I raised my arms in the air, allowing him to remove my thin t-shirt. His eyes traveled across my naked breasts, down to my belly button. I helped him remove his shirt and laid it on the floor next to my own. I admired the curve of his chocolate pecs, the cut of his arms and his chiseled six-pack. Clint latched onto my left nipple, suckling gently before moving to my right one. He sucked and nibbled, moving from one to the other while tugging on the drawstring of my nylon shorts. I elevated my hips, granting him easy access to remove the material. Clint wasted no time in pulling my bottoms off and spreading my legs open. When I felt his tongue on my clitoris, I thought I'd crawl through the floor. He pinched the hood of my clit between his fingers while licking and sucking on my engorged knob.

"Yesss…" I moaned in ecstasy.

I grabbed my own breasts and squeezed my nipples while staring down on the man who was licking my kitty like it was the sweetest treat on Earth. Clint slipped his index finger in my honey pot and made come-hither gestures inside of me.

"Shit!" I screamed.

It felt like there was a raging fire burning inside me, spreading through me with every stroke of his tongue. The sound of my juices comingled with my moans, echoing throughout the room. Clint pushed my legs back until my knees were by my ears. He pulled his finger from my pussy and replaced it with his tongue. I grabbed his ears while I continued rotating on his tongue, grinding on his lips.

"Ohhh…" I groaned involuntarily. I arched my back as a wave rolled from my core throughout my extremities and my creamy liquid filled his mouth.

"So, tell me…how is it that you came to represent Leon?" I asked Clint. I traced the outline of his bicep with my fingertip while awaiting his response.

After Clint had pulled not one, but two orgasms out of me, I'd led him to my bedroom, where he'd sexed me down until I could take no more. The man wasn't bigger than AJ or Gator, but he had a decent-sized rod; for someone who'd gone without as long as I had, decent was good enough.

"I met Leon through a former client," he said.

I pulled myself up against the headboard and tossed my hair over my shoulders. "Are you from Huntsville?"

"No. New York."

"Ah. I love New York," I said. "So what brought you here?"

"It wasn't my choice," he confessed. "I grew up in the 'hood, and my family wanted better for me."

"So they sent you here?"

"Yep, fresh outta high school," he continued. "I enrolled at the University of Alabama and graduated from their School of Law, and here I am."

"A true success story," I said, smiling sweetly.

"I am," he said, "and you can be too."

"What do you mean?"

"You're so beautiful and smart, Diamond," he said. "You're tough too. You could easily go into business for yourself."

"Doing what?" I asked.

"I don't know. What do you like to do?"

"Shop," I said honestly.

"Then open your own boutique," he suggested, rolling over onto his side. "Become a fashion consultant. Do anything. The possibilities really are endless, and there's more to life than being Leon Douglass's trophy wife."

I knew what Clint was saying was true, but that did not stop me from taking offense. "I think you should go," I said, easing off the bed.

"Why?"

"This was a mistake," I said, picking my clothes up off the floor. "I'm sorry, but you've gotta go now." I slipped my t-shirt and shorts back on.

Clint looked at me strangely, then eased out of the bed. "Diamond, do you wanna talk about it?"

"No," I said.

"I'm sorry if I offended you," he said. "That wasn't my intent."

"It's fine," I said, feeling salty. "But you need to go."

The lawyer flashed his eyes at me, then slowly started to put on his clothes. The two of us marched downstairs in silence. At the front door, Clint gave me a peck on the cheek, then left without saying another word. I secured the locks behind him, then headed back upstairs to my bedroom.

"What were you thinking, Diamond?" I questioned myself. I had enough issues and problems, and now I'd added screwing my husband's attorney to the mix. If fucking up had been a sport, I would have been the MVP.

Repulsed by my own behavior, I shook my head and stepped into my bathroom to run a warm bath. After filling the tub, I removed my clothes and slid in till the bubbles were at my neck, hoping it would help me relax my mind. Thoughts of Clint's tongue between my legs sent a warm sensation from my belly button down to my clit. I knew that what we'd done was wrong on so many levels, but it had felt so good. "Won't happen again," I told myself, then grabbed the soap and sponge from the corner of the tub and began to massage and rub my skin.

After I'd had a nice, long soak, I stepped out of the tub, covered every inch of my skin that I could reach with Shea butter, then slipped into my bathrobe and headed to my lonely living room.

As I stepped down the staircase, I thought about calling Venetta but decided to wait until morning. Although she'd apologized for how she'd spoken to me the day she'd decided to move out, I still wasn't in the mood to deal with her. The day had been long and tiring, and all I really wanted to do was unwind and go to bed.

As soon as I stepped onto the landing at the bottom of the staircase, I was immediately knocked to the floor from a blow to the back of my head. I yelped involuntarily from the pain, clutching the knot where I'd been hit. I slowly pulled myself up and faced my attacker, a man in a ski mask, black sweats, and red and black Jordans. I stared into his eyes, trying hard not to focus on the gun he was holding in his gloved hand. My heart pounded in my chest as I contemplated my next move. I took a step back, then made a break for it, attempting to run. He grabbed my arm, jerked me back, and shoved me roughly against the wall. I gasped from the impact, then swung wildly, attempting to keep him away. Pain shot through my jaw when he punched me below my eye.

"Where's the safe?" he demanded, grabbing a fistful of my hair.

"W-we don't have one," I whined, wincing in pain.

"Lying bitch!" he grumbled. He released his grip on my hair, then slapped me hard across my face.

I rubbed my stinging jaw while staring into his cold, dark eyes.

"Upstairs…now!" he said, forcing me back to my feet. He shoved me toward the landing and cocked the gun.

I pushed my hair out face, then looked at the man.

"Move!" he yelled.

I led him upstairs to my bedroom closet and safe. I opened the safe, then stepped back.

"Where's the fucking bread?" he asked, rummaging through the contents.

"I don't have any," I lied. The truth was, I'd placed the money Gator had left me back in the safe under the dining room floor for safekeeping.

He pulled out the jewelry from the safe and dropped it in his bag. "Bitch, don't lie to me!" he said, pointing the gun at me.

"I'm not!" I said. "You have everything I've got. Please leave."

He pushed me out of the closet and toward the bed. "On your knees," he ordered.

"No," I said, shaking. "You got what you wanted, now leave."

He slapped me again. "On your damn knees!"

Feeling as if I had no choice but to obey, I eased down to the floor, never taking my eyes off of his.

"You know what I'm about to do?" he questioned, unbuttoning his pants. He shifted his weight slightly, allowing his sweats to drop to the floor while continuing to aim the gun at me. He slid his hand in the waistband of his boxers and pulled out his limp penis. "I'ma let you eat this dick."

"No!" I argued.

"Suck it, bitch, or I'll put a bullet in your fucking head!"

I closed my eyes, feeling I was trapped inside some awful nightmare.

He pressed the end of the gun against the center of my forehead. "Suck it or die, bitch."

The next morning, I was sitting in my kitchen, staring at the shattered glass covering the kitchen floor, replaying the previous night's events in my head. After Clint had left, I'd forgotten to reset the alarm when I'd gone upstairs to take a bath. My intruder had broken the patio door to gain access. The jewelry the man had taken was worth well over $250,000, but I knew he'd be lucky to get ten grand for it on the street, considering the current state of the economy. I wasn't sure if it felt worse to have been violated or to know that he was getting away with it; there was no way I was going to report stolen jewelry that had been purchased with illegal money.

The sound of the front door opening pulled me from my daydream. I had a lot of questions for Randall, including what was he really doing while I was being attacked, so I was glad to hear that he was home.

"Hey, sis!" he called from the other room.

"In here," I said, staring into space.

"Hey, I was thinkin' the two of us could go to breakfast..." He stopped talking as soon as he entered the room and saw me. "Diamond! What the hell happened to you?"

"Someone broke in last night."

"Are you all right?" he asked as he walked over to the table and pulled a chair up next to mine.

"Where were you last night, Randall?"

"Like I told you," he said with a frown, "I had to make a run to Nashville."

"Did you talk to anyone? Tell them anything?"

"Diamond, what's going on?"

"You tell me," I said flatly. "You suddenly showed up, out of nowhere, after all those years, in the same place I am. Then, a few days after I confided in you about Jonah, the raids happened. Last night, while you were gone, somebody broke in and—"

"Hold up! You think I had something to do with all that?" He stared at me with wide eyes. "Really? You think I'm that damn grimy, Diamond?"

I could hear the hurt in his voice see the pain of betrayal in his eyes, but none of those things mattered at the moment. I was dealing with the evidence and facts I had seen. "I'm asking you if you told anyone anything," I repeated.

"Hell no!"

I pulled my eyes from his, not wanting him to see my expression. "Who can vouch for you?" I pressed.

"Diamond, I'm telling you I had nothing to do with any of this shit!"

"Prove it," I said, craving the truth.

"Diamond, this is *me*," he attempted to reason. "I'd never do anything to intentionally hurt you."

"Prove it, Randall!"

He removed his cell phone from the holster on the waistband of his pants and dialed a number. He shook his head, placed the phone on speaker, and set it on the table in front of me.

"This is real fucked up, Diamond."

The line rang several times before someone finally answered, "Hello?"

"Mama?" I whispered lowly.

"Hey, Ma," Randall said. He raised his finger to his lips, instructing me to be quiet.

"Hey, baby. Did you make it back safely?"

"I just got in," he said. "How you feeling?"

"I'm good, son," Mama said. "I'm a little nervous about the treatment tomorrow, but God knows best."

Treatment? I thought, confused. I stared at Randall, wanting an explanation.

"I coulda stayed with you," he told her.

"I'll be fine," she said. "The nurses are great here."

"They'd better be good to my mama," Randall said.

"I'm gonna get some rest now, honey. I'll call you after chemo tomorrow."

"Talk to you later."

They exchanged "I love you's" before Randall ended the call and slipped his phone back in its holster. He looked at me, then clasped his hands together in front of him on the table. "I was in Nashville with Mama," he explained. "I took her to the Vanderbilt-Ingram Cancer Center to start treatment for her bladder cancer."

"I thought...but you said the two of you weren't speaking," I stuttered.

"We weren't when I told you that. I stopped by to see her about a month ago," he explained. "I was there when the center called to confirm her admittance. You know me, Diamond. I'll bug the hell outta somebody till they tell me what I wanna know. That's the only reason she told me."

"I went to see her yesterday," I said, swallowing, "and she didn't say a word about it."

"I know. I pulled up a few minutes after you left, and she told me about your, uh…conversation."

I rose from the table and walked over to the kitchen island, trying to process my thoughts and attempting to sort through the mixture of feelings boiling inside of me. "How can she afford Vanderbilt?" I questioned, looking at Randall.

He looked away, then looked at me again. "*She* can't." He blew out through his parted lips.

"Gator?" I asked.

"Yes."

It never ceased to amaze me that the very ones we pissed on with our judgment were often the same ones who'd go above and beyond to show that they cared. Mama didn't like my husband's profession or the fact that I was married to him, but she sure as hell didn't have an issue with spending his money. Regardless of who she'd thought had written those checks, all along, she'd known the source of the funding.

"I'm sorry I doubted you," I said sincerely.

"No worries, sis," he said with an understanding smile.

* * * * *

"Do you want out?" Gator asked as we talked on the phone.

I had shared with him, detail for detail, what had taken place during the robbery. The pain in his voice as he apologized profusely for not being there to protect me brought me to tears, but the tears were bittersweet. Part of me hated that he felt guilty, but another part wanted him to. In a way, he'd left me, and I wanted him to feel defeated for failing to protect his wife.

"There's no way out for me," I said softly. "I'm Mrs. Leon Douglass, and running or hiding won't change that. That name will follow me no matter where I go, and I can either let it hold me down, or I can use it to pull myself up. I refuse to live my life in fear of being attacked, and I refuse to be disrespected ever again. I don't want out, Gator. I want in."

"In?"

Diamond

"Yes," I said. "I want them to know that nothing has changed but your location, that we are still a force and a family to be reckoned with, and I want the next motherfucker who even thinks of touching me to consider themselves dead."

"Do you know what this means, Diamond? The risk? I won't be there to protect you, and—"

"You don't have to be," I said, "I got this."

"Be at D'Alessandro's tomorrow night at 8:00," he said before giving me a brief description of who I'd be meeting.

"Thank you."

"Also…Jonah was murdered last night."

"What!?"

"Word is that there was some type of riot at Limestone," he said, referring to the prison where Jonah'd been sent. "He was stabbed over thirty times."

"I can't believe that," I said sadly. "He was a good man, a loyal friend."

"I know," Gator said, clearing his throat, "and he will be missed. Anyway, baby, I've gotta go. Remember that I love you."

"I love you too."

"Loyalty?"

"Always," I said.

"Never forget that," he said firmly.

Chapter 20

Venetta parted sections of my hair as I sat in front of my bathroom vanity, staring at my face, content with the makeup that covered my skin. I applied concealer and powder to cover my bruise and a thin layer of gloss to my lips. Jumping, I shrugged my shoulder as she got too close to my ear with the flat-iron.

"I'm not gonna burn you." She laughed and shook her head.

It felt odd not wearing bundles of weaves, but I actually liked the look and texture of my natural hair. After taking my weave out, I was ready to allow Venetta to cut it in a simple but classy layered bob that would frame my face. I'd once said I'd only stop wearing weaves if they stopped making them or if my husband went broke, so I was now owning up to what I'd said. I'd learned the hard way that life had a way of making me eat my own words and shit my own truths.

"Done." She smiled and laid the iron on the counter.

I admired the style; it made me look slightly younger than I wanted to appear, but it was definitely a good look. "I love it," I said honestly. "Thank you."

"My pleasure."

I stood and ran my hands down the front of my jacket. I'd selected a black pantsuit for the meeting. The short-sleeved, one-button jacket and flared pants were sexy but professional. Under the jacket, I added a hint of color by wearing a slinky red camisole. To make everything really pop, I selected red pumps. My wedding rings and a pair of diamond stud earrings were the only subtle accessories I needed to complete my look.

When I exited the bathroom, Venetta was right on my heels. "Are you sure you don't want me to go with you?" she asked, removing her handbag from my nightstand. "I learned a lot about real estate from Terrance."

I'd told Venetta I was attending a real estate investors' seminar at The Embassy. I'd chosen not to tell her the truth because she was so emotional all the time, and I didn't know how she would react. I was starting a new venture in life, and although Gator had entrusted his sister with some of his business secrets, I felt the less she knew, the better. "Thanks, but I need to go this one alone," I said.

"Well, make sure to let me know how it goes," she said, walking to the door.

"Will do."

She stopped, then turned around and looked at me with a huge smile on her face. "I almost forgot to tell you that I finally had lunch at that restaurant."

"What restaurant?"

"The Ambiance."

"V., isn't that the restaurant Octavia Whitmore owns?"

"It is," she said, "and the food is delicious."

There was no way in hell that Venetta had patronized the place out of just a desire for a good meal. I'd thought she'd let her obsession with the Whitmores go, but it was obvious I was wrong. "Do you think that was a good idea?"

"What?"

"Going there," I said, "where she works."

"I didn't bother her," she said firmly. "In fact, I didn't even see her there. I like good food, and I shouldn't be punished for other people's errors."

"We should talk about this later," I suggested.

"Sounds good, sweetie." She kissed me on the cheek and walked out of the room.

I grabbed my clutch off the bed, turned off the lights, and followed her downstairs.

Randall was sitting in the living room, waiting for me. Although he was not part of Gator's team, he was part of mine, the only man I trusted to stand beside me other than God. He was dressed in a black suit and a crisp white shirt with a red tie; he looked good in my husband's clothes, and he knew it, smiling from ear to ear. "Ready to roll?" he asked, rising from the sofa.

"Couldn't be more ready. Let's go."

* * * * *

The last time I'd been at D'Alessandro's was on one of my many date nights with my husband. I vividly remembered dining in the private, glass-enclosed room, sipping Rosé and toasting to life and love. On this night, I'd be in that same private dining room again, but it would be all business.

"Diamond!" Pauli the owner greeted me as Randall and I entered the restaurant. "It's been too long." He gave me a friendly hug, then kissed my cheek.

"It has, Pauli," I said with a smile, "but you still look good."

A light red flush fell over his olive cheeks, and he ran his fingers over his bald head.

"I try." He laughed. "Not bad for an old man, huh?" He pulled at the cuffs of his suit jacket, then winked.

I laughed lightly. "Not bad at all," I said. "Pauli, this is my brother, Randall."

The two men shook hands and exchanged pleasantries.

"Well, I have your room all set," Pauli advised me. "Alissa will be your server for tonight." He pointed to a pretty brunette standing by the bar, dressed in the traditional D'Alessandro's uniform, crisp white blouse and black slacks. "Whatever you need is on the house."

"Thank you, Pauli."

"I haven't had the opportunity to express my sympathy for your troubles," Pauli stated, staring at me with tenderness in his blue eyes. "Gator has always been like family to us, and he is missed."

"Thank you," I said graciously. "I appreciate your words of kindness, and I know Gator would as well."

"It's my pleasure," he stated. "Enjoy your visit and let me know if there is anything I can do for you."

"Thank you."

Pauli then escorted us through the restaurant to the private dining area. I was surprised to see that all three men I was supposed to meet were already there. One was a brother with a pecan-colored complexion and low-cut hair; he'd attended our anniversary party, and I knew from Gator's description that his name was Tyrese. The other familiar face in attendance was a Caucasian male with dark brown eyes and tattoos covering almost every inch of his visible skin, with the exception of his face. I remembered his name was Ryan, as he worked at the convenience store where I often stopped for gas. Sitting to his left was a husky man with dark chocolate skin and a bald head, a man who I assumed to be Kendrick.

"Hello, gentlemen," I said politely. "I'm Diamond, and this is Randall."

None of them said anything before Alissa knocked on the door, inquiring if she could get us anything. I was thankful for the interruption, because I had no clue what to say next.

"Let me get a bottle of peach *Cîroc*."

I cut my eyes at Randall, none too happy with him for sounding so greedy and needy.

He shrugged his shoulders at me and grinned slightly.

"Anyone else?" Alissa asked.

I could see the apprehension in the other men's faces. "Please order whatever you like," I said with a smile.

"I'll take a glass," Kendrick said, "to help Randall out."

"Make that two," Ryan said.

"Anyone else?" Alissa asked politely.

"Can you bring us two of your sampler platters?" I asked. "I'd also like a bottled water, Coke, and Sprite."

"Sure." She smiled and exited the room.

The tension returned in the room instantly, until I finally spoke up: "So…who's ready to get back to work?" I asked, looking around the table.

"I don't think the question is who," Tyrese said. "We're here. We just need to know when."

In my heart, I knew there were other methods I could've and should've chosen to get myself out of my financial bind, but I chose to ignore the whispers of my heart and focused on the unsettlingly loud voice that constantly plagued my mind, encouraging me, *Get money!* Our team was few in numbers, but they were hungry; due to the drought in the city, some were damn near starved. They were ready and willing, and all I had to provide was the opportunity for them to do the work.

Chapter 21

The Saturday following my meeting at D'Alessandro's, I made the four hour and forty-two minute drive to the Holman Correctional Facility, where Gator was incarcerated. I was thrilled that I was going to see my love but also anxious to discuss our next steps.

"You look gorgeous," he said as soon as he saw me.

We embraced for several seconds before sitting down at one of the plastic tables in the corner of the visiting room.

"So...this is all you?" he asked, stroking my hair with his fingers.

"Yes. You like it?"

"I love it. You're actually wearing makeup," he observed, studying my face closely.

"Only to cover the bruise," I said.

"You're beautiful no matter what."

I smiled. "How are you?" I asked.

"I'm good," he said. "Just taking it day by day. I spoke to Clint about my appeal."

The mention of Clint made me slightly uncomfortable. I hadn't had contact with him since we'd slept together. "And what's the game plan?" I questioned, trying not to sound nervous or guilty.

"To find new representation."

"Why?" I asked, practically holding my breath, praying that I wasn't the reason.

"I don't know." Gator sighed. "It seems Clint no longer has an interest in representing me and that my appeal isn't worth his time."

"Hmm. Did he actually say that?"

"No. He didn't elaborate," he said. "I thought maybe he mentioned something to you."

"No," I said, "but I'll speak with him."

"Thanks, love. I've arranged for you to meet with Luis in a week," he said lowly, changing the subject. "You'll fly into St. Maarten, where he'll have a car waiting for you."

I nodded.

Luis had been Gator's connect for several years, and from the way Gator talked about him, the two of them had a strong business relationship, so strong that Luis was willing to make a one-time exception and front us on our first run.

"Is there anything I should know about him?"

"Just make sure you look him directly in his eyes at all times," he said. "He'll like you because you're beautiful, and that's a plus. Be polite but firm if he makes any advances."

"Gotcha."

"Stay calm. Remember, baby, this is only a meeting. You'll fly out the next day. It'll take him a day or two to arrange the actual delivery, which will more than likely take place in Miami. Also, I have someone sneaking me a phone in, so I'll be able to maintain better contact."

"Great."

"Any other questions?"

"No. I got this."

"I know you do. I told you that one of the many reasons I married you was because I knew what you were capable of, and you have yet to prove me wrong."

* * * * *

I exited the prison with my head held high, stepping swiftly through the parking lot on the way to my vehicle. Once I was safely inside, I retrieved my phone from the dashboard. I had enough things on my mind without Clint attempting to slide out of representing Gator, and we certainly couldn't afford to hire another attorney at the moment.

"This is Clint," he answered on the first ring.

"Hi. It's Diamond."

"How are you, Mrs. Douglass?"

"I'm good, just leaving from visiting with Leon."

"And how was your visit?"

"It went well." I smiled. "However, he tells me you no longer want to represent him, that you don't wanna handle his appeal."

"That is correct."

"Why is that, Clint?" I asked, starting the engine.

"If I remember correctly, *you* fired me."

"If I remember correctly, *you* stated I couldn't afford another attorney."

"Sorry about that. It was a little harsh."

"Sometimes the truth is," I said.

He chuckled.

"It's not funny," I said with a sigh.

"Sorry. To be truthful, at this point, I just feel there's...well, a conflict of interest."

"There's not," I said quickly, "or at least there doesn't have to be."

"There is, Diamond. I have an interest in my client's wife...and that's my conflict."

"Clint—"

"Listen, I need to be going," he said. "I have an important meeting to get to. Let me know if you'd like a referral. I know some excellent lawyers."

"Don't worry about it," I said with attitude. "I know how to use the Yellow Pages."

Chapter 22

I knew my trip to St. Maarten was entirely for business, but I was excited to travel somewhere outside my state for the first time in a long time. The inner diva Gator had once spoiled was in desperate need of a change of scenery. Not only did I select Randall to accompany me on the trip, but per Gator's request, I took Tyrese along too.

Our flight touched down in Princess Juliana Airport at 11 a.m., and Luis had a car waiting for us. The driver, a pudgy man with mocha-colored skin, introduced himself as Stanley.

As we traveled toward our destination, Randall marveled at the sites, reminding me of myself the first time I'd visited the city.

Our chauffeur pulled into the parking lot of the Sonesta Beach Hotel and Casino.

"I'm sorry," I said, slightly confused. "I thought we were meeting Luis at his estate."

"Tomorrow at noon," Stanley said. "Until then, please enjoy your accommodations."

"Word!" Randall said eagerly, looking up at the luxury hotel.

"One moment," I said, concerned. I wasn't aware of any change in the plans I'd discussed with Gator, and I wanted to be one hundred percent sure everything was kosher. I dialed Gator's number, hoping and praying he could answer at the moment.

"You made it?" he answered quietly and quickly.

"Yes, but the driver brought us directly to the resort and said our showing isn't until tomorrow."

"No worries, love. I received the message this morning that there was a change in the appointment. Everything is still a go."

"Okay." I sighed with relief.

"Enjoy your time there and promise that you'll think of me."

"Always."

"Everything okay?" Stanley asked, holding my car door open.

"Yes," I said. "Thank you."

He assisted me out of the car, then retrieved our bags from the trunk. "If you need anything, please feel free to call," he said, handing me a business card.

"Thank you. I will."

"This is sweet," Randall said as we entered the resort. He reminded me of a child on his first trip to Disney World as he looked around the lobby in awe. "Yo, can I hit the casino later?"

"No gambling," Tyrese stated as we approached the front desk. "We're here to make money, not lose it."

I smiled in agreement; he'd taken the words directly out of my mouth.

"You guys are no fun," Randall complained.

We checked in and headed to the Ocean Terrace building of the resort, to our respective rooms.

"You have free rein to everything in your room," I advised them. "The resort is all inclusive." I slid my keycard through the slot and turned the handle when the light turned green.

"Does that include the ladies?" Randall grinned as he watched a petite redhead walk by.

Tyrese looked at him and shook his head. "I'm gonna meditate for a moment," he said, opening the door across the hall from mine. "Call me if you need me."

"Thank you, Tyrese," I said politely.

"That brother's just too uptight," Randall said, shaking his head.

"That brother is about his business," I advised him. I was beginning to wonder if bringing Randall into the business was a wise decision. Although I trusted him, his outlandish and wild sense of humors seemed to rub the other team members the wrong way. "I'm going to take a power nap. Let's meet in the lobby at seven o'clock for dinner."

"Sounds good," he said, then walked into the door next to mine after trying three times to successfully slide his keycard through.

I stepped in my room and set my luggage down. The room was modest compared to the one I'd stayed in the last time I had visited the island, but it was nice nonetheless. It offered an ocean view from the private balcony and was furnished with a king-sized bed. It was exceptionally clean and nicely decorated with vibrant colors and a variety of hardwoods.

After taking a quick shower, I slipped on a short sundress and decided to go for a walk and enjoy the beautiful sunshine. I strolled along the shoreline, allowing my toes to dig into the warm, white sands with every step. Staring out at the crystal-clear waters, I watched the waves with admiration, while flashbacks of the last time I'd visited the island danced in my head. My honeymoon had been one of the happiest times of my life, but I'd taken those moments for granted, and now I wanted them back. I continued my stroll along the beach until my stomach began to rumble.

I returned to the hotel, hoping to grab a light lunch at Bay View Restaurant. In the restaurant, I spotted Tyrese, sitting at the bar. "Hey," I chimed, climbing on the chair beside him.

He was staring at a book, open on the bar in front of him. "Hey," he said, closing the book.

"How was your meditation?"

"Good," he said. "Nice and peaceful."

"How often do you meditate?"

"At least once a day."

"That's cool." I picked up one of the menus lying on the bar and glanced through it. After making my selection, I flagged down a waitress and placed my order.

"Are you ready for tomorrow?" he asked.

"I am," I said confidently.

"If all goes well, we'll be back up and running by the first of next week."

"I definitely hope so," I said, thinking about the stack of bills I needed to pay. "So...how did you meet Gator?"

"Through my brother," he said, "Jonah."

I looked at him and suddenly felt somewhat guilty. "Oh. Jonah was a good man."

"Yes, he was."

"How is your family? Do you need anything?"

"Only prayer," Tyrese said, looking at me. "I can handle the rest."

"Prayer, huh? I can do that."

"I appreciate it."

There was an uncomfortable silence between the two of us until Tyrese stood up then picked his book up off the bar.

"Well, I'm gonna do a little sightseeing," he said. "Have a great evening."

"You too," I said with a smile.

* * * * *

Randall called to advise me that he wanted to skip out on dinner. He'd met one of the locals earlier in the day and had been invited to some "bad-ass beach party" that was to be thrown by the resort. I knew I couldn't stop a grown man from doing his thing, and he would only drive me insane if I tried, so I advised my brother to have a good time and to call me as soon as he got in.

I was still full from my lunch at the Bay View and quite restless, so I slipped on my bathing suit and hit one of three pools at the hotel for a night swim. There were several couples lounging around, each lost in their own romantic worlds. I felt somewhat like a third wheel in their presence, but I was determined to enjoy myself. I found an empty lounge chair and set my towel and sandals down.

"Diamond?"

I turned around and instantly locked eyes with Clint. He was wearing swimming trunks and slip-on sandals, and there was a beach towel slung across his broad shoulders. "What are you doing here?" I asked, surprised.

"Vacation," he said.

"Wow," I said. "What a coincidence. When did you get here?"

"Three days ago," he said. "I just packed my bags and left. I needed a breather and this is one of my favorite spots."

"So you were here when we talked?"

"Yes."

I was on the island to partake in criminal activity, and I'd run into a lawyer who knew me quite intimately. Either I had the worst timing in the world, or the universe loved throwing me into awkward situations; I was beginning to think it was the latter.

"What about you? Who are you here with?" he questioned, raising his eyebrows.

"Um...my brother," I said nervously. "Randall decided to treat me to a mini-vacation."

"Wow. That was nice of him. Where is he?" he asked, looking around.

"At the beach party, with a date."

"He dumped the prettiest woman I've seen on the island for a pretty girl?" he flirted.

"Something like that," I said.

"Not to talk shop, but did you manage to find other legal representation?"

"Not yet," I said. "I just started looking."

"Well, my offer still stands," he said. "I'll get those referrals together for you as soon as I'm back in town. Enjoy your stay," he said, then casually turned to walk away.

I had faith that Clint would keep our secret, but only if he had something to lose. I needed to keep the man playing on our side, at least for the moment. "Clint, wait," I beckoned.

"Yes?"

"I-I need you," I said, "and not just for the case. I just need you to be understanding and patient with me right now."

"What are you saying?"

"I'm saying I want you. I really do, but I just need patience and a little space to figure it all out. I've been through a lot."

He smiled and opened his arms.

I stepped into his embrace and wrapped my arms around his neck. Scandalous as it was, I planned to give the man just enough attention and affection to keep him wrapped around my little finger. Keeping him happy was a win-win situation; he'd be smiling, and I'd be able to save my own ass and maybe Gator's with his help.

Chapter 23

The next morning, Gator called to let me know the plans had changed yet again. "You need to stay at the resort during the showing," he said. "Let Ty and Randall know to take their bags with them. The car will be there for them in an hour," he advised me. "Stay at the resort until Tyrese calls you. When he does, catch a cab to the airport, and they'll meet you there. "

"What? Why—"

"Just do it, Diamond," he barked, then hung up, showing me no love whatsoever

I was pissed and tempted to do the exact opposite of what Gator had demanded, however, I set my phone on the counter and went to Tyrese's room to let him know the game plan. I knocked lightly, still fuming from the tone Gator had taken with me over the phone.

Tyrese opened the door, wearing jeans and a crisp polo. "Morning," he said, stepping back to allow me inside his room.

"Good morning." I gave him a breakdown of our change of plans.

He just nodded his head and kept a straight face the entire time, taking it all in. "I'm ready," he said.

"Great."

Once he was filled in, I left him alone and knocked on Randall's door once, then twice. He hadn't called me when he'd returned from the party the night before, and I was hoping he was actually in his room rather than shacking up with some beach blanket bimbo somewhere else in the hotel.

After a few seconds and my fourth knock, I finally heard him on the other side of the door.

"Coming!" he called.

He opened the door, wearing nothing but his boxers. His eyes were thin slits, completely bloodshot, with luggage-sized bags beneath them. He reeked of alcohol and sex.

I stepped past him, only to see that the beautiful room was destroyed, as if a frat party had been thrown in it, and there were two naked women sleeping peacefully in the bed. On any other occasion, I would have given my brother a high-five for his obvious conquests the night before, but this occasion called for me to get in his ass. "Are you fucking serious?" I ranted. "This is a damn business trip, Randall! You've got one hour to get ready before the driver gets here!"

"What?" he asked, scratching his bare chest. "Dude said noon, and it's only, like, 9:00 in the morning."

"I don't care what time it is," I stated, walking over to the bed. "Shower, get dressed, and take your bags with you." I jiggled the sleeping women. "Excuse me, ladies, but it's checkout time for you," I said.

They looked at me like I was crazy, and I gave them a look that confirmed that I was. Slowly, and without a word of complaint, they crawled out the bed and started retrieving tiny slivers of glittery, skimpy clothing from the floor. Once they were dressed, I escorted them to the door.

After filling Randall in on my conversation with Gator and reminding him how important the meeting was to all of us, I returned to my own room to hold my breath and pray that things would not go horribly wrong.

Two hours later, I was sitting in the hotel lobby, a nervous wreck, waiting for Tyrese's phone call. I had a sickening feeling in the pit of my stomach that something was not right, such an unsettling feeling that I called for a cab well in advance and offered the driver $300 to wait for me. He graciously accepted, which was no surprise, since the normal rate from the resort to the airport was a measly $15.

"Hey, you," Clint said, entering through the lobby doors.

"Hey," I said, staring at my phone anxiously.

"Leaving paradise so soon, angel?" he questioned, staring at my bag.

"Yes," I said. "I'm just waiting on my brother to get back from saying goodbye to his friend," I lied, feeling even more uncomfortable and vulnerable in the lawyer's presence.

"Okay. Well, I'm here for three more days."

The sound of my phone ringing caused me to jump. "Excuse me," I told him. "Hello?"

"Ready," Tyrese said quickly. "Meet us at the curb."

I quickly grabbed my purse and luggage. "I have to go, Clint," I said, flashing him a smile. "Call me when you get back in town."

"All right. At least let me get your bag for you," he offered, reaching for it like some kind of lovesick bellhop.

"No, it's okay. I got it." I hurried out the entrance of the hotel with him trailing behind. I handed my driver my luggage and opened the cab door.

"Diamond," Clint called, "what's the rush, sweetie?"

Damn it! I thought, as he was quickly becoming a royal pain in my ass. "My brother's meeting me at the airport instead," I lied.

"What time is your flight?"

"He has the tickets," I said. "Look, I'll see you when you get home." I leaned in and kissed him hard on the lips, hoping it would be enough to coax him out of my business. I stepped back and smiled.

"I'll call you as soon as I'm settled in," he said.

I climbed in the back of the cab, slammed the door, and asked my very patient driver to hurry the hell up.

Gator had advised me that we were only meeting with Luis and that the actual exchange would take place at another time. I quickly discovered that was not true when I saw Randall and Tyrese climbing out the back of the limo, each carrying leather duffle bags with a gold "L" on the pockets, luggage that clearly didn't belong to them.

"What the hell's going on?" I whispered as Tyrese approached at the curb.

"Be easy," he said. "Luis said it's now or never, so we chose now."

Randall smiled like a Cheshire cat, his hangover obviously gone. "Let's move," he said.

My chest began to tighten, and my stomach gurgled. *Now is not the time for the shits,* I told my body, but the butterflies continued to dance.

"When we get to TSA, stay in the left lane," Tyrese instructed me. "Look for a female with short, spiky black hair and pink reading glasses. She'll get us through."

"Are you sure?" I asked.

"No," he said, looking at me seriously, "but we've got no choice but to take his word for it."

"You should have left it there," I stated, getting cold feet.

"Diamond, that wasn't exactly an option," Randall piped up. "When dude said it was now or never, I think he was referring to more than the goods."

"I agree," Tyrese replied, and the cold tone in his voice made it clear that it had been a life-or-death decision; fortunately, they'd chosen life.

We arrived at the security checkpoint and saw the female Luis had mentioned. She was in the left lane, guarding the monitor. I clenched my thighs together as the urge to pee surfaced in my lower body. I was the first to go through the scan. Glancing up at the woman's nametag, I saw that her name was Mandy. I grabbed my items from the plastic bin and stood, trembling slightly and trying to look casual as Tyrese approached.

As he prepared to set his bag on the roller, a tall, hefty agent approached Mandy and ordered her to switch lanes. Tyrese's normally calm demeanor immediately took on the look of a shaken man.

Oh my God! We're so busted, I thought frantically. My pulse raced as visions of us being taken down by security bombarded my head. I watched as Mandy and the man went back and forth briefly, until she finally turned to step away. *No! No! No! Damn it, Mandy!* I screamed in my head.

The man motioned for Tyrese to drop his bag on the conveyer belt, and I saw the defeat in his eyes as he obeyed.

"Ugh!" Randall suddenly screamed.

I shot my eyes past Tyrese and gawked at my brother, who was hunched over lying against the conveyor belt, clutching his chest. His antics caused an uproar amongst the staff and the waiting passengers. I watched as several people sprang into action to help him.

"I-I can't...can't br-breathe!" Randall cried loudly.

The man who'd come over to relieve Mandy was the first agent to step up and advised the passengers to step back. "Give us some room here, people!" he shouted, trying to maintain crowd control in the busy place.

Mandy resumed her position at the monitor as Tyrese's bag, followed by Randall's, rolled through the scanner.

After several minutes, Randall begin to breathe normally. "Sorry. Panic attack," he said, panting. "I'm so, so sorry. Doc says it's PTSD, flashbacks from the war."

I stood in one place, stunned speechless, my urge to potty now gone.

Tyrese quickly grabbed both duffle bags and his shoes from his bin. "Go," he mouthed to me. I nodded and proceeded to walk in the direction of our gate. It was five minutes before we were supposed to board, and Randall was still nowhere to be found. "Maybe I should go back for my brother," I said.

"No," Tyrese stated. "He'll be here."

When the boarding agent called for our flight, Randall was still nowhere to be found. When our section was called, Tyrese and I got in line. I handed the man my boarding pass, worried that we were about to leave my brother behind.

"I'm comin', Ana Mae!" I heard Randall call out.

I turned around to see my brother, sitting in a wheelchair, being pushed by a brown-skinned, extremely top-heavy airport employee. The female rolled him up to the counter and stopped so Randall could get out of the wheelchair.

"Thank you, sugar," he said, reaching for her hand. He pressed his lips to the back of her hand like some kind of British gentleman and smiled. "If you're ever in Texas, be sure to come see me," he said with a wink.

Jackass, I thought, trying hard to suppress my smile.

The woman blushed slightly, then walked away, her large chest bouncing with every step.

We managed to board the plane without further incident, but I would not be satisfied until we were safely in the air. When we took off, I exhaled softly. I couldn't wait to get back home and give Gator's ass a piece of my mind.

We had a two-hour layover in Atlanta before our next flight departed for Huntsville. Not wanting to risk any further skirmished or close calls with airport security, we opted instead to rent a car and drive back. We rode in silence for the three-and-a-half-hour trip. When I saw the green "Entering Madison County" sign, I was relieved, but I was also anxious for the next chapter to begin.

Chapter 24

Luis had provided Tyrese and Randall with fifteen kilos of cocaine each, on consignment, at the rate of $15,000 per brick. The agreement was simple: If he didn't get his money within ninety days, the next ninety days would be their last. I was concerned with the stipulations, but both Gator and Tyrese assured me that it was more than enough time to settle our debt, and they ended up being one hundred percent right.

Word spread like wildfire that the purest coke our city had ever tasted was once again being served, and business started to bloom. The increase in traffic and clientele led to the recruitment of new workers to join our team and forced me to choose a second-in-command.

Although Randall had proven himself to be a valuable asset to the team and had handled the east side of the city without a hitch, I felt that when it came to the business end of things, Tyrese was a more favorable candidate. I chose not to address the subject with either of the men, but I was sure just from looking at the responsibilities and assignments given to both that my choice was obvious.

Clint was once again working on Gator's appeal, and while we hooked up from time to time, he did not pressure me for a commitment.

My relationship with my mother was still rocky, but at least we were on speaking terms again. I continued to pay for her medical treatments at Vanderbilt and vowed to do so until her cancer was in remission.

* * * * *

To keep from making the same mistakes as my husband, I decided to take a portion of my profits and invest in a legitimate business. There was an empty building for sale on the corner of Madison Boulevard and Hughes Road that had caught my eye, the perfect place for my legitimate venture, Diamond's Lounge. The location offered an abundance of parking, and the building was a comfortable 9,000 square feet. Although I planned to make some renovations to suit my personal taste, the establishment was already in perfect working condition. "What do you think?" I asked Randall. I already had my heart set on the location and was ready to make an offer, but I thought it best to ask my brother's opinion anyway.

"Nice," he said, running his hand over his head. "Yo, I can see the deejay booth bein' right over there." He pointed to the right corner of the room. "And the bar over there."

"Yep, and my office there, overlooking the dance floor," I said, pointing to the second level.

"I can definitely see you sitting up there like a boss." He laughed. "I love it, sis. I think you should go for it."

I suddenly had an idea that I felt would help solve one of my issues. "I think *we* should go for it, big brother. What do ya say we make it happen together?" I asked.

"Whatever you need me to do, I got you."

"No, I mean *we*, as in partners." I smiled slyly.

"Me and you?" Randall asked excitedly.

"Yes!"

"Hell yeah, we can make it happen."

"Great!" I said, happy that Randall was excited about the business venture, even though it was an offer I'd made on a whim. It resolved the issue with declaring Tyrese my second-in-command in my other line of business and gave Randall an important job too.

I glanced over at the flamboyant RE/MAX agent who was patiently waiting by the door as Randall and I did our walk-through and conversed. "Draw up the contract," I advised the gentleman.

"Fabulous!" he said, absolutely beaming. "Have we already secured financing?"

"Do you accept cash?" I asked, already knowing the answer.

Diamond

He looked at me and smiled like a whore in a room full of paying dicks. "Oh, we love cash!"

Chapter 25

Renovations on Diamond's Lounge took just under eight weeks. Once they were done, the end result was breathtaking. The lower level of the club had wooden floors and an elevated stage where musicians could perform live, as well as a booth for my on-staff deejay. In the middle of the stage was a diamond cut and a large "D." I installed two bars, one on each side of the dance floor, and, much like at Club Delight, there was a runway running the perimeter of the dance floor, with stripper poles on each side. The décor we selected was simple but classy, with wooden tables and high-backed leather chairs. Installed in the ceiling were rows of purple and yellow track lighting, casting a funky but sensual glow. There were six flat-screen monitors in the walls, so I could showcase fights and other sporting events. In the back was a large dressing room, complete with lockers for the dancers we planned to feature on Friday nights, and there was a fully equipped kitchen with its own separate entrance.

The second level housed my office and a full bathroom, and a service elevator and staircase led to a private back exit of the club. In the office were two desks, with glass tops, and executive chairs in Italian leather, as well as a large, matching leather sectional. The front wall faced the dance floor and was made entirely of glass. Remote drapes went from the floor to the ceiling, in case privacy was necessary.

I made sure to install an extensive security system, as well a security booth enclosed in bulletproof glass. I wanted my patrons to have a good time but before they went inside to party, clearance would be reminiscent of some government events.

I chose not to have a VIP section for the simple fact that every patron was going to be treated like a celebrity. My security staff included a former Navy SEAL, a retired police officer, and an active officer of the Huntsville PD, who wanted to make some extra money when he was off duty. I'd learned from my husband that it was always good to have at least one lawman on our team.

My requirement for my waitresses and bartenders was simple: They had to look good. I hired only the sexiest men and women I interviewed. It might have seemed narrow-minded or unfair to some, but in such a business establishment, I knew people would be ten times more likely to spend money with a sexy woman or man than they would be with the ugly broad or goon down the street.

I was out wrapping up the final details for our grand opening when Venetta popped in for a visit. I hadn't seen her in weeks and had come to the conclusion that she had a new man in her life; whenever I called, she was always busy. Even Gator had mentioned a change in her personality. She walked through the front door in a pale blue, off-the-shoulder blouse and tan slacks. Her brown skin was radiant, and she looked happier than I'd seen her in years.

"Look at you!" I smiled and gave her a friendly hug. "Lookin' good, boo."

"Thanks, sis." She smiled, stepped back, and took a look at me. "So do you, as always."

"Meh, I try," I teased.

"This place looks fabulous too," she said, looking around the room. "I'm so proud of you."

"Thanks, V. That means a lot," I said sincerely. "C'mon. I'll give you the tour."

After I showed her all around the place, we sat in my office, playing catch-up.

"So…who is he?" I asked.

"Who's who?"

"The man who has you glowing," I said.

"I don't have a man," she said, blushing.

"I know that look, girl. You've either run up on a good man or some good di—"

"Diamond!"

"I'm just sayin'," I said with a shrug.

She laughed, then shook her head while looking at me. "Someone new has come into my life," she admitted, "but I don't wanna talk about that now. I just wanted to stop by and personally congratulate you on your accomplishments."

I was anxious to hear all about the new person in Venetta's life and was tempted to demand that she give me all the juicy details right then and there, but I still had to go home and get ready for the opening later that night. "Okay, but you've gotta promise to fill me in later," I said. "I wanna hear all the good stuff."

"Absolutely," she said, standing. "I'm afraid I won't be able to make your opening tonight though."

"Aw! Why not? It won't be the same without you here."

"I completely forgot that I made prior plans," she said. "Please don't hate me."

"I could never, but whoever this guy is, he'd better be worth it!"

"Trust me," she said, grinning shamelessly, "he is."

* * * * *

The theme for my grand opening was "All White Everything." For the occasion, I purchased a one-shoulder, asymmetrical, chiffon cocktail dress with ruffles and beading. It hugged my body in a sensual but elegant way, as if it had been made only for me. I kept my hair natural but changed the look for the occasion by asking my stylist to set my strands in layers of curls. I looked and felt unstoppable. I couldn't help but smile as I looked out the office window and saw that my building was packed to capacity.

"Look at that crowd, li'l sis!" Randall cheered, walking through the office door. He was stunningly handsome in his all-white suit with platinum tie and bright white alligator shoes. His traditional twists were gone, replaced with a clean-shaven head.

"I'm looking at them right now." I grinned.

"That's right." He laughed. "Yo, sis, this is gonna be the hottest spot in the city before long."

"It already is," I said proudly. "You did an amazing job with the promotions, Randall."

I'd left the responsibility for advertising the grand opening up to him, and he'd also coordinated the deejay and after-hours entertainment. At first I was nervous about giving him so much responsibility but it was apprehension wasted. He was proving to be an excellent partner and an even more savvy businessman, than I ever would have thought, had I not given him the chance.

"I told you I got you, sis," he said, "and I meant it."

"Well, I'm gonna go mix and mingle for a little while," I said.

"Have fun," he said. "Let your hair down."

I exited my office then moved through the crowd, greeting my patrons and bobbing my head to Fantasia's "Lose to Win." It was the perfect song for the occasion, the perfect song for my life. I had taken loss after loss, but now I was finally winning again.

As I approached the bar, I spotted Clint on the dance floor, holding a champagne glass, talking to a tall female with a model-like figure. She had long hair that stopped at the top of her ass and was wearing a body-hugging, above-the-knee little number that looked two sizes too small. I was curious if they'd come together or if he'd just met her there. As I moved in closer, I noticed that she had a pretty, round face and very full lips, and she looked somewhat familiar. "Welcome," I said loudly as I approached them.

Clint's eyes lit up slightly as his gaze traveled from my head down to my six-inch heels.

I smiled, feeling slightly cocky that he'd given me the onceover in front of the other woman.

"Diamond," he said, extending his hand to me. "You look lovely."

"Thank you," I said, ignoring his hand and instead extending my arms for a hug.

Clint gave me a safe church hug, then stepped back.

Humph, I thought. "Hello," I said, politely addressing his friend.

"Hello." She smiled, batting her eyes.

"Diamond, this is London. London, this is Diamond," Clint said, introducing us. "This is her place."

"You have a beautiful club," London said, staring at me. She had a thick accent, a combination of a Southern drawl and something else I couldn't put my finger on.

"Thank you so much. I'm happy you were able to come."

"I wouldn't have missed it for the world," Clint stated.

"I love that dress," London stated, casting a glance over my physique.

"Thank you."

She took a sip from her champagne glass, never taking her eyes off me.

"Well, thanks again for coming," I said, looking from one to the other. "Enjoy."

Thirty minutes later, the lighting softened, and the music slowed down. Randall hopped onstage and announced that we had a special treat for our guests. The door leading to the back of the club opened, and out stepped four exotic dancers, all dressed in white bikinis and clear platform heels. I stared at the last dancer to take the stage and noticed that it was London. She winked at me, then flipped herself up and around the pole effortlessly. The patrons inside the club cheered and clapped, and I felt my panties grow moist. I continued to watch her for a few more minutes before excusing myself to my office.

It was 2 a.m. when the last of our customers finally made their departure. I sat at my desk, going over the figures for the night, more than satisfied with our profits. Just as I was wrapping up, I heard a light knock on the office door. I secured all the cash in the safe and said, "Come in."

Randall popped his head in the office door and smiled.

"Hey, you. What are you up to?"

"Thought I'd toast to my partner in crime," he said. He pushed back the office door, revealing a bottle of Rosé and two long-stemmed glasses.

"I can use a drink right about now," I said, rising from my desk. I walked over to the sofa, kicked off my heels, and plopped down.

"I know that's right," he said, walking over and sitting down next to me. He filled the glasses and handed one of them to me. "To change," he said.

I clinked my glass against his and took a long sip of the liquid.

"So…what's on your agenda for the rest of the night?" he asked.

"I'm gonna go home and curl up with my sheets," I said. "This has been fun, but I'm tired as hell."

"What!? Are you serious? You just had one of the most successful openings ever in this town, and you're going to bed already?"

"Yes, sir. It's past my bedtime," I said, finishing off my drink.

"I'm headed over to Kendrick's for the after-party. It's from 3 until… well, whenever, so if you change your mind—"

"After-party? Do I even wanna know?" I questioned.

"Nope." He laughed. "All I'm gonna say is, don't wait up for me."

"I won't." I laughed, shaking my head.

"You do look tired, sis. Why don't you take off?" he suggested. "I'll lock up here."

"You sure you don't mind?"

"Positive," he said.

I was more than ready to get out of that dress and enjoy being in nothing but my skin. I gathered my things and hugged my brother goodbye.

Outside in the parking lot, I saw Clint leaning against his car, talking to London. She'd replaced her bikini with fitted jeans and a white wife-beater, and her hair was pulled up in a high ponytail.

I pretended not to see them until London called my name. "Hey," I said, walking up to them, just to be polite.

"We were just talking about you," London said sweetly.

"All good, I hope," I said, looking at Clint questioningly.

"Of course." He smiled.

"That's all that matters," I told him. "Well, I'm headed home to relax, but thanks again for coming...and, London, I really enjoyed your performance."

"I can come back anytime," she said. "Your brother knows the number."

I'm sure he does, I thought, laughing to myself. "Sounds good," I said, then smiled graciously.

"Hey, we were just thinking about heading to breakfast," Clint said. "Would you like to join us?"

"That's a very tempting offer, but I'm not in the mood for another crowd right now."

"Breakfast at my place," he added.

I looked from him to the woman.

"Come on," London said seductively. "It'll be fun. We all know you want to."

"Just breakfast?" I asked, looking at Clint.

"Yep. Toast, eggs, bacon...the works!"

"You got orange juice?"

"Of course...and champagne."

"Then it's a deal," I said.

Diamond

* * * * *

After eating the scrumptious breakfast Clint had prepared, the three of us cozied up in his living room to enjoy a pitcher of mimosas and the sounds of Maxwell crooning through his stereo speakers. I sat on his soft leather sofa with my feet tucked under my ass, sipping my fourth glass of the champagne and orange juice concoction, listening to London and Clint go back and forth about baseball. London sat on the small loveseat across from the sofa, while Clint reclined in the matching leather recliner. I laughed lightheartedly, pretending I was entertained by their conversation and banter, as if I knew anything at all about pitchers and steroid busts and the damn World Series. I hated sports with a passion and had never taken the time to learn any of the technicalities of the actual game. Of course, if they'd asked me how much a baller made in a year, it might have been another story.

"You look lonely," London stated, looking at me and calling my bluff, "or bored."

"Nah, I'm fine." I laughed lightly and held up my glass. "Just feeling a little tipsy."

"I think that was his mission." She giggled, looking at Clint. "Less OJ, more champagne."

"He's a man. I wouldn't have expected anything less," I joked.

When I eyed Clint playfully, he smiled sweetly back at me.

"Hey! It's more innocent than you think. After such dedicated, hard work, I thought you might need a little something to help you unwind," he said, still smiling. "Is that so wrong?"

"Not entirely," I said honestly. "I did need something to help me relax. Opening a business is very stressful."

"Well, you look extremely good doing it," London complimented.

"Thanks," I said appreciatively. I set my glass down on the table in front of me and began rubbing the back of my neck with my free hand. My muscles were tight, and I desperately wanted to go home and hop straight into a hot bath.

"Tense, huh?" London asked, watching me.

"A little," I confessed.

"No worries. I give the best massages." She eased off the loveseat, set her glass on the table next to mine, then walked over to the sofa and eased down beside me. "Turn around, mama," she instructed.

I did as she told me and faced the chair where Clint was sitting, leaving my back facing London.

London instantly hit the spot, as she began to knead my neck lightly with her warm palms.

"Mmm…that feels so good," I moaned, closing my eyes.

"You like?" London asked lowly, stroking her fingertips down the curve of my neck across my collarbone.

"Yes."

London spread her legs on each side of me, leaning back and allowing me to recline between them. I felt light heat coming from her body, and it turned me on slightly. Slipping her hand under my chin, she guided my face back and upward. I opened my eyes and stared directly in London's. The corners of her lips turned up into a sensual smile before she leaned in to give me a full kiss. In that moment, the two of us were completely oblivious to Clint's presence as she sucked on my bottom lip and tongue like my mouth held the source of her life. Her hands traveled down the front of my dress, cupping my breast; at the same time, I extended my arm, grabbed her by the back of the head, and pulled her closer to me.

"Mmm…" she moaned, running her fingers through my hair. She kissed me again, then pulled away, easing from behind me.

I glanced over at Clint, who was sitting in the chair, mesmerized, watching the two of us intently with an obvious bulge pressing against his pants.

London pulled me to my feet and took her time helping me out of my dress and panties. When I stood before them wearing nothing but a smile, her eyes cruised down my body, then back up again. "Up there." She pointed, instructing me to sit on the back of the couch.

I stepped up on the sofa and eased down with my back up against the living room wall.

London tossed her hair to one side, then slowly started to peel off her clothing. Her body was beautiful and flawless, with the exception of a red butterfly tattoo with its wings spread, covering her hairless kitten. She knelt before me on the sofa, rubbing my thighs with both hands, the admiration on her face was making me even wetter. London guided my legs further apart, then dipped her head, covering my clit with her lips.

"Damn" I whispered, staring down at her head.

Diamond

London traced the lips of my pussy slowly with her tongue before lapping my heated juices like a dog drinking from a bowl.

Clint sat with his pants open and his pole at full staff and rock hard. When I motioned with my finger, inviting him to come join us, he obeyed. He stood, then stepped over to the sofa.

London gave me an erotic show while she stripped Clint down to his birthday suit. They kissed passionately before kneeling on the sofa, side by side. Clint spread my lower lips open, and together they pushed me beyond the brink of passion, taking turns licking and sucking on my honey pot. I felt the warming sensation breaking through as I exploded, covering their lips with my creamy liquid. Grabbing my waist, Clint guided me down from the sofa on to the floor. London engaged his lips with a kiss while I maneuvered my tongue up and down his dick, making it nice and moist.

"Shit," he said with a moan.

I bobbed up and down on his stick, going lower each time, until I had every inch of him in my mouth and halfway down my throat. I watched in admiration while Clint sucked and nibbled on London's tight chocolate nipples while rubbing her protruding clit between his fingers. Grabbing his rod, I stroked him slowly. I pushed Clint on his back, then eased down on his dick as London assumed the position over his lips, spreading her legs wide. I cupped London's soft breast, gazing in her eyes.

"Mmm," she moaned in pleasure. She rocked and rotated her hips, riding Clint's face and drenching his lips with her juices while I drenched his rock-hard stick at the same time.

Chapter 26

*D*iamond's Lounge had been open for a month, with a packed house every weekend. The income I received from Diamond's, combined with the money I received from the streets was beyond sweet, although not nearly as much as my husband had once been able to give me. I wasn't worried; I knew it would all come in time.

When the time came to re-up with Luis again, he agreed to have his people meet us in Miami. I was grateful for the cooperation and thankful that I'd be paying upfront this time. I selected Tyrese, Ryan, and Kendrick to make the run.

Meanwhile, Randall had been gone for five days, accompanying my mother to Vanderbilt for one of her treatments, leaving me to run the business alone. I handled my business and never complained about hard work, but I was looking forward to his return over the weekend. It was hump day, Wednesday, and that meant happy hour would pack the place with guests who were eager to take advantage of our 99-cent drink specials. After putting in eight long hours, I wished my staff a good evening and departed.

It was a beautiful August day, and I hadn't seen Venetta since the day of the grand opening, so I decided to drop in to pay her a visit.

"Diamond!" she squealed, standing in her doorway. "What are you doing here?" She gave me a long hug, then stepped back to look at me.

"I left the club early so I could stop by and see how you're doing," I said, waiting for her to invite me in.

"Oh, okay."

"Well? Can I come in or not?"

"Sorry. Of course you can," she said, stepping back.

I stepped inside and was impressed to find her place immaculate, spotless and clean. I walked over to the sofa and sat down, then quickly noticed a baby monitor and bottle sitting on the table. "Are you babysitting?" I questioned.

"Yeah, kinda," she said, running her hands down the front of her dress. "Actually, I signed up to be a foster parent, and I'm considering adoption."

"Adoption? Really? That's great."

"Yeah. It was kinda sudden, but I thought it'd be a good idea. I mean, I've got a lot of love to give and all this room to share, right?"

"Right." I knew Venetta was receiving money from her insurance policies on both her son and husband, so she could afford to take care of a child for a while, but I didn't know for how long. I was also curious as to how she got approved to be a foster parent so quickly, as I had always thought it was a long process. Her emotions were rather up and down, and I was surprised that a caseworker or someone like that hadn't bothered to check her mental stability before trusting her to take care of a baby. "When did you sign up to be a foster parent?" I asked.

"A few years ago, but I didn't decide to pursue it until recently."

Soft cries flowed from the monitor, interrupting our conversation.

"Excuse me," she said, then hurried upstairs.

I waited a few seconds then finally decided to follow her. I walked in the direction of Venetta's voice, stopping at the room that was formerly Emerson's. I pushed the door open, since it was no longer padlocked, and immediately noticed an extreme change in décor. The room was now a nursery, decorated in blue.

Venetta was standing there with her back to me, rocking and cradling the baby in her arms.

"Can I see?" I asked, stepping closer.

"Oh!" she gasped, spinning around. "You scared us."

The baby she held in her arms was a beautiful boy who looked to be no older than a few months .

"This is that special someone I was telling you about," she cooed, "the new man in my life."

"He's a little younger than I expected," I said, and we both laughed. "What's his name?" I asked.

"I haven't picked one yet," she said, staring into the baby's face.

I found that strange and immediately asked, "Didn't you say he was in foster care? What did his birth mother name him?"

"His birth mother is dead!" she snapped. "She's a nonfactor! Dead, dead, dead as a doornail!" Just like that, she'd flipped out again.

"Calm down, V." I said gently. "You don't want to upset the baby."

"You're right." She sighed. "I'm sorry, but the mere mention of that awful witch does something to me. She was such a terrible woman, Diamond."

"Understandable," I said softly.

The tension in the room was thick and slightly scary, and I decided it was time for me to go, before something else I said had her going into another outburst and frightening the little one.

"Well, I guess I should get going."

"Okay," she said, still gazing at the baby. "Please lock the door behind you."

"Sure." I looked at her and the child again and left the room.

Out in my car, I sat behind the wheel, replaying her odd words and vague explanation over in my head. Something didn't' seem to add up. I would have been the last person to pass judgment on another woman's ability to be a good mother, but ever since she'd lost her own son, her husband, and basically her brother, Venetta had been a whole special kind of crazy all her own. I pulled my cell phone from my purse and scrolled through my contacts, looking for a number for Dan, the cop I'd hired to work security at the lounge.

An incoming call halted my actions.

"This is Diamond," I answered.

"Hey. It's Fitz." He was one of the newest members on my team. He worked the south side of the city and was responsible for handling two of the stash houses we had in the area.

"What's up, Fitz?"

"The cat caught a mouse," he said. "Things got, um…a little ugly."

"Really?"

"Yeah. I'm 'bout to clean up now, but I wanted to let you know to watch your step when you walk in the kitchen."

"Will do," I said. "I'll see you in forty minutes."

All thoughts of calling Dan suddenly flew out the window after Fitz's bad news. He had spoken carefully in code, but he'd basically told me he'd caught someone trying to steal from me. I maneuvered my car down the curvy road as fast as I could without losing control. I had two things on my mind: getting to the spot as quickly as possible and wondering who'd been stupid enough to attempt to steal from my family.

I made the drive from Limestone County, where Venetta lived, to the warehouse Gator owned in the town of Triana. When I pulled up to the building, I saw Fitz standing outside, smoking a cigarette and holding an aluminum baseball bat. "Hey, Fitz," I greeted as I stepped out of the car.

"What's up, Boss Lady?" he said, flicking the cigarette butt in the gravel. He had a gash on his forehead and a small cut on his cheek that was still bleeding a bit.

"What happened?"

"I just came from making a drop over in New Projects," he said, "and this fucker came at me from behind. I took care of him right quick, though, stuffed his sorry ass in the trunk, and drove him out here."

"You look a little banged up. You sure you're all right?" I questioned.

"Yeah, I'm good."

I followed him inside the warehouse and saw a man tied to one of the metal beams in the middle of the room. The building was completely empty, with the exception of a metal shelf that housed several tools. When Fitz had told me over the phone that things had gotten messy, he hadn't been exaggerating. There was a swollen gash on the side of the man's head, revealing his pink flesh. Blood trickled from the gash, down the side of his brown face, onto the white t-shirt he was wearing.

He looked at me and grinned, revealing a bloody, chipped set of teeth. "Couldn't finish the job so you called your bitch?" He snorted as spit and blood flew from his lips.

"You think you're a funny motherfucka, don't ya?" Fitz said, walking over to the man. "A regular ol' Kevin Hart up in this bitch, huh? Ha-ha, motherfucka." He swung the baseball bat and hit the man hard in the gut.

When he could breathe again, the man hollered; cried in agony and pain.

"You attempted to steal from me," I said, staring at him. "That was a mistake, and now we're facing a dilemma."

"Fuck you," he coughed out. "How's that for your dilemma?"

"So disrespectful," I said, shaking my head. "Do you even know who I am?"

He looked at me and smiled. "Yeah. You're the bitch who I let eat my dick!"

Flashbacks of the night I'd been attacked in my home temporarily paralyzed me as those same words echoed in my head. "Pull down his pants," I instructed Fitz.

"Say what?"

"Do it."

Fitz shook his head, then did as I requested.

I stared at the man's leg and saw the same oddly shaped mole, the one I'd seen the night I'd been violated.

"Come on!" The man laughed and taunted, "Get on your knees."

"Who sent you to my house?"

"It ain't hard to find a ho."

I looked at Fitz, and he swung again, hitting the man roughly in his already bruised abdomen. "Now, I'm gonna ask you one last time," I said through clenched teeth. "If you don't answer me this time, I'm gonna saw it off and let *you* suck on it before I make you eat it."

"Go to hell."

"You first," I said. I calmly walked over to the metal shelf against the wall and removed a small handsaw. Fitz watched me closely as I stepped up to the man and grabbed his limp penis. I jerked on the skin roughly, then dug the rusty edge of the saw into him. Blood squirted from his member, covering my French manicure and hands, but the sound of his cries played in my ears like music.

"Aw, shit," Fitz mumbled.

"Stop! No! Please stop!" the man begged. "Please stop! I'll tell you anything you wanna know, you crazy bitch!"

I released my grip on the man's severed member and stepped back. "Well? Who sent you to my house that night?" I asked again.

"She came up to me on the block and…" He paused and began crying hysterically. "I don't know her name, but she was driving a Ferrari, a real thick, dark-skinned chick."

Venetta, I thought in disbelief.

"The bitch paid me a stack in advance and told me I could keep anything I found, as long as I left you alive." His body begin to tremble uncontrollably from pain, fear, and blood loss. "I'm sorry. Please, lady!" he pleaded. "I'm so, so sorry."

"So am I," I said, dropping the saw on the ground. I then looked at Fitz. "Kill him." The sounds of the man's frantic screams echoed behind me as I walked through the warehouse doors, but they didn't bother me one bit.

* * * * *

"Diamond, what happened? You look like you been—"

The impact of my fist connecting with Venetta's jaw silenced her; she stumbled backward and fell to the floor. I stood in the middle of her living room, shaking, still covered in the man's blood.

"What are you doing!" she screamed, clutching her face.

"I know it was you!" I yelled, standing over her.

"What are you talking about?"

"You sent that sick fucker to my home to rob me."

She looked at me, her eyes filled with so much conviction that there was no way she could possibly deny it.

"Why?" I asked. "Why'd you do it? Do you even know what he did to me?"

"I was mad, angry at you," she said slowly. "It was like you didn't even care about what was happening to my brother, to your own husband!"

"Because I chose not to agree with your vendetta against that family? Because I chose not to go after the Whitmores?"

"Yes," she agreed. "Yes! We stand together in this family, Diamond. If one of us goes down, we all do. If one of us has an enemy, we all do."

"As of today, you're no longer part of my family," I said firmly. "You're nothing to me."

She began laughing like a hyena and pulled herself to her feet. "Ha! Do you think I care? I don't need you. I have him now," she said, referring to the baby.

"It's not official yet, bitch," I threatened. "I'm sure I can have him removed from your house."

Diamond

"I dare you! Do that, and I'll tell Leon I saw you sucking AJ off on the patio. I was there Diamond."

"Pssh. He'll never believe you, and even if he did, what can he do to me now?"

"Anything he wants," she said, lowering her eyes. "Don't let the prison whites fool you, Diamond. My brother is just as powerful in as he was out."

I rolled my eyes. "Venetta, I meant what I said. You wanna keep that baby, you best stay away from me and anyone associated me. If I even see you again, I'll have you committed." I walked out leaving the door open behind me.

Chapter 27

It had been over a month since I'd visited Gator, and I was looking forward to sitting down with him face to face. My team had made it back safely from Miami, Randall was home, and everything was business as usual.

I stepped into the visiting room and smiled at my husband as I approached. Out of the corner of my eye, I felt someone watching me. I nonchalantly cut a glance to my left and saw a female guard with low-cut hair and a medium build watching me. She rolled her eyes, then cast her attention to the other side of the room. *Hater,* I thought to myself.

I made it my pleasure whenever I visited Gator to make sure I wore something eye catching and provocative, and this was no exception: a chiffon blue jumper and animal-print heels.

"My love," Gator greeted me with open arms and a kiss.

"Hey, baby."

We held each other for a moment, then sat down.

"How was your drive?"

"Good," I said. "I'm used to it by now."

"How are things at the club?"

"Wonderful." I smiled. "All business is good."

"That's great," he said, leaning forward. "Venetta told me the two of you had a bit of a falling out. You need to make up immediately."

"A falling out?" I laughed that she'd put it that way. "Did she tell you what she did?" I asked, agitated.

"Yes."

"And you think I need to make up with her?" I asked, my eyes wide.

"She felt it was necessary to protect me."

I couldn't believe he actually thought his sister's actions were justified, and it pissed me off.

"I personally would have used other methods, but sometimes when it comes to loyalty, we can't take chances."

"What?"

"Jonah," he answered, staring at me.

"What about him?" I asked, confused.

"I assumed you were asking me if I was aware of what Venetta did in regard to Jonah."

I looked at him and shook my head. "No," I said, studying his expression. "She was the informant?"

"What were you referring to then?"

"Never mind," I said. "She threw Jonah under the bus, one of your most loyal workers, and you're all right with that?"

"I would have chosen other methods," he said, "but my sister loves me and was only doing what she felt was in the best interest of the greater good."

"And just what did she accomplish? We still lost almost everything. Jonah died inside because your sister sold him out."

"Jonah died inside because he crossed the wrong man," he said coldly. "That was his decision."

It was in that moment that I came to the shocking realization that I knew nothing about the true character of the man I'd married. "Who did he cross?" I asked softly.

"Let's not trouble ourselves with things of the past," he said, changing the subject.

He didn't have to answer the question, for I already knew what he meant: Jonah had allegedly crossed Gator, and Gator was responsible for his death.

After my visit with him, I was confident that Gator knew nothing about my affairs before or after he went to prison, or I probably would have been laid to rest as well. I decided it was in my best interest to hop back into psychotic Venetta's good graces, at least enough to keep her pacified and for her to keep her mouth shut about me and AJ. I said a silent prayer that she would keep my dirty little secrets.

Diamond

I was less than an hour from my home when I received a call from Clint. "Yes?" I answered, still agitated.

"Where are you?"

"Almost home. What's up?"

"Can you meet me at Venetta's?"

"Why? What's Lizzie Borden done now?"

"She's dead, Diamond," he said solemnly.

"What!?"

"Octavia Whitmore shot her...presumably in self-defense."

"What happened?"

"Did Venetta mention anything about a child?"

"Yes, a baby boy," I advised him, "a foster child she planned to adopt."

"It wasn't a foster child. The baby is Octavia's son."

"Oh my God," I said, realizing my intuition had been correct and that something about the baby wasn't as it seemed. "I'll be there as soon as I can," I said in a daze, realizing that my prayer had, in a way, been answered. After all, now Venetta's lips were permanently sealed.

Chapter 28

Venetta had been dead set on blaming the Whitmores for our issues, and it had cost her her life in the end. The authorities informed me that Venetta, with the help of a doctor and two other women, had kidnapped Octavia's newborn son, telling the Whitmore woman that her baby had died. It was sick, desperate, and something I never would have imagined Venetta capable of.

Although he was granted permission, Gator chose not to attend Venetta's memorial service. I laid her body to rest next to her husband as Minister Golston said a brief prayer, and I stood hoping I would not have to bury another person for the rest of my life.

Despite how I felt about Venetta selling Jonah out, the responsibility of handling her estate fell in my hands in the absence of her brother. I sold her home and vehicles and donated the proceeds, as well as all of her belongings, to charity, in the hopes that from all the pain and wrongdoing, someone would benefit and some good would come of it.

I pulled into the reserved parking spot outside of Diamond's Lounge and noticed a limo parked beside Randall's Hummer. It was just after 9:00 a.m., two hours before we opened for lunch. I entered through the front doors and locked the doors behind me. I could hear voices as I walked up the stairs to my office, and before I reached the landing, the door opened. "Hello," I said, staring at the olive-skinned man who opened the door.

He waited until I was completely inside the room, then slammed the door hard. There were two other men in the room, along with Randall.

One was leaning against the window, holding a black leather bag. Randall was sitting on the sofa with his hands clasped tightly together, and a bronze-skinned man was sitting behind my desk. He had silky, jet-black hair and dark brown eyes, and he was dressed in an expensive suit with no tie.

"What's going on?" I questioned, looking around the room.

"You must be Diamond," the man behind the desk said in a heavy Italian accent.

"And you are?"

"Have a seat, Diamond," he said.

"I prefer to stand," I said boldly.

"Diamond, sit down," Randall whispered. There were tiny beads of sweat glistening on his bald head, and there was a look of terror in his dark eyes. "Please," he said.

Only because my brother asked me to, I eased down beside him on the sofa.

"Diamond, I see why Leon wanted to keep you out of my sight," the man said, licking his lips crudely. "I must commend a man who knows what he's got."

"Luis?" I concluded.

"Yes," he said. "I apologize that we are meeting so unexpectedly, but I'm sure you understand the urgency of my visit."

"I-I don't understand," I stated, confused.

"Diamond, after such a wonderful start, I took for granted that you and your partner understood the importance of compensating me in full and on time."

"I sent the money with Tyrese," I explained, confused. "There was fifteen grand per key."

"You did." Luis nodded. "However, another delivery—a rather large one at that—was made to one of your associates later. For that one, I have yet to receive what is owed to me."

I shot Randall a look, begging him to tell me the man was lying.

"It wasn't me, Diamond," he said. "I don't know what he's fucking talking about."

Memories of the days Randall was gone, accompanying my mother, replayed in my head. *Is it possible that he just used that time as an excuse?* "I-I didn't know anything about that," I said truthfully.

"I assumed as much," Luis stated. "This is why it's important to choose your associates carefully."

"How can we make this right?" I asked calmly.

"I think we both know I'm not interested in negotiating," Luis said, clasping his hands together on the desk. "I have only engaged in the conversation thus far out of respect for Leon as a business partner...and the pleasure I find in looking at you pretty face." He looked at one of the men and nodded.

The man pulled Randall off the couch and shoved him to the floor. I watched in horror as the man removed a chrome-plated gun from a holster inside his jacket.

Randall shook nervously but remained quiet.

"Please!" I begged when the man pointed the weapon at my brother's head. "Tell me how much he owes you, and I'll pay it!" I looked at Luis with tears in my eyes. "Please just tell me how much."

"You must understand my position," Luis said. "Your partner has no respect for a man's possessions. I can't let such disrespect, such disregard, go unnoticed and unpunished, or others may follow suit."

"He didn't mean it," I said. "Randall, please tell him! Tell him!" I pleaded.

"It wasn't me!" Randall snapped.

"Then who was it, hmm?" Luis questioned.

"I already told you that I don't fuckin' know!"

"My sources say you were present for the exchange," Luis said. "Are you saying they're lying?"

"Yes!" Randall blurted.

The man standing over him with the gun hit him across the head with the butt of the weapon.

Randall moaned in agony; clutching his head.

"Please, Luis! Whatever you want me to do, I'll do it," I said, still attempting to negotiate. "Please don't kill my brother. Please!"

He stood and walked around the desk. "Come to me, bella," he ordered.

I did as he requested. I stood, toe to toe, with him as he stroked my cheeks with his fingertips. I was willing to do anything if it would spare Randall's life, including giving up my own.

"The wonderful thing about doing business with women is that they're strong inside," Luis said, staring me in the eyes, "but they are also tender and humble enough to do whatever is necessary for those they love, even if it means sacrificing their own lives. Diamond, are you willing to take your brother's place?"

"Yes," I said, sobbing softly.

Luis nodded, then pressed his lips to my forehead.

I knew death was next.

"I salute you," he said. "You remind me of my mother, strong and resilient and willing to die for those she loved. Someday you will, Diamond, but not today."

I looked at Luis, studying the seriousness in his stare.

"Including my interest and late fees, it's $480,000," Luis said.

I stared at him in disbelief. I didn't have near that amount, even if I gave the man every dime to my name.

"Is there a problem?" he asked.

"But I don't have that much," I whispered.

"Hmm. Then it appears we have dilemma," he said, exhaling, "don't we?" He motioned at the gunman.

"Wait!" I said quickly. "I'll get it. Just give me some time." I looked from him to the shooter to my brother. "Please just give me some time."

Luis waved his hand for the man to lower his gun, and I felt slight relief as the man stepped back from my brother. There was a rush of relief in Randall's face, as he rose from his place on the floor and sat back down on the edge of the sofa.

"Four days," Luis said. "I'm being generous, Diamond, so please don't make me regret it. If I don't have my money by the deadline, you can kiss your brother goodbye." He then touched his fingers to my cheek before walking to the door with his men in tow.

As soon as they were gone, Randall cried out, "It wasn't me, Diamond. I swear I was set up."

"By who?" I snapped, pacing.

"I don't know, but Mama's my witness. She'll tell you I was with her that entire week Diamond, I never left her side!" He ran his hands over his head, then screamed. "Fuck! I shoulda known some shady-ass shit was up. It was too easy."

"Who do you *think* is responsible?"

"Gator," Randall said without a second thought, tapping his hand on his knee nervously. "He's probably been plotting on me the whole damn time."

"But why? It doesn't make any sense, Randall. You've never done anything to Gator."

"I know it don't make sense, Diamond!" he blurted. "But look who we're talking about. I'm telling you, this shit has his name written all over it. If it wasn't him, it was that crazy-ass dead bitch he called his sister."

What would Gator have to gain from hurting my brother? I had to wonder. It didn't make any sense whatsoever. Randall, however, had already proven himself to be a thief.

"Of course you'd blame me right off," Randall stated, reading my mind. "You think I don't know that? You think I don't know I'm the most likely candidate to steal from a mofo? I know I am! Hell, if I was on the outside lookin' in, I'd blame me, too, but I'm telling you I didn't do that shit. I was nervous and scared as hell dealing with those bastards the first damn time. Why would I take from a fucker who threatened to kill me, in not so many words, during a so-called friendly visit?"

I looked at my brother, staring at his tear-filled eyes. In my heart, I knew he was telling the truth, but the truth didn't matter. Luis had given me four days to come up with the money, money I knew was impossible for me to make in such a small amount of time. If he didn't get it, though, Randall would be a dead man, and there wasn't a doubt in my mind that I'd be dead right along with him. "I believe you," I said, running my fingers through my hair.

He sighed in relief.

"Randall, I need you to go check in with the crew, see how much they've made thus far."

He nodded his head in agreement.

"And, please don't mention a word of this to anyone—not a damn soul," I added. "Right now no one can be trusted."

"I'm on it," Randall replied, then exited the office in a hurry.

I sat down behind my desk, consumed with my thoughts and fears. The chirping of my phone momentarily disrupted the thoughts running through my mind. "Hello?"

"My love," Gator greeted, "I understand there's a situation, a bit of a problem."

"'A bit of a problem'? Well, ain't that the freaking understatement of the century?" I blurted, breathing heavily. "Luis is threatening to kill my brother, Gator—all for something I know he didn't do, obviously something someone linked to your team did! I've got four days to come up with $480,000 or it's over."

"Diamond, baby, you and I both know no one had the opportunity to make that meeting but Randall. Can you not vouch for every member on the team during that time except him?"

He had a point about the team, because during the time of the alleged transaction each and every member was in our city and accounted for. However, I knew there had to be some other feasible explanation besides the one implicating Randall. "Mama will tell me if he was with her or not," I said defensively. "I gotta believe him, Gator. He's my brother."

"Your mama? Are you talkin' about Anna?" he replied, blowing loudly. "The same mother who disowned you for marrying me but graciously accepted every check I sent her? Baby, what you gotta do is look at things clearly. Family or not, they're playing you, my love."

I listened in heart-wrenched silence as Gator continued to present his argument. Yes, my mother had turned her back on me then willingly accepted God only knows how many checks with my name on them. Yes, the two of us were back on speaking terms, but that had only happened after the conviction of my husband, the man she knew would protect me and my interests at all cost. Painful as it was to accept, the thought of my own mother and brother playing me wasn't really that farfetched. I knew that money could turn a nursing mother against her own child, so I could only imagine the hold it could have on a woman whose children were grown.

"Diamond, how do you plan to flip that amount of money in four days?" Gator asked tenderly. "You can't, baby," he said, stating the obvious when I couldn't bear to say the words out loud.

I sniffled, feeling utterly defeated. "What do you suggest? Can you talk to him?"

"I tried, my love, but I'm afraid it's outta my hands. I can't protect Randall, and, to be honest, he's not my responsibility. I couldn't save my sister, but I'll be damned if I'm gonna lose my wife too. What do I suggest? Sweetheart, my best suggestion is to let Randall go. He's Luis's problem now. Just let him handle Randall as he sees fit."

"Gator, Randall is my brother, and—"

"It's the only way, Diamond."

I took a deep breath, then slowly expelled warm air through my parted lips. "You're right," I agreed, definitely defeated. "I love him, but there's nothing I can do. It all makes sense now, Gator. The two of them, my own mother and brother—"

"No matter what, baby, you still have me," he reassured me. "Love and loyalty."

"For life," I added, sobbing lightly.

"Where is he now?"

"He's gone," I whispered, dabbing at my tear-stained cheeks.

"Tonight, have Luis meet him at the warehouse," he urged. "Luis will handle the rest."

"Are you sure?" I asked. I wanted to be completely certain that it was the path Gator and I should take and that we both wholeheartedly agreed.

"It's the only way."

"Fine. You're right. I-I'll do it," I said, weeping at the thought of losing my only brother to his own damn stupid antics.

"I love you, Diamond."

"I love you too." I disconnected our call while mentally acknowledging Randall's notion that Gator was guilty as hell. I immediately called Randall. "Where are you?" I questioned as soon as he answered.

"Almost on the south side. Why?"

"Turn around," I said. "There's been a change in plans."

"What's the change, sis?"

"Go home and wait for me. I'll be there within the hour."

"I'm on my way now."

"Randall…" I blurted before he could disconnect the call.

"What's up?"

"Pack a bag," I stated, opening the safe hidden in the floor under my desk.

"Huh? Why?"

"We're leaving town, gettin' the hell outta here."

"What about Mama?"

I detected sincere concern in his voice, concern that I also felt myself. "I'm on my way to see her now," I explained, stuffing the money from the safe in my bag. "Just go home and do what I asked."

"I'll be home when you get there."

I scribbled a quick sign, letting everyone know that the lounge would be closed for the day, taped it on the front door, and locked the doors before jumping in my car and peeling off. I didn't bother contacting my employees; I hated to leave them hanging, but my departure was a matter of life or death.

＊＊＊＊＊

I'd heard every word Gator said about my mother and brother and their possible plot against me and I'd pretended to fall for it. True, his story was not farfetched, but I wasn't buying it. I was on to him, and I was willing to take my chances with my family. Gator was out of his damn mind if he thought I'd fall for that bullshit he'd told me over the phone. I refused to hand my brother over to be slaughtered by wolves he would have never known in the first place if it hadn't been for me. My husband was eager to turn my brother over to Luis, which meant one thing to me: It was him against us. I could not forget that he was the same man who'd allowed his psycho sister to snitch on his right-hand man.

I climbed out of my car and hurried up to my mother's front door. I knocked rapidly on the door until she answered.

"Diamond?" She smiled brightly. "Come in, sweetheart."

"Got no time for visiting, Mama. I need you to pack a bag," I said, stepping inside her living room and closing the door behind me.

"Why?" She asked, staring at me with innocent, confused eyes.

"We have to go. Something's happened, and we're leaving town," I stated frantically. "Please just trust me on this, Mama. We have to go…immediately!" I stared in her eyes, begging and pleading for her to understand.

"Wait just a minute, child. Calm down and talk to me." She grabbed me by the hand, guiding me to the sofa and pulling me down with her. "Tell me what happened, Diamond."

I didn't want to waste a minute, not even to explain, but I knew there was no way my mother would let me get away with that. I poured out my heart, from start to finish, bringing her up to speed on everything that was going on.

"My Lord," she whispered, pressing her hand to her chest. "Oh, Diamond."

"I'm sorry, Mama," I said sincerely. "I know I messed up, but I have to get Randall out of here, and we want you to come too. We're going to go to Houston for a few days, until we can figure out our next move. You have to come with us."

"I'll be fine," she said, shaking her head in disbelief, "but you can't run for the rest of your life, and you shouldn't have to, honey. No one should." She stood slowly, clasping her hands in front of her.

"There's no other option, Mama."

"There has to be another way," she whispered, removing the cordless phone from its cradle on the end table.

"Mama, tell me you're not trying to call the police," I sputtered, jumping up.

She looked at me and shook her head. "No," she said, putting the phone back down in its cradle, "I suppose you're right." She eased back down on the sofa next to me and placed her shaky hand on top of mine. "Diamond, there's a lot I need to tell you and your brother about my past. I haven't always been so good. I, too, made my share of mistakes growing up and disappointed my own mother." She shook her head as her mind strolled through her painful, shameful memories. "That's why I should have been more understanding and less judgmental about your decisions. I apologize for that. Maybe if I had opened up, you wouldn't have chosen such a destructive path and—"

"Mama, we'll have plenty of time to right our wrongs," I said, hopeful. "We can't go back, but hopefully we'll all have the opportunity to start anew."

Chapter 29

During the drive home, I replayed my conversation with Mama over and over in my head. I was curious and slightly confused, but I didn't have time to let those emotions take over, and cloud my judgment. I would sort through it all once we reached our destination and my family was out of harm's way. Mama agreed to let me send for her when Randall and I were settled in our new state. Although, I was completely displeased with her decision to stay behind, I knew once her mind was made up, there'd be no changing it, so I gave her enough money to cover a couple months and told her I'd be in contact as soon as we reached our destination.

Once I had my bag packed, Randall and I loaded up my car, and we hit the road. I stared out the passenger window, watching everything pass by in a blur.

"Diamond, are you all right?" Randall asked, breaking my train of thought.

"I will be," I declared. My phone chirped, indicating an incoming call, and I stared at Gator's number on the screen. I thought about sending the call to voicemail, but decided it would be better to talk to him, so as not to arouse any suspicions. I advised Randall to be quiet before I answered.

"Will he be there tonight?" Gator questioned as soon as I answered.

"Yes," I lied. "It's done."

"Where are you now?"

"I'm just pulling up to the house," I fibbed. "I'm gonna take a long, hot bath and try to get some rest."

"Sounds good, baby," he said lowly. "Call me later."

"I will."

"I love you, Diamond."

"I love you too." I rolled my eyes, still disgusted with what my husband had become.

"You still cool?" Randall questioned when I ended the call.

"Now that I'm getting away from the bullshit? Ten times better."

"What do you say we hit up the West Coast?" Randall suggested, maneuvering along Highway 72. "You can enjoy the sun, and I can give the beautiful ladies of LA some of this deep-fried Southern comfort." He smirked mischievously.

"We're on the run, and you're thinking about women?" I said, rolling my eyes. "Shit, leave it to you, Casanova."

"I'm a man, Diamond. It's in my DNA to think about women all the damn time. Besides, I know we're going to make it. We'll be fine," he added seriously. "We're like Thelma and Louise in this bitch! Only both of them were women...and white." He cut his eyes at me, causing me to laugh slightly.

"And those crazy-ass bitches drove off a damn cliff in the end." I chuckled, looking at him.

"What the hell? You sure?"

"Yep."

"Damn. I knew I shoulda watched the ending," he stated, sucking on his teeth. "Bonnie and Clyde, only sister and brother? That any better?"

"Their fate was just as bad," I mumbled, staring at the battery life on my phone; it was only at ten percent, but I'd been in too much of a rush to charge it. "Stop at the next store," I stated, setting the phone in the center console. "I need to pick up another travel charger."

"That's cool. I need to grab something to drink before we get going."

Just then, I received another call, this one from Mama.

"Where are you two?" she asked, sounding worried.

"We're on 72," I stated.

"Is everything all right, baby?" Mama sounded like she was holding her breath with worry.

"Everything is fine. We're just pulling off at the gas station. I need to get another charger, and your son is thirsty."

"Hey, Mama!" Randall screamed.

"I swear, the boy sounds like he's going on a field trip," she huffed. "He just don't understand the meaning of trouble."

"I know," I said as we came to a complete stop at the traffic light and sat in the turn lane with our blinker on.

"I want both of you to know I love you," Mama said solemnly, "and that everything is gonna be just fine."

"We love you too," I said, watching the traffic. "I'll figure out a way to make this right, I just need some time right now."

"Of course you will," she said lovingly.

Less than five seconds after I hung up with my mother, Gator called again.

"Hello?" I answered, trying desperately not to sound annoyed.

"Diamond, why do you continue to lie to me?" he questioned with anger and aggression in his voice.

"What are you talking about?" I asked naïvely.

The light turned green, letting us go, and Randall pulled out made a left toward the Shell station on the corner.

"You know exactly what I'm talking about!" Gator responded. "Have you forgotten that I know your every move, that I have eyes and ears everywhere?"

Suddenly, my thoughts flashed back to the night he'd been arrested, the night when Jonah had warned me about the tracker on my car. *He has someone following us,* I thought frantically.

"Shit," Randall blurted, slamming on the brakes as an SUV with tinted windows cut us off.

I turned in my seat, looking out the windshield at the cargo van behind us. The van had barely missed hitting us when Randall had made his abrupt stop.

"Where the hell did these idiots learn how to drive!?" He honked the horn for the vehicle in front of us to move.

The van cut to the left, pulling up on the driver's side of my car. Once the van was beside us in the lane, the SUV sped off, almost fishtailing in the process.

"It didn't have to be this way," Gator said softly.

I felt a queasiness in my stomach as my heart rate increased. "Randall!" I screamed, dropping my phone and watching as the passenger side window of the van slowly crept down. I placed my hand on my door and grabbed the handle in an attempt to escape.

"Shit!" Randall screamed.

Shots rang out like fireworks, exploding inside the car.

I felt the cold, jagged scrapes of glass raining down on my body as the window shattered. A burning sensation penetrated me from my back to my abdomen, sending me, face first, up against the door. An involuntary yelp escaped my lips as another bullet struck me, this time in my left arm. I fell on the pavement and landed on my back. Wincing from the pain that coursed through my body, I struggled to catch my breath. Tears rolled down the sides of my face while I stared up at the light blue sky.

Voices mingled together around me in a combination of chaos and fear. I heard a woman scream, "He's got a gun!" That was followed by the sound of squealing tires. The sunlight on my face disappeared behind the shadow of the man now standing over me. Blinking several times, I finally focused on the barrel of the gun he was clenching between his hands. I closed my eyes to let go of life and all the pain that came with it and welcomed the dark, peaceful abyss called death.

Chapter 30

Gator

"I've set up an account for you, so if an appeal is granted in your favor, you'll be comfortable," Clint stated, looking across the table at me.

I could tell from his mood and tone that he was in his feelings over the things that had transpired with the murder of my wife. Earlier, he'd provided me a copy of the obituary from Randall's and Diamond's memorial services. I chose not to attend; much like the burial of my sister, because I refused to pay my respects in shackles. I would have addressed Clint's issues, but the truth is that I didn't give a damn about his feelings. He worked for me, and he, of all people, should have known that business was business. "*When* an appeal is granted in my favor," I corrected.

"When," he blew out loudly.

"Is there a problem, Clint?" I asked, ready to address what I saw and heard as disrespect.

"Yes," he grumbled. "As a matter of fact, there is."

"I'm listening."

"I didn't take this position to become a criminal," he grumbled through clenched teeth.

"That wasn't part of the deal."

I smiled, amused with the frustration the man was clearly feeling. "Should I remind you of how great your debt is to me?" I questioned. "Fucking a client's wife has gotta be reason enough for disbarment."

He adjusted his tie, then ran his hand across his head. "That was a one-time thing," he whispered. "The night of the opening, I had too much to drink and—"

I raised my hand, silencing the lies I knew were going to drizzle from his lips.

Granted, I only had proof that he'd slept with Diamond at the grand opening of her lounge, but I could tell from the look in Clint's eyes at the mention of my wife's name that something had transpired before that night. A man can deny many things, but seldom can he hide when he's been pussy whipped to the point where he thinks he's in love.

"The details no longer matter," I stated. "What's done is done."

"What if those maniacs who gunned down Diamond and Randall come back for me?" he breathed out nervously. "Who's going to protect me?"

"That would be between you and the God you serve," I advised. I understood Clint's passion and concern with being terrified that Luis's soldiers would come looking for him. After all, Clint had gotten Luis for almost half a million in product. When Venetta addressed her concerns with Diamond's loyalty to the family business, I found it necessary to secure a back-up plan. Yes, I had my local team in the streets who were once again passionate about getting money, and I had Diamond's beautiful face to thank for that, but I needed someone to hold it down on another level. That was why I contacted London, a true go-getter, a hustler in platform heels, whose actions spoke volumes about her loyalty. I wished I could take credit for her work ethic, but that was something she'd gotten from her sister Lisette and her brother Tabious. It wasn't a coincidence that Clint was in St. Maarten at the same time as Diamond; I made that happen, too, just like I had London contact Luis to tell him she and Clint wanted to make another deal on Diamond's behalf. The two of them met with Luis's delivery man, and it was a done deal. When Luis contacted me about who had his money, I dropped Randall's name in the pot. I would say I felt guilty for robbing Luis merely out of selfish gain, but in my industry, there was no room for guilt or shame.

Diamond

My only regret was the way things went down with Jonah. I wished I could have been the one who'd stared him in the eyes when he took his last breath. I think we both deserved that honor. He was a good soldier, one I trusted with my life and my wife, so I was quite disappointed the morning of my arrest when AJ advised me that he'd seen Diamond leaving the abortion clinic. The abortion meant only one thing: There was no possibility that that the child was mine. My instincts told me there was only one person who had enough time alone with her to invest in conceiving a baby, and that man had to be Jonah. There was also the issue and concern of an informant within my team tipping the authorities off about the abductions. When I put two and two together, I kept coming up with Jonah, which was why he had to die. I'd always followed my instincts, right or wrong, and if Jonah's blood had been shed in error, I'd have to deal with karma myself when the time came.

"That's it?" Clint asked, disrupting my thoughts. "I'm just shit out of luck?"

"Clint, you know how these things play out," I said calmly. "We do what we have to and pray for the best. Thanks for your diligence, but now I no longer require your services."

He stared at me with low, angry eyes. "I can still destroy you," he threatened. "I'll tell what I know."

"Do that." I laughed loudly, chuckled a few seconds longer, then lowered my voice. "We both know you'll be dead by morning if you do." I stood and gave him a stern look, daring him to so much as whisper another word, then walked off toward the guard to exit the room.

* * * * *

I thought I was finished receiving visitors for the day, but then I was called down for another guest. When I saw Anna, I was pleasantly surprised. "Mom!" I said, standing as she sat down.

She gave me a vile look of disgust, letting me know she wasn't happy to see me.

"How are you, Anna?" I asked seriously.

"How do you think I am?" she snapped. "I buried a daughter and a son in one day, all because of you!"

"I can imagine the pain you must be feeling," I stated, leaning forward against the table, "but your children chose their own destinies. I know you want to hate someone over it, but I'm not your enemy, Anna. I believe family should take care of family. That's why, in spite of your disapproval of me, I continued to make sure your bills were paid."

"Was it because of that or because you didn't want Diamond to know you were present the day her father died?"

"Come again?"

"I did my research Leon," she stated. "I know you were with Oscar moments before he took his last breath."

I had never mentioned it to Diamond, but I was very familiar with my would-have-been father-in-law. When Oscar was living, he'd been my primary mechanic until he quit, after discovering drugs hidden in the fender of a mule's car. I respected the man for wanting to maintain his reputation and earn an honest living, but I didn't feel comfortable with him knowing so much when he wasn't part of my team or on my payroll. "Your sources are correct," I stated to his widow, "but what does that matter now?"

"Tell me what happened," she demanded.

"Anna, why dwell on the past?"

"Tell me!"

I decided to indulge the woman, as she was clearly looking for some form of closure. "Oscar made a…well, a discovery in the vehicle of one of my employees," I explained, "and he requested that we no longer do business with him, fearing the trouble it would bring for his family. When I was informed of this, I went to the shop in the hopes of having a decent conversation, man to man and face to face. Unfortunately, your husband became disrespectful and expressed his distaste for my occupation. One thing led to another, as they say, and one of my soldiers had to restrain him." I paused, giving her time to digest the information. "As it turned out, your Oscar had a weak heart—a good one but weak nonetheless."

"So you left him there to die?" she questioned. "Why didn't you call for help?"

"That's not what I do, Anna," I said, staring into her eyes.

"You let my husband die and had my children murdered," she mumbled.

"Again, your husband had a weak heart," I corrected. "As for your children, they died at the hands of another man."

She wiped her eyes, catching the tears flowing over her lids. "Did you ever love her, my Diamond?" she finally asked.

"Of course I did," I stated. "I wanted to give her the world, but I guess fate had other plans." I refrained from divulging the fact that her daughter was a whore, as there are some things a mother doesn't need to know about her child.

"She loved you," she said, "and you destroyed her. I hope you live with that for the rest of your miserable life." She rose standing on her feet.

"Is there anything else?" I asked respectfully.

"Yes. When death comes for you, Leon, I pray I'm alive to witness it."

"I pray you are too," I stated seriously. I watched Anna as she exited. She was nothing more than a broken-spirited woman looking for sympathy and compassion, two things that were foreign to my soul.

Epilogue

I was perched in a chair next to the small metal bed, watching Diamond move her head slowly from left to right until finally fluttering her lashes and opening her eyes.

It had been six weeks since Luis's men had opened fire on her and Randall, leaving his body riddled with bullets and his brains seeping from his skull. When I arrived on the scene, I saw Diamond lying on the pavement. I climbed out of my vehicle with my gun in hand, creating more chaos at an already chaotic scene, but I was determined to save her if I could. When I'd received the call that Randall and Diamond were in trouble, I'd wasted no time springing into action. I wished I could have saved Randall, but some things are out of our hands, and his life was one of them.

I reached Diamond and found her bloody and wounded but still alive. I lifted her up in my arms, carried her to my vehicle, and fled the scene as quickly as possible to get her the medical attention she desperately needed. It was touch-and-go at first, but the doctor advised me she would survive.

"Wh-where am I?" she groaned, looking at me with cloudy eyes.

"You're in a safe place now, Diamond," I said, leaning forward in my chair.

She flinched, then used her right hand to push the cotton sheet and fleece blanket I had covered her with down to her waist, until her naked breasts and stomach were exposed. I watched as she stared at the gauze bandage covering her side and a portion of her stomach.

"The bullet entered your back and went out your side. You also took a shot to your left bicep," I explained. "You lost a lot of blood, but you're going to be fine."

She nodded, then pulled the sheet back up to cover herself. She stared at me, studying my face intently, undoubtedly trying to remember where she knew me from.

"I'll go over details of what happened later. Right now, you just need to rest and regain your strength."

"My brother?" she asked, clearing her throat.

I shook my head, acknowledging the thoughts I knew she was thinking. She started to cry softly.

I felt uncomfortable, not knowing what words to say, so I said nothing at all.

After several seconds of sobbing, she looked at me again. "Who are you?" she questioned. "I-I know you, don't I?"

"You do," I confessed. "You know me as Z, but you can call me Lawrence."

G STREET CHRONICLES
~ PRESENTS ~

DAMON
AND
Octavia

"THE FINAL LIE"

PART 7 OF THE *"LOVE, LIES & LUST"* SERIES

MZ. ROBINSON

G STREET *Essence*

G Street Romance

G STREET CHRONICLES
~ PRESENTS

Heels of Love

Part One of
"From Love to Loathe"
Series

Phoenix Rayne

G Street *Romance*